All that ever mattered to me was you. I knew what it was going to be like when we saw each other after four years apart. That's why I stayed away and never tried to call you or write you. It would've been too hard on both of us. If you came back to me of your own free will, then that was a different matter. And you did...

But I've brought you pain, Stefanie.

Long ago, Mother put the fear in me that I'd go off the deep end like my father. I've been haunted by that ever since she came to Mackenzie, but I couldn't tell you.

All I seem to do is bring you pain. Because of me, you didn't stay in California. Without me you could've had a Hollywood career.

My gorgeous, sweet wife. Oh, Lord—the fire's dying. I can barely see to write.

Dear Reader,

EVERLASTING...

To me, that word connotes something marvelous, precious, above and beyond the norm. *Forever.*

Who wouldn't want to enjoy a marriage defined in those particular terms?

In my book *The Vow*, Stefanie and Nick Marsden are one of those blessed couples who have an everlasting marriage. In that case you, the reader, might well say, "I'm not so sure I want to read about perfection."

May I remind you that I never said anything about their marriage being perfect? It's the imperfections they struggle with and overcome that make their battles heroic—until one day they discover they've arrived at that state of bliss called "everlasting."

Quite a feat for two imperfect mortals in an imperfect world!

Rebecca Winters

THE VOW

REBECCA WINTERS

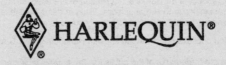

TORONTO • NEW YORK • LONDON
AMSTERDAM • PARIS • SYDNEY • HAMBURG
STOCKHOLM • ATHENS • TOKYO • MILAN • MADRID
PRAGUE • WARSAW • BUDAPEST • AUCKLAND

To my beloved father, Dr. John Zimmerman Brown, Jr. During World War II he was a lieutenant colonel and flight surgeon in the army-air force who headed the military base in Clovis, New Mexico. During those dark, fearsome days he took care of the men who were burned in action and had been flown to New Mexico for treatment. He, himself, had to parachute out of a plane when the engine died. When he had no choice but to bail out into nothing, he told me he got down on his knees first and prayed to God his life might be spared to take care of his wife and children once again. His prayer was answered. He lived to rear six children in an EVERLASTING marriage. He will always be my hero.

ISBN-13: 978-0-373-65426-0
ISBN-10:   0-373-65426-X

THE VOW

www.eHarlequin.com

Printed in U.S.A.

ABOUT THE AUTHOR

Rebecca Winters, an American writer, mother of four and grandmother of five, lives in Salt Lake City, Utah. When she was seventeen, she went to boarding school in Lausanne, Switzerland, where she learned to speak French and met girls from all over the world. Upon returning to the U.S., Rebecca developed her love of languages when she earned her B.A. at the University of Utah. She did postgraduate work at the Alliance Française in Paris, then became a junior and senior high school French teacher in Salt Lake, where she taught for twenty-two years.

At the same time as she enjoyed her teaching career, she turned to writing. Her first book was published in 1978. Today she has written ninety-seven books, ninety-four of them with Harlequin Enterprises (seventy-four Harlequin Romance and twenty Harlequin Superromance novels). The publication of *The Vow* marks her debut with the Everlasting Love line.

Rebecca has won a National Readers' Choice Award, a B. Dalton Award, many *Romantic Times BOOKreviews* Reviewers' Choice nominations and awards, the RIO Award for excellence and was named Utah Writer of the Year. Her books have appeared numerous times on the Waldenbooks bestseller list. She welcomes feedback and invites her readers to e-mail her at becky485@msn.com.

Books by Rebecca Winters

HIGH FLIGHT

Oh, I have slipped the surly bonds of earth
And danced the skies on laughter-silvered wings;
Sunward I've climbed, and joined the tumbling mirth
Of sun-split clouds—and done a hundred things
You have not dreamed of—
wheeled and soared and swung
High in the sunlit silence. Hov'ring there,
I've chased the shouting wind along, and flung
My eager craft through footless halls of air.
Up, up the long, delirious burning blue
I've topped the windswept heights with easy grace
Where never lark, or even eagle flew.
And, while with silent, lifting mind I've trod
The high untrespassed sanctity of space,
Put out my hand and touched the face of God.

by John Gillespie Magee, Jr.

John Gillespie Magee, Jr., was an eighteen-year-old American
when he entered flight training in 1941. Within the year,
he was sent to England and posted to the newly formed
No 412 Fighter Squadron, Royal Canadian Air Force.

On September 3, 1941, Magee flew a high altitude (30,000 feet)
test flight in a newer model of the Spitfire V. As he orbited
and climbed upward, he was struck with the inspiration
for a poem— "To touch the face of God."

Just three months later, on December 11, 1941 (and only
three days after the U.S. entered the war), Pilot Officer
John Gillespie Magee, Jr., was killed. The Spitfire V he was flying,
VZ-H, collided with an Oxford Trainer from Cranwell Airfield
over Tangmere, England. The two planes were flying in the clouds
and neither saw the other. He was just nineteen years old.

Chapter 1

I love you, darling.

   I love you, too.

   My life began the day I met you.

Nick Marsden made a noise in his throat.

The two besotted passengers he'd dropped off in Cranbrook, BC, had sounded like a pair of lovesick teenagers.

During the flight from Mackenzie, Montana, on this cold January day, he'd caught snatches of conversation between the bride and groom headed for the Canadian Rockies. The newly married couple might be staying at a ski lodge, but it was obvious that any honeymoon suite would do.

He grinned.

Forget words. It was the physical part of lovemaking you could depend on. With two bodies coming alive to each other, there could be no mistake about what you were doing and feeling.

Nick needed the scientifically proven, like the solid cushion of air beneath the plane's wings—a law of physics he could always count on to cradle him above the earth. Once on terra firma, another equally binding law of physics took over in the bedroom: one can't touch without being touched.

Animate objects exerting force on each other.

That was what he craved, what he received, from his wife, the only woman for him. Nick had made up his mind about Stefanie Larkin the moment he'd seen her long legs in one of those tiny skirts. Between that and her driving by his house after school, not much else had registered on the first day of his senior year at Clark High back in 1973.

Once the teacher had assigned him a seat behind her, he'd fixated on the glistening dark hair that cascaded down the middle of her back. Then she'd turned around to check him out.

Compared to her expensive *everything*, his cheap blue shirt had told its own story. So had her piercing green eyes that he'd assumed were judging him.

Though her hello had been friendly—he'd give her that—his ever-ready defense mechanism had shifted into overdrive. Whatever he'd muttered provoked the desired response. She'd turned around again and ignored him from then on. That was good. Better to leave well enough alone. At seventeen, he'd recognized immediately that Stefanie Larkin was out of his social class.

Luckily for him, *she* never knew it. Another smile broke out on his face.

He still couldn't believe she hadn't given up on him. At

first he'd tried to freeze her out. Cease and resist. But the more he refused to respond to her—the more he resisted even the slightest overture on her part, like the way she watched him during lunch—the more he ended up getting caught in his own trap. Pretty soon she was all he could think about. She'd become his obsession.

But Nick had been a surly SOB back then. Her sweetness managed to bring out the worst in him because he didn't trust it to be real. Not at first. Odd how such a long-buried memory would surface on this frigid January afternoon. Because of the honeymooners, no doubt.

He reached for his thermos, drinking the last of the hot coffee he'd replenished in Spokane, Washington, where he'd gone through customs. It had only taken twenty minutes.

Tonight when he took her to bed…

Anticipating the pleasure they gave each other, he glanced out the cockpit window of his four-seater, eager to get home early. The trip they'd returned from the day before yesterday had spoiled him.

He already had plans to take her someplace exotic next year. His old friend, Todd, from their Montana Air National Guard days had been in the Maldives recently and couldn't stop talking about it.

"You wouldn't believe how beautiful those islands are, Nick. Some of them aren't even on the map—they're uninhabited. You and Stefanie will have the place to yourselves. All you have to do is rent a boat and find your own paradise. I swear I'll never go anywhere else. At first Joanne was kind of nervous about playing Robinson Crusoe, but her tune changed when we got there."

Todd's excitement had infected Nick.

After trimming the plane to hold altitude, he made a few corrections, then contacted his assistant, Dena, over the radio to tell her he'd be landing in fifteen minutes. Flying VFR meant winging back to Mackenzie without a flight plan. When visibility was good, he liked the freedom.

"Did any more bids come through today?" They were looking for someone to resurface the parking area in front of the office.

"As a matter of fact, we received two. The one from Perma-Seal came in lower than the others, but Grant says you shouldn't go with them. Apparently they did the parking lot over at Carter's Shopping Center—and you know what happened *there* last winter."

"I remember it well." Stefanie had been driving out of the lot around eight-thirty one night when the car hit a sinkhole big enough that it popped both front tires. "Tell Grant to run it by Dries." That was Nick's nickname for Andries, the man he loved like a father. "When I get back, we'll talk it over and make a final decision. See you soon, Dena."

He was nearing the northern Cabinet Mountains, which were covered in snow from past storms. Might as well enjoy the view while he continued to entertain intimate memories of his wife on their private stretch of beach. Nick had made sure his bookworm bride of thirty years hadn't wanted to read any of the novels she'd brought along on their trip.

On the first afternoon, when the sun was its hottest, she'd gotten up from the sand to go inside and take a shower. He'd waited until she'd entered their rented villa, then he'd joined her beneath the spray and insisted on washing her hair.

Her shocked little cry had quickly turned into low moans of desire, their passion taking them back thirty years to the first time they'd made love. Throughout the rest of their second honeymoon they'd communicated in the most elemental of ways, experiencing the joy of being together without deadlines or interruptions.

Whoever said life began at forty was crazy. Being fifty-two was a liberating experience. For one thing, his cute little grandson, Jack, gave them all the pleasure of having a young child around without any of the problems.

So far no prostate problems. Better yet, his very fertile wife had sailed through menopause. No more months when they had to worry about her being late.

No more agonizing whenever Nan was out with a boyfriend, wondering if she was doing what Nick had wanted to do with Stefanie from the first moment he'd laid eyes on her. If Nan was the next pregnant woman in the family, he'd be thrilled. His daughter had always wanted to be a mother. Being an elementary school teacher was perfect for her.

No more worry over David's needless fretting about going into the banking business in Kalispell instead of becoming a pilot like his dad. He'd been afraid he'd hurt Nick's feelings. But secretly Nick was glad; he couldn't have handled either of his children being pilots.

No more concern over Dries, who'd pulled out of his depression since his retirement. These days he was using that razor-sharp brain of his to write his memoirs of life in Holland prior to World War II.

After that, he'd write about his experiences as a fighter pilot during the war. Stefanie was helping him decide on the best photos to include. It had become a family project.

No money worries. He'd had to turn away business for a long time now.

Nick's only worry was that he was feeling too damn good lately.

He hoped the vacation had hastened his wife's recovery from empty-nest syndrome. With their son and now their baby girl married and making homes of their own, he was rediscovering his twenties without fear of getting her pregnant again.

Spare him the agony of their first child's stillbirth twenty-eight years ago. He'd never forget Stefanie's sobs coming from the delivery room while their OB stepped into the hall to talk to him.

"Stillbirths are as random as raindrops, Mr. Marsden."

"But my wife's perfectly healthy!"

"She is, but these tragedies can occur for no apparent reason. Rarely is a stillbirth caused by something the mother did."

Nick shook his head in a daze. "That's not a good enough explanation, Doctor."

"I agree. But until autopsies are routinely offered to all stillbirth families, the causes, and thus any new risk-reduction measures, will continue to elude us. I'm sorry. Your wife needs you. Go on in."

On legs of lead, he entered the delivery room, still gowned.

"Nick—"

He bent over and put his arms around her, pressing his lips against her wet face. Tears ran down his cheeks into her hair.

"Our baby died," she wailed in anguish. "I can't stand it."

Nick couldn't either. So many hopes and dreams for

their little Matthew, whom they'd already named for the deceased father Nick had never known.

He held her tighter, attempting to draw all her pain into himself. No words could ease her suffering or his.

Be strong for her now, Marsden. Fall apart later when you're alone.

A quick crescendo behind the instrument panel jerked Nick back from that hellish time. He blinked the moisture from his eyes, alert to a clattering noise in the engine.

Within five seconds, he heard a loud explosion followed by a metallic sound that blew through the cowling. It created a large wound in the metal. He'd lost a piston!

Dear Lord.

For a second he couldn't think for the shock of what had just happened. Only the sound of the wings cutting the air accompanied his thoughts.

He took a moment to contemplate the gravity of the situation, then years of emergency training kicked in. He eased the yoke toward his stomach, slowing the aircraft for the best glide while he watched for a decrease in airspeed.

Realizing the heavily forested terrain offered few options for a smooth landing, he began searching for a suitable crash site. When he saw a patch without trees, he committed himself and lined up for a downwind.

The ground was rising faster than he'd expected. He barely had time to do it, but he dialed 121.5 and called in his position.

"Mayday. Mayday. Mayday—"

"Stefanie?"

The sound of the familiar voice made Stefanie Marsden

pause at the front entrance of the building where she worked as head photographer for *Northwest Trails Magazine*. She turned to find one of the staff chasing after her.

"Hi, Janet. How's it going?"

The blond woman puffed a little as she came up to Stefanie. "Not as good as you look with that tan."

"We just got back from the Caribbean." Civilization had intruded on their honeymoon spot of thirty years ago, but it was still a paradise.

"I couldn't tell," she teased. "Some people have all the luck."

Stefanie *was* lucky. If something was still missing after all these years, she'd made up her mind on this trip to let it go. Nick couldn't help that he'd always kept his deepest thoughts and feelings to himself.

Who knew how much happier he'd be if he could ever unburden his soul to her? But it wasn't going to happen. The only important thing was that she knew Nick loved her. That had never been in question.

"Could I get a recipe from you?" Janet asked.

"Which one?"

"The Christmas cookies you brought to the office party a couple of years ago."

"Do you mean the cherry winks?"

"Those are delicious, but I'm talking about the chocolate squares with the mint centers."

"Oh…my grandmother's recipe. I'll get it for you. It's in one of my journals."

"You still keep them up?"

"Off and on."

Soon after Stefanie turned sixteen, her mother had died

of a brain aneurysm. To help her deal with the grief, her Grandma Dixon had bought her a journal and urged her to write down her feelings. She'd filled a number of those notebooks over the years.

They'd served as scrapbooks, too. She'd taped in the odd photo or newspaper article or postcard. There was a three-page spread of the postcards she'd written to Nick from Hawaii when she was seventeen. She'd never sent them.

Every time she'd attempted to write him something profound, it sounded trite and foolish. She'd wanted him to think of her as a woman uniquely eloquent, given to lofty thoughts and pursuits. Stefanie dreamed big in those days.

"Luckily I know where to lay my hands on that recipe, Janet. Do you want me to e-mail it to you?"

"That would be great. I'd like to make them for a dinner party I'm having for Clint's boss the day after tomorrow."

"I'll get right on it."

"Let's hope they turn out as good as yours."

"Of course they will."

"Thanks." Janet hurried down the opposite corridor.

As Stefanie left the building, she zipped up her parka against the wind. When it blew from the west, a storm wasn't far behind. Cold gusts molded the black wool skirt to her legs.

She still had the legs of a young woman—or so her married daughter, Nan, had confided to her over the New Year's holiday.

"While Dad was in the bedroom packing for your trip, I heard Dave tell him he was a leg man, and Dad said he was a leg man, too. He must've been talking about you, Mom."

The revelation that Nick had been discussing women's

legs with their son brought a smile to Stefanie's lips. But right now her own legs were freezing. She rushed along the walkway to the parking area reserved for staff and found her car. The leather seat felt like ice. So did the steering wheel.

Their comfortable ranch-style house was five miles away. In summer she occasionally walked home for the exercise; winter was another proposition altogether. The weather forecast had predicted snow by nightfall, so she'd decided to play it safe and wear her warmest coat.

Shivering, she quickly turned on the engine and drove out of the lot without waiting for the interior to warm up. Once she'd negotiated the downtown traffic, it didn't take her long to reach the area known as Huckleberry Creek, where they lived. She was eager to get home.

Her husband ran the North Country Flying Service out of Mackenzie. She hoped he'd arrived ahead of her, but as she pulled into the driveway and pressed the remote, an empty garage greeted her. Stefanie loved it when he managed to beat her home from work. There was something special about knowing he was in the house waiting for her, but his job didn't allow that to happen very often.

She brought in the mail from the porch, swearing she wouldn't go outside again tonight, no matter the reason.

In their bedroom she took off her coat and changed into a comfortable pair of jeans and a soft sweatshirt. Nick should be home any minute, and he'd be hungry.

Some newlyweds had chartered a flight to British Columbia. Stefanie would never have planned a skiing honeymoon, in the Rockies or anywhere else. Her idea of heaven was a beach on Tortola, a hot sun and her husband. *Not* in that order, she mused.

With her thoughts on Nick—who, at a lean fifty-two, looked better than any groom in his twenties ever could— she hurried into the kitchen to get their meal started.

When her maternal grandparents had passed away, neither her brother Richard nor her sister Liz were living in Mackenzie, so it was decided they'd receive the money that was left, and Stefanie would inherit this house.

Six months ago, she and Nick had the kitchen and family room totally redone and the ceiling vaulted in preparation for Nan's wedding in August. It had meant a month of eating out and a constant layer of dust on everything.

But the results had been a spacious, modern great room and kitchen in knotty alder with accents of cream, sage and plum. Little pots of African violets in the recessed window over the sink stood out against her French lace curtains. Now when she entered the house, she marveled at the beautiful transformation reflected in the gleam of the honey-toned hardwood floors.

A large, framed Monet still life hung on the wall next to the French doors leading to the patio. The colors tied everything together, including the French country print on the couch and love seat.

Of course, these days, only she and Nick were here to enjoy it. First David, now their daughter, Nan, had married and moved out. A different phase of life had begun for them. Stefanie was still trying to adjust.

She and Nan had always been close. Even with her away at college in Seattle, they'd found time to talk on the phone every day. More often than not, Nick flew Stefanie to Seattle at least once a month for a quick visit with their daughter.

But now that Nan had a husband, it was different.

Stefanie didn't want to intrude on their marriage and make Ben wish he didn't have her as a mother-in-law. For that matter, she always went through Amanda to talk to David, just to be careful. Maybe she was being too careful.

As she put potatoes in the oven to bake, the grandfather clock in the hallway—an heirloom from Nick's family—chimed quarter past five. Where was he? The steaks were ready to grill.

After fixing a spinach-and-avocado salad with mandarin orange sections and Nick's favorite poppy seed dressing, she decided to find that recipe for Janet before she forgot.

She walked around the island separating the kitchen and dining area from the family room, with its floor-to-ceiling bookcase. Besides their many books, which represented a lifetime of reading and could have stocked a small bookstore, a collection of family pictures filled an entire shelf and included the recent wedding photos Stefanie had taken, plus a new picture of her father with his second wife, Renae, to commemorate their wedding anniversary last summer.

Another shelf housed Nick's prized first-edition encyclopedia of World War II. Twenty volumes' worth. Nobody loved flying more than he did. He spent hours poring over rare combat photos of vintage Dorniers, Messerschmitts and the British flying boats.

On a third shelf she kept her journals, a personalized bible with beautiful pictures, which her parents had given her as a child, and ten of her all-time favorite books. They were held in place by two alabaster bookends of Rodin's *The Kiss* and *The Thinker.*

Stefanie had bought *The Kiss* at Laguna Beach with her babysitting money when she was fifteen.

While on a trip there with her family, she'd read a novel by Catherine Cookson called *The Fifteen Streets*. Her mother had seen it in a bookstore and told her she had to read it.

It was a beautiful yet painful love story about two people living in northern England in the early 1900s who found their way to each other despite all odds.

What Stefanie loved best was the wealthy, educated young heroine moving across the hall from the impoverished, uneducated young man. His mother wants the two of them to get together, but she's afraid the people in the Fifteen Streets, deeply rooted in Catholicism, won't accept this high-class woman in her son's world.

Since then, Stefanie had read the book every year, with the exception of this year. It was her number-one keeper on the shelf. She would've read it on the trip last week, but Nick hadn't left her alone long enough to do anything but play with him and make love. It had been heavenly....

Eager for tonight when he'd be home, she reached for the first journal and hurried back through the house to their home office, where a print of his grandmother's favorite painting—Pellegrini's *Rebecca at the Well*—hung on the wall opposite the desk.

Stefanie had matched the blue of the woman's dress in the painting to the tiebacks on the off-white sheers. Combined with the walnut desk and moldings, she felt it achieved a striking effect. The rest of the walls in the office and the hallway displayed Stefanie's photographic artwork.

With a flip of the light switch, she crossed over to the desk and began to leaf through her journal, looking for the recipe. Since Nick hadn't returned yet, she might as well do this now.

It took a few minutes to wade through her teenage cursive before she discovered what she was searching for and typed it into the computer. One of the drawers contained the magazine's staff directory. She looked up Janet's e-mail address and sent her the recipe.

While she was at it, she printed off a copy to put in her recipe book, something she'd meant to do the last time she'd had to dig this up for her sister, Liz. If Stefanie's grandmother hadn't dictated it to her from memory and she hadn't written it down in her journal, it would've been lost.

Just as she was about to go back to the kitchen, the phone rang. She picked up the receiver, thankful to see that the call was coming from Nick's office. He'd probably had some business there before driving straight home from the airport.

"Nick?"

"Afraid not, Stefanie. It's Dena. Obviously you haven't heard from him either," she said without preamble. Dena Livsey was the office administrator and the wife of one of the mechanics; both of them had worked for Nick the last ten years. Her worried voice gave Stefanie an uneasy feeling.

"No. Not on this phone or my cell." She got up from the chair and peered out the window to see if his four-wheel drive was in sight yet, but there were no headlights. To her dismay, it had started snowing. "I expected him home by now."

"I heard from him at quarter to four saying he'd be back in fifteen minutes," Dena explained. "It's five-thirty and a storm front's moved in. I can't raise him."

Stefanie's heart sank at those words, but Nick was an excellent pilot. She closed her eyes tightly for a minute. Of course he was all right.

One day a few years ago, he'd been three hours late because his passenger went into labor during the flight and needed immediate help. They were too far from a hospital or clinic, so he'd set the plane down in a pasture and delivered the baby himself.

Fortunately it had happened in the summer and he'd been able to radio for an AirMed helicopter. When Stefanie threw her arms around him later, praising him for his heroics, he'd said, "Don't give me any medals. It was part of our Air Guard training."

She'd asked his buddy Todd about that and he'd grinned. "Nick's conning you. The guy can do anything. He's a top pilot, you know, what they used to call an ace."

Stefanie *did* know. But her husband would argue that the only "ace" was Dries, who'd seen combat in World War II and shot down seven enemy planes.

"He must've landed at another airport for mechanical reasons, Dena." Though she couldn't understand why he hadn't phoned either of them yet. "I'll try Coeur d'Alene while you call Kalispell."

"I'll do that right now. I'm also going to call Spokane. Maybe he went back there for some reason without telling me."

"Ring me the second you learn anything. I'll do the same."

She hung up with Dena, then flipped through Nick's Rolodex for the number. But a call to the Idaho airport revealed no news. Stefanie refused to believe anything had happened. There'd been many times in their marriage when he'd been overdue, causing her anxiety. It went with the territory of being a pilot—and a pilot's wife.

Maybe that was the problem. After all these years of his coming home safe…

When Dena didn't answer, Stefanie left the news on her voice mail. Maybe she was more unnerved than usual because she'd known where he was every second of their recent vacation.

She went back to the family room with the journal, praying the phone would ring and she'd hear Nick's voice.

By now a different kind of cold had filled her veins. She turned on the gas log in the marble fireplace, but knew she wouldn't warm up until he walked through the door.

Her gaze lingered on the model of a Curtiss JN plane sitting on the traditional carved-wood mantel. Through the aviation museum at Wright-Patterson Air Force Base in Ohio, she'd tracked down an expert to create a perfect replica. Her wedding present to Nick after they'd returned from their honeymoon.

The "Jenny" as it was nicknamed, had become famous as a primary trainer for the American pilots of World War I. Nick had spent a good half hour looking at it when he'd taken her to see an airplane exhibit on their first date.

The replica had been very expensive but worth it when he'd opened her present wrapped in heavy white paper with gold ribbon. His eyes had lit up like hot blue stars as he'd pulled it from the box and examined it for what seemed like hours. Just when she thought he'd forgotten about her, he put it on the table and tightened his arms around her. That was thirty years ago….

Turning sharply away, she started to reshelve the journal

when it fell to the floor. She was shaking. As she crouched to retrieve it, her gaze fell on one of the early entries, compelling her to read.

September 3, 1973.
"He's taller than anyone else, and you notice his glance, where it turns, as though it were keener, clearer and brighter than anyone else's, lit with a more intense fire. What could I say to him? Anything I might say would be trivial and superficial, like pink frosting flowers. I felt the whole world before this to be frivolous, superficial, ephemeral...."

I've stolen those words from Anne Morrow Lindbergh's description of Charles, but they could be mine about Nicholas Marsden.

She's one of my favorite authors. I wish I could express myself the way she does. I wish I wasn't a silly girl who ruined something yesterday I can't fix.

It's because I'm the kind of girl anyone can walk over. When I'm with Penny and Sara, I don't know how to say no to them. I don't know what I'm afraid of. I guess I don't want them to be upset with me. I hate causing trouble, so sometimes I don't say what I really think.

They always say what they think and they don't worry how I'll feel. My brother, Richard, never liked Penny or Sara very much. A long time ago he told me I'd need to get a spine if I kept hanging around with them.

After what happened yesterday, I can see he was right. But it's too late. Even if Mom were alive, she wouldn't be able to help me. Because I think Nick hates me. How come I feel as if I've already lost something precious?

Emotion tightened Stefanie's throat. Her eyes blurred. She stood up, realizing that from those first days as a senior at Clark High Nick had been the center of her life.

Chapter 2

September 3, 1973

"**G**ood morning, class, I'm Mr. Detweiler." Her homeroom World History teacher had come in with a sheaf of papers in his hands. "Until I learn your names, I'd like you to sit in alphabetical order, starting right here." He pointed to the first seat in the row nearest the windows. "Jack Andrews, Carrie Briggs, Brad Foster, Philip Hamilton…"

Turning to the back of the room, Stefanie saw someone interesting at the end of the next row.

He seemed older than the boys she knew. A transfer from Lewis? It was the alternative high school in their town of ninety-five hundred people.

He had a remote look on his face, as if the classroom proceedings were far from his thoughts. But if he smiled…

Her heart beat faster.

"…Stefanie Larkin." Mr. Detweiler gestured to the first seat in the row she was in.

Picking up her books, she moved to the front, wondering who'd be sitting behind her.

"Nicholas Marsden." The teacher pointed to the seat.

She watched anxiously. She didn't know anyone named Nicholas. When the guy she'd been admiring seconds ago sat down behind her, she couldn't have been more pleased.

Turning to face him, she smiled. "Hi, Nick," she said, taking the liberty of shortening his name. "I'm Stefanie. Looks like it's going to be a fun year."

He shot her a glance that could have been irritation or annoyance before he acknowledged her greeting with an offhand hello. Then he sat back with his arms folded, waiting for class to start.

Her smile faded slightly. She wasn't used to getting this response from a guy and wasn't about to let him put her off. "Have you always lived here?" she asked.

"No."

Mr. Detweiler stepped to the front of the room. "Okay, class, may I have your attention." Immediately the chatter ceased.

Stefanie turned away, surprised Nick had shown no interest in her. It shouldn't have hurt, but it did.

The teacher passed out a class outline and launched into an overview of the course. He was reputed to be an old eccentric, crazy about the subject he was teaching. The remaining half hour passed by quickly. Stefanie had always loved school and figured that once she could get Nick to talk to her, she'd like her World History class.

As soon as the bell rang, everyone raced out of the room, including Nick. She followed a little more sedately.

"Stef?" She saw her best friends waving to her from where they stood next to the far wall. Penny flipped her long, straight blond hair over her shoulder. "Meet any cute guys yet?"

Stefanie would never describe Nick as cute. "There's an *interesting* guy in my homeroom. He sits right behind me. His name's Nicholas Marsden, but I called him Nick." Maybe that was what had ticked him off. "He looks like a Nick to me. Dark hair. Blue eyes."

"You're lucky. Joey's behind me in German." Sara rolled her eyes.

The girls sympathized. Joey Johnson could never sit still. Though he was one of the cutest boys at Clark, he drove everyone crazy; nonetheless, Stefanie had been friends with him for years.

The crowd in the hall had begun to thin out. Penny said, "We'd better hurry if we're going to get to English on time."

They started down the stairs to their next class. This teacher didn't ask them to sit alphabetically, so they sat next to each other while Mrs. Yotz read over the disclosure of class rules she'd be sending home with them. Stefanie looked around the room, eager to see if Nick was there so she could point him out to the girls. To her disappointment, he must've been assigned a different time or a different English teacher.

At lunch she saw him sitting three tables away. She quickly nudged Penny. "There's Nick," she whispered. "He's the one talking to Frank Willis." Her heart raced.

Penny twisted her head around. "With those shoulders, he should be on the football team—if he isn't."

Nick wasn't conventionally handsome, but he had an all-male look that made her keep watching him.

Sara stared at him across the lunch tables. "Wow. He's a real bad-boy type, isn't he?"

Stefanie didn't think of him that way, but she kept her thoughts to herself.

"I wouldn't mind going to the Hello Day dance with him," Penny murmured while she munched on potato chips.

"Stefanie saw him first," Sara said. "I'm going to the dance with Frank. Do you want me to find out if he already has a girlfriend?"

"No." The possibility that he was taken had been bothering Stefanie all morning. If he liked another girl, that could be the reason he'd been standoffish. But she didn't want her friends getting involved in her life.

"Why not?" Sara said.

"Because I'd rather you didn't. That's all."

"Well, it's only the first day. You don't usually have a problem getting boys to like you."

"I wonder where he lives," Penny mused.

Stefanie wondered the same thing. "It's none of our business."

"Don't be silly. If we knew, we could accidentally drive by his house and maybe talk to him and his friends while he's out in front or something." Penny picked up her sandwich, then laid it down again. "I know who could tell us. My mother's volunteering in the school office this afternoon. I'll ask her to look up his file."

"Don't." Stefanie wished she hadn't said anything about Nick.

"I don't have anything planned after school," Sara said,

excitedly. "We could walk to my house. I'll ask Mom if I can drive you guys home. We'll take a detour on the way."

Stefanie had her reservations but ended up giving in.

The lunch bell rang. "Let's meet at our usual place," Penny said before they made their way to their next class. Stefanie had Chemistry, then Latin. But during the last period of the day the three of them would be in Gym together.

After school, Sara and Stefanie waited by the flagpole and talked to their friends. Penny came running up to them. "He lives at 343 Spruce Street, and his birthday's March twenty-second. That's as much as I could see before Mother had to look up information on someone else."

Nick was a few months older than Stefanie.

Sara's brow furrowed. "I think Spruce is on the other side of the stockyards."

If she was right, he didn't live in the best part of town. Stefanie couldn't have cared less what area of Mackenzie he came from, but maybe *he* did.

So many authors wrote about class struggles. Stefanie had practically memorized *The Fifteen Streets*.

"…and so Blaine Farr had to move to Nebraska with his mom and her new husband."

Stefanie blinked. She frowned at Penny. "I didn't know Mrs. Farr got married again."

"According to Mom, it happened fast."

Poor Blaine. Stefanie couldn't imagine her own father marrying another woman, let alone having to move somewhere else.

Once they were at Sara's house and she had the keys from her mom, they piled in her family's station wagon. She turned on their favorite music station, which was playing a song by the Carpenters, "I Won't Last a Day Without You." Stefanie avoided the girls' eyes as Sara backed the car out of the driveway. Across town, Penny asked directions from several people until they found Spruce Street.

"Number 343 must be that way."

"This isn't a good idea, guys," Stefanie said, but Sara had already turned onto the street.

The houses were a dingy white with small front yards. One of them was fenced. "I think that's it," Penny said.

Sara slowed the car as they drove by, drawing the attention of a German shepherd, who ran over to the fence, growling.

"Speed up, Sara! This is so embarrassing." Stefanie hadn't felt good about it from the beginning and wished they hadn't come. If Nick saw them…

"Why? We have every right to be driving on this street," Penny reasoned. "No harm done."

Stefanie disagreed. "Sara? Would you mind dropping me off at my grandfather's office?"

"No problem."

Her Grandpa Dixon was an internist, and her grandmother worked for him part-time. Since the death of Stefanie's mother a year ago April, it was arranged that Stefanie would get a ride home with her whenever she wanted. Otherwise it was a long walk.

But as fate would have it, her grandmother had left, so Stefanie waited for her grandfather. He'd probably have to make rounds at the hospital before driving her home. That was okay. She could get a head start on reading *Macbeth* for her English class.

The Larkins lived near the outskirts of Mackenzie in a two-story Colonial house of red brick with white trim and shutters, which her father had inherited from his deceased parents. Giant horse chestnut and catalpa trees surrounded it. Stefanie and her siblings felt as if they'd spent their lives picking up the prickly green-covered chestnuts and cigar-shaped pods so their father could mow.

Her twenty-four-year-old brother and twenty-one-year-old sister were away at college now. Except for a cleaning lady who came in once a week, she and her dad were on their own and usually made dinner together.

He was the owner of the Northwest State Bank of Montana, a business built by Stefanie's grandfather, Robert David Larkin. Stefanie hardly remembered him or her Grandmother Larkin. They'd both died when she was small. But she did remember how hard her father had worked to keep the business growing and make it prosper.

Since her mother's death, her dad had been working harder than ever. She didn't tell him or her grandfather Dixon about Nick. Only giggly little idiots would've driven past his house, and she was embarrassed by her behavior.

The next morning Stefanie was eager to see Nick—and nervous, too. She wanted him to notice her, so she dressed in her pink sweater and matching A-line skirt. In front of her bedroom mirror she pinned her hair up, then let it down, trying to decide which was the more attractive.

In the end she left her long dark brown hair to swing casually over one shoulder, then asked her dad to drive her to school early.

Ages seemed to pass before Nick came into their homeroom. He headed for her desk, frowning at her.

"What did you think you were doing outside my house yesterday?"

Her breath caught, and she stared at him, feeling helpless. He must've been in the yard with the dog, but she hadn't seen him. She should have obeyed her instincts and told Sara to drive her straight to her grandfather's office after school.

"I don't know what you're talking about." She felt the blood rush to her cheeks.

"I wouldn't come around again if I were you." With those words he wheeled into his seat.

Stung by his rejection and feeling guilty, she quickly faced the front. Toward the end of class, she wrote him a note.

Dear Nick,
Did you know there's no revenge as complete as forgiveness? If my friends and I upset you by driving past your house, I'm sorry. It was a dumb thing to do. Haven't you ever done something you regretted? By the way, you have a beautiful dog. Is it a male or female?
Stefanie

She folded the note in her lap so Mr. Detweiler couldn't see what she was doing. When the second bell rang, she slid out of her seat and dropped it on Nick's desk before darting from the classroom. Normally she told her friends everything, but not this time.

Stefanie had to wait through the whole weekend until Monday to find out if he'd read it. But he was absent that day and her spirits fell. Even when he came back to school on Tuesday, it made no difference. He ignored her all week. When the bell rang for the end of History class Friday morning, she paused by his desk. He was gathering up his books.

"Didn't you read my note?"

"I don't know what you're talking about."

Oh, yes, he did, but Nick was paying her back with her very own words. Not to be daunted, Stefanie said, "Then I guess I won't write you another note asking you to the Hello Day dance."

He stood up abruptly, locking gazes with her. "I don't dance."

"You're welcome, Nick," she said to his retreating back.

The second he disappeared from the room she approached the teacher. "Mr. Detweiler?"

"Yes, Stefanie?" He was at his desk recording test grades.

"Would you change my seat please? I did something stupid and now Nick doesn't like me."

He raised his head. "Mr. Marsden made a similar request."

That hurt.

"What did you tell him?"

"The same thing I'm going to tell you. *No.* I don't allow seat changes until the next report-card term."

"But—"

"If the two of you are having a problem, it's better that you solve it, don't you think?"

"I don't know if I can."

"Then ignore him."

That wouldn't be hard since Nick seemed determined to have nothing to do with her.

The room was filling up. She was going to be late for

her next class. Mr. Detweiler had already returned to correcting papers.

She started for the exit.

"See you on Monday, Miss Larkin."

On the phone Sunday night, she broke down as she told Penny about her frustration over Nick. A few minutes after they'd hung up, Penny called her back. "I looked for Nick's zodiac sign in my sister's astrology book. He's an Aries. Listen to this—

"'You often find that an Aries is a doctor, an athlete, an astronaut or a pilot. They have daring instincts and a love of adventure. You'll notice they're quiet, but when they do talk, they're blunt and candid.'"

Nick had been all of those things, Stefanie mused. In fact, he was brutal.

"'They love to make love.' Apparently they have a big sex drive."

"Penny!"

"'On the other hand, they're quite easily upset by other people because deep down they're sensitive. But you wouldn't necessarily know it since they can ride roughshod over other people's feelings without realizing it.'"

"Are you making this up?"

"No! I'll bring the book to school tomorrow and you can read it for yourself."

"What else does it say?" Stefanie was too intrigued not to listen.

"'Their strong sex drive tends to lead them into an early marriage. Unfortunately most early marriages don't end well.'"

At this point Stefanie wished she hadn't asked.

"Here's something interesting. 'Aries are crazy about their own children and will do anything for them, even die for them without worrying about themselves.'"

After a slight hesitation Stefanie asked, "What does my sign say?"

"Just a minute. You're a Libra. Let's see… 'You find Librans in the world of successful artists, composers and health-care givers.

"'Libras are able to be empathetic and can understand another person's views. They're willing to compromise and will do anything rather than have a confrontation that would end the relationship.'"

"Makes me sound like a pushover."

"You are."

"Thanks," she said wryly.

"And guess what else? A female Libra likes men and *could* be promiscuous because Libras are romantic."

Stefanie's face went hot.

"You'll probably have a successful marriage."

"That's nice to hear."

"This is why. When you're a Libra, you're so nice your husband will forgive you if you have a fight. He won't be able to complain because you have the ability to handle his imperfections, even if they're bad. Yours is the nicest of all the signs in the zodiac."

"It sounds like I'm a doormat."

"Well, if you and Nick ever date, for sure he'd be getting the better deal, so don't say you haven't been warned."

Stefanie didn't believe in all that astrological stuff. By the next morning she'd decided to take her teacher's advice and give Nick the silent treatment. Of course, she was constantly aware of him, but she avoided eye contact and made certain they didn't walk out of class at the same time.

Three weeks went by, including the Hello Day dance. Much to Sara and Penny's disapproval she didn't end up going. They told her Joey was upset that she hadn't asked him to the dance. Stefanie didn't know why. Joey was a friend, nothing more. He knew that.

That weekend she decided to go to Great Falls with her father. He had bank business that took her out of school on Friday and prevented them from getting back to Mackenzie until Monday night. She did her homework in the car to keep up her grades.

When she took her seat in History class Tuesday morning, a voice behind her said, "I thought you'd withdrawn from the class." She was shocked that Nick was speaking to her.

She half turned in her seat and said, "I'm sorry you're so disappointed." When she looked ahead again, her glance met the teacher's. Too late she remembered his advice.

The next week she found a note on her desk when she walked into History class. Assuming Penny or Sara had put it there, she picked it up and unfolded it to read.

A World War I airplane exhibit is coming to the fairgrounds on Halloween. There's going to be a haunted house set up next to it. You have to wear a costume. Want to go?

Airplane exhibit on Halloween? Who'd be interested in that? But the haunted house sounded like fun.

She forgot she wasn't talking to Nick and turned to him. "Did you see who put this note on my seat?"

"Count Dracula," he said in a Bela Lugosi voice.

How did *he* know what was in that note? Unless he'd read it…or *written* it.

A certain conversation with the teacher came to mind. *Why don't you ignore him?*

Stefanie had been doing that for weeks. She stared straight at Nick. "Tell the count I'll have to check with Vampira, but I'm sure she'll want to go."

She'd spoken before thinking. She was definitely a pushover, but she didn't care because this note meant he'd forgiven her.

As Stefanie turned the page, the clock chimed six. She clutched the journal to her breast. Still no call from Dena… The other woman had a list of all the airports and knew where to phone. Stefanie would give it five more minutes, then call her again. Unable to think or move, she looked down at the next journal entry.

October 31, 1973
I can't wait until tonight. Today after school I went shopping with the girls. I bought some stage makeup but couldn't find an outfit I liked. So I picked out a pattern with long flowing sleeves and bought some black material. Grandma Dixon is sewing it right now. She used to make a lot of her own clothes. I want to look like an elegant Vampira for Nick.

That evening Stefanie stood next to Penny in front of the full-length mirror, admiring their costumes. "I love your blond wig. In that cape you look exactly like Little Red Riding Hood."

"You should've bought a wig, too. It'll take a lot of shampooing to wash out that black rinse."

"Tomorrow I'll tell you if it was worth it. I've always wondered what it would be like to have black hair." *I wonder how Nick will like it.*

"No one'll know it's you under all that makeup."

"Good. I want to surprise Nick. I have a feeling he's going to be a scary Dracula."

"I wish you guys were coming to Sara's party. Everybody's going to be there."

"I know, but this is our first date. He's got his own plans."

"It's weird that there's going to be a haunted house on the fairgrounds."

"I know. He said it's in the building where they put the art exhibition during the fair. I found out from Dad it's being put on by the bankers' wives for a charity fund-raiser." Her mom would've been involved if she were still alive.

"Are you nervous?"

"Yes." Nick got top grades and exhibited a keen intellect, yet he was an enigma to her on many levels.

"Well, I'd better get going. Beware the Aries man," she teased.

Stefanie knew exactly what she was talking about. "I'm Vampira, remember, so he'll have to be careful around *me*," she asserted. "Let's go." She walked Penny out of her bedroom and down the wide staircase.

Her father was at the front door handing candy to trick-or-treaters. When they'd gone, he turned around, took one look at the girls and began laughing. "Good and evil before my very eyes."

"Oh, Dad." Stefanie smiled.

"Don't let the wolf eat you up, Penny," he told her.

"I'll be careful."

"Tell Sara I'm sorry I can't come," Stefanie said.

"No, you're not," Penny whispered in her ear, "but she understands. It's Joey who's going to have a problem. You keep breaking his heart."

Stefanie wished Penny wouldn't say that. Her friend knew how she felt about Joey, and it was beginning to annoy her that Penny insisted on pressing the point. How would Penny like it if Stefanie did the same thing to her?

"Good night, Mr. Larkin."

"Good night, Penny."

After the door closed, her father said, "Your mother wouldn't recognize you."

Her eyes smarted with tears. "Don't get me started, Dad."

The doorbell rang again before he could respond. He grabbed the candy bowl from the hall table and opened the door. A half dozen little kids in costume crowded around the entrance. In the background she saw the black caped figure of an adult. At first she thought it was a parent, then she let out a gasp.

Nick's hair was slicked back from his forehead like that of someone who'd just surfaced from the water, displaying a natural widow's peak. His head gleamed a dark sable in the porch light, reminding her of a picture of Rudolph Valentino—the dashing hero of the silent movies—she'd seen in one of her grandmother's many scrapbooks.

He wore no makeup except a ring of red lining his eyes. Yet the effect with his fangs gave him a pallor that was at once startling and lifelike. She could understand why the kids made a wide circle around him before running off.

"Hi, Nick. Come in and meet my father, John Larkin. Dad? This is Nicholas Marsden."

Nick removed his fangs before stepping inside. "Mr. Larkin." They shook hands.

Her father stood a little shorter than Nick, who had to be six-one. "My daughter tells me you're not originally from here."

"No, sir. Eureka."

"The Banana Belt of Montana."

Nick nodded.

"Welcome to Mackenzie, Nick. I wonder if I've met your parents. Who's your father?"

Oh, Dad—not one of your unsubtle inquisitions.

"Matthew Marsden. He died when I was four."

"I'm sorry," her father murmured. Stefanie loved him, but this was one time she wished he'd just leave things alone.

"My mom and I went to live with his parents," Nick explained further, as if he wanted to get it all said now. "She left when I was eight to find work somewhere else, and I haven't seen or talked to her since. I still live with my Marsden grandparents. He ran a grocery store until he retired."

"I see."

"When my great-uncle Walt got cancer, we moved here this past summer to help take care of him and his dog. He's always worked for the railroad and lives alone. We'll stay until he's passed on."

Stefanie's moan coincided with the ringing of the doorbell.

"Excuse me for a minute," her father said. While he handed out more candy, Stefanie looked up at Nick. That was the most information she'd ever heard from him. In a few seconds he'd given her father the story of his life, leaving her imagination to fill in the painful details.

That white house with the fence flashed through her mind, stabbing her with fresh guilt. Behind those walls lay a sick man.

"I'm sorry he's so ill," Stefanie said.

"It's life." Nick studied her for a minute. "Shall we go?"

She could hardly blame him for not wanting to talk about it. "I'm ready."

As they walked out the door behind the little kids, she said, "Good night, Dad."

Days before, she'd informed her father of their plans. Other than saying he wished they were going out with her friends, he'd kept any other thoughts to himself. After hearing what Nick had told them, she was sure her dad had a lot more concerns, which he'd discuss with her later.

His hazel eyes serious, he studied the two of them. "Have fun tonight."

Nick nodded. "I'll bring her home by midnight." At the end of class yesterday she'd told Nick her curfew.

They drove to the fairgrounds in what turned out to be his grandfather's blue car. Chet Atkins was playing on the radio.

"Sorry about Dad, but you know parents. He's been more protective since Mom died last year."

He stared straight ahead. "You're lucky he cares."

"I know," she whispered.

Nick's mom had just left him at his grandparents'? She couldn't comprehend it.

"If you were my daughter, I probably wouldn't let you go out with me."

She suspected he meant it.

The fairgrounds parking area was packed with cars. To her surprise, throngs of people had come to the exhibit, some in costume, some not.

"How did you know about this?"

Once he'd found a space, he shut off the engine and angled his head toward her. In the dim light he looked almost sinister. "One day I'm going to be a pilot."

You often find that an Aries is a doctor, an athlete, an astronaut or a pilot.

Stefanie felt a shiver run down her spine.

"You mean like with United Airlines or TWA?"

"No. I'm going to run my own flying service. That way I can go where I want, when I want." He eyed her intently. "I'll 'be like the bird who halting in flight on limb too slight, feels it give way beneath him, yet sings, knowing he has wings.'"

"That was beautiful. It sounded like poetry. Yours?"

"I wish. Victor Hugo. Have you noticed everything he wrote had to do with flight?"

"I've only read *Les Miserables*. But you're right. Jean Valjean was always in flight to escape Javert and the ugliness of his past life."

Very few of the boys she knew had figured out what they wanted to do in the future. The ones with ambition couldn't wait to leave Mackenzie. She doubted any of them liked poetry, let alone could quote it.

Stefanie had felt a physical attraction to him on the first day of class. Since then, his mind had fascinated her. Now that she knew something of his suffering, the tug on her heart was stronger than ever. "When did you realize you wanted to fly?"

"Forever."

While she pondered the emotion behind that statement, he put his fangs back in his mouth. "I especially like to fly at night." He said it in a chilling imitation of Bela Lugosi. When she'd been a little girl, she'd seen the 1931 film version of *Dracula* on TV. It had given her nightmares…

A nervous laugh escaped. "You've convinced me."

He reached out an index finger to the blood-red lipstick covering her mouth. His touch, though brief and light, felt strangely intimate. Then he rubbed it on his lower lip and licked it. "I like the taste of you, Vampira."

Stefanie knew he was teasing her, but her body quivered. People under the sign of Aries love to make love. Afraid he could tell what she was thinking, she got abruptly out of the car.

The next two hours were instructive as Nick showed her around the vintage planes flown during World War I. It was a new language to her. A Fokker triplane, a Sopwith Camel, a Spad, a Jenny. He probably knew more than the people running the show. The energy radiating from him told her she was in the presence of someone rather extraordinary.

He intrigued her so much, in fact, that when he suggested they leave to go through the haunted house, she didn't want to tear him away from something he clearly loved.

"Actually, I'd rather see the films. The one on the Red Baron sounds interesting."

"Liar." But he softened it with a slow smile.

"I'm serious. Mr. Detweiler has a thing for World War I, and I'd love to impress him. Wouldn't it be funny if we bumped into him here? He thinks I'm a dumb brunette."

"With your grades?"

Stefanie was pleased Nick had noticed. "I'm talking about his opinion that young people aren't observers of life."

Nick's eyes traveled over her straightened black hair. "He doesn't give us much credit, does he?" He grinned. "We'll get him started on his favorite subject and he'll forget to teach."

"Exactly."

Like partners in crime, they sat through three absorbing documentaries and ate popcorn and chocolate-nut sundaes on a stick. Before tonight, she'd known virtually nothing about William Boeing or Donald Douglas. As Nick explained, the Wright brothers' invention would've gone relatively unnoticed without the vision of the other two men.

At ten to twelve they started back home. Her father had left the porch light on. The last thing she wanted to do was go in the house.

"Thanks for tonight. I learned a great deal and had a wonderful time."

He cocked his head as if pondering the veracity of her words. "I'll see you in class," was all he said. She knew the aircraft show was important to him, but maybe he wished he'd gone alone.

"Okay." She put her key in the lock and opened the door. "Good night, Nick."

"Keep your window locked tonight." Dracula had resurfaced.

Stefanie let out a little laugh. He didn't reciprocate; instead he melted into the darkness. She entered the house on the stroke of midnight.

But the clock had only chimed six times.

In shock, Stefanie lifted her head. This wasn't Halloween night. She'd been so immersed in the past she felt as though she was between two worlds. It didn't seem possible there'd been no word about Nick yet. Her glance fell on the next entry.

November 1, 1973
This weekend has gone on forever. I've been waiting in the hope Nick might phone me. After church, Dad asked if I wanted to drive over to the grandparents with him. I told him I needed to stay home to study for a Chemistry test. But the truth is, Nick doesn't have my grandparents' phone number. I'm going to have to wait this out until tomorrow.

The next morning, Stefanie sat at her desk, heart pounding, watching for him. He walked in as the bell rang. Was it on purpose so he wouldn't have to talk to her? Her spirits sank at the thought that he might never again reveal that secret part of his psyche she'd glimpsed for a few precious moments.

Mr. Detweiler started marking roll. She raised her hand.

"Yes, Stefanie?"

"Did you happen to go to the aircraft show at the fair-grounds over the weekend?"

He nodded. "I'm assuming you went, too?"

"Yes."

"What did you think?"

"I don't see how anyone had the courage to fly those planes. They looked like oversize toys."

"That's what they were. The men who flew them had a

daring most people can't even grasp. Are you familiar with *The Little Prince?*"

"We read it in French class." This was her sixth year of French. She loved that book.

He adjusted his glasses. "If you read one of Saint-Exupery's other books, you'll gain some insights into flying. Did you watch any of the documentaries at the show?"

"All of them," she answered and was pleased to see the surprised look on his face. "What I don't understand is why William Boeing was demonized after the contributions he made to aviation."

The second she put forth her comment she felt a subtle tug on the hair she'd washed half a dozen times to get rid of the black dye. Nick's touch set off an explosion in her stomach not unlike a burst of fizz. The bubbles just kept popping in every part of her body.

Mr. Detweiler got out of his chair. "You bring up an excellent point that characterizes the climate of the country during the Great Depression."

Several of the students flashed her looks of approval as their teacher launched into a monologue that got everyone off the hook for the rest of class. She didn't hear much of what he said. She was too mesmerized by Nick, who'd stretched out his long, muscular legs, allowing his foot to nudge the heel of her right shoe beneath the chair.

When the bell rang, a note fell into her lap. *You had him going, Miss Larkin. What will your encore be tomorrow?*

She turned to tell him, but he'd disappeared.

Deflated that he wasn't waiting for her in the hall, she made it through the day—barely. By the next morning she was so anxious to see him she walked into class feeling feverish.

Nick had gotten there first. He nodded to her, but he was doing his homework and only said hello. It set a pattern for the weeks that followed. They'd say hi coming and going, but he kept conversation to a minimum. No mention of another date. Something had gone wrong, but she didn't know what. Or why.

Something was wrong with Nick—

Stefanie jumped up and phoned the office. She got voice mail. Maybe Dena was talking to someone who knew Nick's location.

She checked her watch. Too much time had passed with no news.

She bowed her head. *I can't stand this*—

Her grief echoed the next entry.

Chapter 3

December 22, 1973

Tomorrow's the last day of class before Christmas break. I've given up any hope of Nick's being interested in me. I know I haven't done anything, so it's a case of his not being attracted, after all.

There've been times I went on a first date with a guy, only to discover I didn't want to repeat the experience. But this is the first time I've been on the receiving end of that situation.

The girls have told me to get over it. Sometimes they've seemed quite cruel, and I feel like they're mocking me. I don't talk about Nick around them, but they make their little remarks anyway. I wish Mom were here to confide in.

Last night I broke down and called Liz. I told her

about Nick. She listened and commiserated with me, but she didn't have any advice. I could tell she wasn't really that interested because she's in love with Don and wants to talk about him.

It's so hard to sit in front of Nick every day and not exchange more than a few words with him. When school starts again in January, Mr. Detweiler will assign new seats. I can't transfer out of the class, but at least I'll be able to sit in another part of the room.

She'd walked halfway to the flagpole the next day, where her friends were waiting, when a hand reached out to slow her down. She turned to see Nick standing there, wearing a black-and-gray parka. "Hi."

Stefanie stared up at him, uncomprehending.

"The weather's going to be perfect tomorrow. Do you want to go tubing with me and Fred?"

It wouldn't matter to her whether they slid down a snowy hill on a sled or on an inflated inner tube. All she wanted was to be with Nick. Keeping up with his moods was like riding The Rocket at the amusement park. Upside down and around in a dizzying circle. "Who's Fred?"

"Uncle Walt's dog. I've got him trained so he'll drag the tube back up the hill and save me the trouble."

Their smiles caught and held. She didn't know if he was teasing her or not. Almost four months had gone by since she'd written Nick that apology and asked about the dog's gender.

"If I wasn't going to Hawaii with my family for the holidays, I'd like that a lot."

Last year, she and her dad had made the mistake of

staying home for Christmas. Neither of them wanted to go through this one without her mother, so they'd decided to fly to Maui with the grandparents. Richard and his wife, Colleen, would be coming, too, and Liz of course. She was bringing her fiancé.

Nick was quiet for a moment before he said, "Then I guess I'll see you when school starts."

How did he do it? After endless weeks of seeming indifferent to her, what was going on? If this was some kind of game he was playing, it hurt too much. Worst of all, why did she want to be with him now more than ever? It simply made no sense.

"I'll be back in time for New Year's Eve day," she said. "Do you want to go tubing then?" she blurted. When would she ever learn?

"I have to work."

He didn't give an inch.

"How's your uncle Walt?" she asked to smother her disappointment that Nick wouldn't suggest another time.

"Not good."

"That must be hard on all of you."

Nick looked grim. "He never complains."

She believed him. Being the tough, silent type obviously ran in the Marsden genes. "I guess I'd better go. My friends are waiting." Instead of walking to her grandfather's office, as she usually did, she was getting a ride from Sara.

Before she and Nick parted, he pulled a small wrapped present from inside his parka and handed it to her. It felt like a book. "Merry Christmas, Stefanie."

He must have assumed she wouldn't go tubing with him, otherwise he wouldn't have been prepared to give this to her now. Why, oh why, hadn't he asked her sooner? She didn't have anything to give him!

"Thank you, Nick. Merry Christmas."

He nodded, then walked off in the opposite direction.

The girls waited until they'd reached Sara's car before badgering her with questions. She wouldn't tell them anything. They didn't understand what was happening to her. Not even she did. In truth, she was too conflicted by emotions to talk and preferred to open his gift when she could do it in privacy.

Once home alone in her room, she dumped her books on the bed and tore off the wrapping paper.

Night Flight. Antoine de Saint-Exupery.

With trembling hands she opened the front cover. Nick had written a comment on the title page. *This is one of the books old man Detweiler was referring to. Enjoy.* He'd signed it with his initials.

Wonderful as Hawaii turned out to be, Stefanie couldn't wait for New Year's Eve. They flew into Mackenzie from Seattle on the morning of December thirty-first.

The sun shone, although it was only five degrees above zero. As soon as she'd unpacked and changed into jeans and a sweater, she looked up the name Marsden in the phone directory. There was only one. Walter Marsden on Spruce Street.

Maybe it was forward of her to call Nick, but he *had* asked her out and had given her a present. It couldn't hurt to let him know she was home again. Without wasting another minute, she dialed the number.

"Hello?" an older woman's voice answered.

"Hello. This is Stefanie Larkin. I'm a friend of Nick's

from school. I'd like to speak to him if I could, but he told me he'd have to work today. When will he be home?"

"Not for a while. He left for his job at nine."

That was six hours ago. Closing her eyes, she said, "Could you tell me where he works? I've been away on a trip and brought him some presents that won't keep long."

A prolonged silence made her think his grandmother wasn't going to give her the address. "Just before you reach the airport," the woman finally said, "there's a road that turns to the left. It winds back a mile and then you'll see Van Langeveld's Air Cargo Company."

Of course. Where else would Nick be working? Stefanie remembered driving there with her mom to pick up a crate of tulip and daffodil bulbs that had been shipped from Holland. Her parents had spent a lot of time working together on the garden.

"Thank you very much."

"You're welcome."

"Mrs. Marsden?" she said at the last second. "How's your husband's brother? Nick told me he'd been ill."

"We buried him two days after Christmas."

An emptiness for Nick's sake welled up inside Stefanie. "I'm sorry for your loss." How was he dealing with the pain? His life was so hard and had been from childhood. When Stefanie had lost her mother, she'd had her father and siblings. Her grandparents.

Of course, he had his grandparents, but otherwise he was alone. It made her heart shiver.

"He's gone to a better place," the older woman said.

"I believe that, too." Walter Marsden was released from his misery. Stefanie suddenly felt as if she'd been punched, because this meant Nick and his grandparents might be leaving Mackenzie before long. That was what he'd told her father on Halloween night.

"Thanks again for the information. Goodbye."

She pulled on her parka and ran through the house. "Dad? I need the car for a little while!"

"Go ahead!" he called from his study, where he was catching up on the mail. They'd been sent a ton of Christmas cards. "On second thought, take the truck."

"Okay." It handled better in the snow, and there'd been a storm the day before.

Stefanie made a detour to the kitchen and pulled a box out of the fridge. Then, grabbing the big sack she'd placed on the counter, she hurried into the garage. The truck had already been warmed up by their drive home from the airport.

She retraced their tracks, taking the turnoff Mrs. Marsden had told her about. After another mile, she came to Van Langeveld's, where she saw an unfamiliar truck parked outside the WWII wooden structure that needed new paint.

Beyond it she noticed the hangar and runway. Someone was operating a snow-removal machine. Though her pulse rate had increased, she sat for a few minutes trying to decide if she recognized him.

The machine drew closer, making a sweeping arc to push the snow into a huge embankment. She caught sight of a black-and-gray parka. Without hesitation she jumped down from the truck's cab with her gifts and started waving. "Nick!"

After a moment he waved back, then drove the machine into the hangar. Stefanie made her way over the newly plowed parking area into the warmth of the office. Holding the box under one arm, she put the sack on the counter. There were two desks behind it and lots of maps on the wall opposite the windows.

From the hallway she heard a door open and close. By the time Nick appeared, bringing the cold in with him, she could scarcely stand still, she was so excited to see him. He came closer, removing his parka and gloves, which he tossed on one of the chairs. The long-sleeved flannel shirt in a blue plaid looked new and suited him. Something he'd received for Christmas?

"I called your house," she said, speaking first. "Your grandmother told me where I could find you. I hope you don't mind."

"I don't mind." The freezing cold seemed to have turned his eyes a deep cobalt as they roved over her. "Your skin's golden. You look like an ad for Florida orange juice."

He made few personal remarks, but whenever he did, her legs went weak. "You've got your fruits mixed up." She pushed the sack in front of him. "Merry Christmas."

Nick glanced inside, then raised his eyes. "We'll have to celebrate."

Her heart rate accelerated. "Are you sure it's all right? I wouldn't want to get you in trouble with your boss."

"Dries is taking the week off."

"That's an unusual name."

"It's short for Andries. Only his closest friends call him Dries. He's a Dutchman who was a crack fighter pilot in 1942."

"Why did he come here?"

"When the Dutch government went into exile in London, they decided to form a flying school in the States. He'd lost his parents in the war, so he agreed to go to Sioux Falls to train other pilots."

"How did he end up in Mackenzie?"

"On a chance flight. He took one look at the mountains and decided that when he got out of the service he'd settle here. Most people call him D.V.L.," he added.

"You must've been thrilled to get a job with him."

He nodded. "I hung around until he agreed to give me flying lessons in exchange for working for him."

Flying lessons—so *that* was why he never had time for anything else, why he often seemed tired during class.

"Except for sweeping up, everything's done for today," he was saying. "Lock that door, then come with me."

She turned to do his bidding, but excitement made her clumsy and she fumbled with the lock.

Nick joined her. "It's stubborn," he muttered. "I'll do it."

While he performed the simple task, she opened the box and held out the yellow-and-white lei she'd brought him. "Aloha, Nick."

Its sweet perfume filled the air. In the hushed silence he said, "Why don't you put it on me."

"L-lower your head," she stammered.

When he obliged, she placed it around his neck. The moment she started to draw away, his arms pulled her into his body. Her own arms slid around his waist, and she looked up at him, startled.

Nick gazed at her in a way that pierced her to her soul. "I've never worn a lei before, but I do know I'm supposed to say aloha back."

Something in his husky tone sent a voluptuous warmth through her body. While she waited to hear him say the word, she felt his breath on her lips, then his mouth descended.

She'd kissed other boys. In fact, she'd made out with several and had enjoyed it.

This was different.

The only way she could describe it was that this was a man's kiss. Once her mouth opened to the masterful pressure of his, she forgot where they were. Like a firework that shot sparks higher and higher, sensation upon sensation bombarded her.

Nick knew what he was doing every second to provoke such an intense response. He didn't use words, yet he made her feel new and wonderful things. Exciting things. She would never, ever be the same again.

His lips traveled over her face as if he loved the taste of her skin. "Better than pineapple and coconuts," he murmured.

She should've been the one to call a halt sooner. Afraid he thought she was out of control, Stefanie eased away from his arms and picked up the empty box and lid. He reached for the sack.

She followed him around the end of the counter and down the hall to a makeshift kitchen. Besides a sink, there were a few cupboards, a card table and two chairs next to a window, a hot plate for coffee and a refrigerator. He put the sack on the counter and pulled out the pineapple.

"This smells so sweet I think I have to eat some of it now. We'll save the coconut for later."

Later when? Tonight? Tomorrow?

After locating a knife in the drawer, he put the pineapple on a plate and set it on the table. Stefanie watched him get two more plates and napkins. He knew his way around this kitchen.

She took off her parka and hung it over the back of the chair. "I brought you something else." One more dip into the sack produced a can of macadamia nuts. With the little attached key, she unwound the band and put the nuts on the table.

Nick popped a handful of them in his mouth while he sliced off the outer layer of pineapple. In another couple of minutes they were both eating mouthwatering chunks of the fruit, juice dribbling down their chins.

"Umm," was the only sound she heard from Nick as he finished off what she couldn't eat. "You've done a terrible thing."

Stefanie understood what he meant. "I know. There's nothing like it fresh from the fields. I picked this one myself."

His eyes bore into hers. "There's nothing like it at three above zero when all you've eaten is a ham sandwich before work. It's the perfect gift. Thank you."

"Thank you for yours." Since receiving her Christmas present, she had a greater understanding of why he was different from the other guys at school. "I loved the book, Nick."

"You read it?"

"Of course."

His eyes flared.

"I could *feel* the sensation of flying. When I finished the book, my father and then my brother read it, too."

Nick nodded. "In my opinion, Exupery described flight better than anyone has before or since."

"After going to the aircraft show, I could picture him in

one of those open-cockpit biplanes, facing the elements. I gained new perspectives not only on flight but on the human condition."

"He had a real skill, didn't he?"

Stefanie nodded enthusiastically. "Thanks to my mom in particular, I've always been a big reader—and I have to tell you, it was one of the most wonderfully written books I've ever read. Saint-Exupery was a pilot with a poet's soul. I've found a new favorite author."

"If you liked him that much, you should read *Southern Mail*."

"I read it on the trip. I also read *Wind, Sand and Stars, Airman's Odyssey* and *Flight to Arras*," she confessed. "I bought them at a bookstore in Waikiki."

"*Flight to Arras* is my favorite," he said.

It had been hers, too. "I can see why. He saw France's decline from a unique vantage point. I was interested to learn he married a South American."

"That's right. He called her his tropical bird."

Stefanie chuckled. "After having read *The Little Prince,* I wasn't surprised he'd say that."

"The rose represented his wife, you know."

She nodded again. "The sentiments in *The Little Prince* were so sweet and insightful they made me laugh and cry at the same time." She took a deep breath. "But *Flight to Arras* helped me understand *you*," she added quietly.

His body stilled. "When did you have time to enjoy Hawaii?"

"Oh, I found ways. Give me a book to read in the sun…"

Just when things felt natural and they were sharing their thoughts and feelings, he glanced at his watch, breaking the spell. She could've wept to see him get up from the table and begin clearing it. Over his shoulder he said, "I'm afraid it's too late and too cold to go tubing."

Tubing hadn't even occurred to her. She didn't want this moment to end. "When you're through working, would you like to come over to my house and listen to records? Bring some of your own if you like. Or we could watch TV and see the new year in."

"I can't." He'd begun to wash the plates and had spoken with his back toward her.

Was he warning her off? Now that she'd delivered her gifts, she could leave?

Don't beg. This is where he works. She knew he was probably breaking the rules to let her be here with him. She shouldn't have come, but she hadn't been able to help herself.

Maybe he worked as a night watchman, too, in order to make a little more money. There was so much she didn't know about him. What she learned had to be found out in bits and pieces when he felt like confiding in her. She had to constantly wait for the next time. It was unbearable.

"Well, it's getting dark, so I'd better go." Since he was standing at the sink, she wiped her hands with a couple of napkins, but they were still sticky when she put on her parka.

"I'll walk you out."

He was going to let her leave just like that? No questions asked?

"It's okay, Nick. I can find my way. I realize you still have work to do."

She made it to the front door of the office before he

caught up to her. Though her eyelids prickled, by some miracle she held back her tears.

"I promised my grandparents I'd help finish packing. We're driving to Eureka tomorrow."

She gasped despite herself. Tomorrow?

She'd known it would be soon, but *tomorrow?* "I…I heard about your uncle Walter."

"It was for the best."

Everything was for the best.

How did he hold it all in without screaming? But maybe he didn't want to scream. Maybe he was one of those people whose life experiences had closed him off to feeling.

"Can't they stay a bit longer for your sake? Pulling you out of school now will be hard on you."

He averted his eyes. "They're anxious to get home. Uncle Walt was renting that house. The landlord already has someone else lined up to move in on Tuesday."

"I see." She took a shuddering breath. "Does that mean I won't be seeing you again?"

"Probably not."

Probably not?

Adrenaline helped her unfasten the difficult lock and open the door. She welcomed the frigid air. "Considering the circumstances, *aloha* does appear to be the appropriate word here. Goodbye, Nick. Take care."

She made her exit with as much grace as possible. It wasn't until she joined the main road leading into town that she began to cry. She sobbed all the way home.

Though there was a big New Year's Eve party at Joey Johnson's house, Stefanie couldn't bring herself to go, not even when Penny and Sara begged her. She was too heart-broken to be around other people, and the long flight had tired her. Her father had decided to turn in early, too.

After her mother's death, she'd been inconsolable, but she'd had her father and siblings who'd needed her, just as she needed them. Along with her grieving grandparents, they'd all gotten through the experience together and were doing better these days.

What she felt tonight was a different kind of pain. No one could ease her suffering. No one except Nick. With one thrust of the knife he'd been cut out of her life. It was always going to be winter for her now.

"Nick!" she cried.

Once again the grandfather clock chimed, sounding the half hour. She could hear the wind blowing the snow against the windows, increasing her anguish. Six-thirty already.

Stefanie tried Dena again without results. She was still on the phone trying to track Nick down. When Stefanie rang Dena's cell phone, she was told to leave a message. Maybe her husband Grant was helping her. The two of them knew the right people to call.

Keep reading, Stefanie, before you jump out of your skin.

January 2, 1974
Tonight I wish Anne Morrow Lindbergh's words could help me. She's been where I am right now.

"It is when we desire continuity of being loved alone that we go wrong. For not only do we insist on believing romantically in the one-and-only—the one-and-only love, the one-and-only mate, the one-and-only mother, the one-and-only security—we wish the one-and-only to be permanent, ever-present and continuous.

"The desire for continuity of being 'loved' alone seems to me the error bred in the bone of man. For there is no one-and-only, as a friend of mine once said in a similar discussion. There are just one-and-only moments."

Is that what I've experienced with Nick then? A one-and-only moment never to be repeated?

Once the bell rang Wednesday morning, Mr. Detweiler said, "Welcome back to reality. Before we get started, who wants to change seats? Speak now or forever hold your peace."

Six students raised their hands.

Knowing the significance of the empty desk behind her, Stefanie didn't see the point of moving. Her teacher sent her a curious glance as he told them to find new seats. "Any students who aren't here this morning will have to take what's left when they decide to show up."

Carrie Briggs slid into Nick's desk. She chatted with Stefanie, who had no idea what the other girl was saying because she was in too much pain. The rest of the short week passed in a blur. When her dad had to go to Kalispell for a bankers' convention that weekend, she went with him because she couldn't bear her own company.

When she entered class Monday morning, she wasn't prepared to see a familiar male body at his usual place behind her desk. The tardy bell hadn't rung yet. There was no sign of their teacher.

She moved up the aisle toward him, half disbelieving. *"Nick?"*

He turned his dark head. The intensity of his gaze made the blood pound in her ears. "Aloha."

"A-are you here just for today, or—"

"For the rest of the year."

Joy.

She sat sideways at her desk "Where are you living?"

"With Dries. He offered to let me stay with him."

She loved that man without even having met him.

"Uncle Walt gave me his truck before he died, so I'm set."

That explained the truck she'd seen outside D.V.L.'s office. "How are your grandparents taking it?"

"I always planned to move out when I turned eighteen. What's two months?"

Nick's birthday was March twenty-second. With the date indelibly impressed in her memory, she was already planning something special for him. She would tell him now so he'd have no excuse not to remember it. But before she could speak, Carrie appeared.

"Hi, Nick." She leaned close to him as if she had the right. "Did you know you're sitting in my seat?" Her over-friendly demeanor brought out Stefanie's jealousy.

His glance swerved to the other girl. "Since when?"

"Since Wednesday, when Mr. Detweiler let us choose new ones."

Nick glanced back at Stefanie. "You didn't want to move?"

"No. You did say *probably* not."

For some reason her answer seemed to satisfy him, because he smiled at her before standing up. Ignoring Carrie, which pleased Stefanie, he walked to the back of the class. After the bell rang, he found an empty seat on the opposite side of the room.

Mr. Detweiler came in late. "Nice of you to join us, Mr. Marsden," he said, looking around. "Please see me after class."

"Yes, sir."

Stefanie wrote him a note.

Chapter 4

Nick, I'm so glad you're staying in Mackenzie. I know you have to work a lot of hours, but I'd like to plan something special for Valentine's and your birthday. If you tell D.V.L. now, there shouldn't be a problem getting the time off. Let me know. Stefanie. (550-0555)

Once class had ended, she waited outside the door for him. Four minutes passed before he emerged. They were both going to be late for their next class.

"Here." She handed it to him.

He studied the note, then tucked it in his jeans pocket. "Meet me in the parking lot after school and I'll drive you home."

Her heart did a kick. "You don't have to rush right back to the field?"

"Not today. Dries knows I've got some homework to catch up on. Mind if I borrow your notes from Detweiler's class?"

"If you'll do your homework at my house, I'll let you copy them."

He smiled. "Sounds like a bribe."

"It is."

The bell for second period rang. Tardy slips for both of them.

He stared at her for a moment, then nodded.

She thought three o'clock would never come. Toward the end of Gym, when the class had gone to the shower room, Sara caught up to Stefanie, who'd showered quickly without getting her hair wet.

"You want to come with me and Penny after school? I have to go to the dentist. Afterward we could stop for a Coke."

Stefanie dried off and started to get dressed. "I would, but I can't."

"How come?"

"Nick's back in school."

"You're kidding!"

"No. He's living with the pilot who owns Van Lange-veld's Air Cargo. The uncle who had cancer gave him his truck before he died, so Nick's going to drive me home."

"Joey's not going to be happy when he hears that."

"Sara, how come you keep talking to me about Joey? You know we're just friends."

"He'd like to be a lot more," she said with a sigh, "and I told him I'd try to help him out. He's planning to ask you to the Valentine's dance, and he says Frank is going to ask me."

Suddenly it dawned on Stefanie that Sara was crazy about Joey and was pretending to be his friend to stay close to him.

She shut her locker and turned to her. "I'm hoping Nick will want to spend Valentine's with me. When you're in German class tomorrow, let Joey know without hurting his feelings that I've already got plans."

"It's going to hurt him, Stef."

"I can't help that."

"I know. Just be careful, okay?"

"What do you mean?"

"I'd hate to see *you* get hurt."

"Why do you say that?"

"You've changed since you met Nick. Penny says the same thing."

That comment stung. "How?"

She shrugged her shoulders. "You just have. How much do you really know about Nick?"

"Enough."

Sara's eyes frosted over as she put on her parka. "Got to go."

Hurt by the way her friend had talked to her, Stefanie pulled on her winter coat while she waited for Sara to leave the gym first with some of the other girls. Picking up her books and the bag with her gym suit, Stefanie hurried through the rear exit of the school toward the parking lot.

At first she didn't see the faded red truck. A horn honked behind her. When she spun around, she discovered Nick at the wheel. Knowing he'd been waiting for her drove every other thought from her mind.

He jumped out and assisted her into the passenger seat. A bunch of students saw them drive off, including Sara and Penny.

"How come they didn't wave to you?"

Nothing got past Nick. "They wanted me to go with them."

Nick slowed the truck to a stop. "You still can."

"Have you changed your mind?" she asked anxiously.

"No."

"Neither have I."

With a resolute jaw, he put the truck in second gear and they pulled onto the main street. Casting her a sideways glance, he said, "Ever been to Naylor's?"

"No."

"It's a drugstore over by Uncle Walt's house. The soda fountain is famous for a drink they make. I always get one on my way to work."

She smiled. "What's in it?"

"Cola with cherry, chocolate, lemon and lime flavorings."

"All at once?"

"I promise you'll like it."

As soon as Stefanie had her first taste of one, she could understand why Nick was hooked. She'd never drunk anything so delicious. Maybe that was because she'd never been happier in her life.

The drive to her house didn't take long since the streets had been plowed since the latest storm yesterday.

"Come on in." She led Nick to the living room off the foyer and through the French doors to the library. Her house had tall ceilings and deep cornices. "This is where I usually study." Books and record albums, mostly operas, filled two walls of the floor-to-ceiling bookcases.

Two gold damask chairs and a cherry-red overstuffed chair had been arranged around the room by her mother with real flair. Since her death, her dad hadn't wanted anything changed. Stefanie agreed.

She sought out the comfortable velvet couch a few shades darker than the forest-green carpet. A flowered chintz covered the windows behind it. When they'd taken off their parkas, Nick looked all around with obvious interest.

"The material is called Shakespeare's Garden. As you can tell, my mom loved color. When Eldredge's came to lay the carpet, Mr. Eldredge said it was too overpowering, but she just smiled—and she was right. Dad always said my mom was a great romantic."

"This room explains you," Nick murmured, but he was studying the titles of books as he said it. "Milton, Shakespeare, Chekhov, Hemingway, O'Neill, Melville, Hardy, Emerson, Molìere." He turned to her. "Have you read all these?"

"A lot of them. Mom read to us all the time growing up. She loved novels, short stories, plays, biographies. Anything. Of course, it's what she taught at school." She gestured at the shelves. "Every Saturday morning we had to clean. Part of our job was to dust all the books. She'd put on an opera like *La Bohème* and we'd get busy while she explained what was going on. My sister Liz and my brother Richard couldn't wait to be done."

Nick flashed her a lopsided smile. "But not you."

"No." She smiled back. "If it hadn't been for her, I would never have understood opera. Or novels like *Hedda Gabler* and *The Fountainhead*—to mention only two."

He returned to his scrutiny of titles. She loved watching him to see what captured his interest. "My grandfather liked to climb when he was young. He collected Westerns and mountain-climbing stories. I've read *The White Tower.*"

"That's one I haven't read."

"It's good."

"*The Treasure of the Sierra Madre* is in there somewhere."

Nick nodded. "I've read that, too."

"Excuse me for a minute while I get us some snacks."

She hurried through the house to the kitchen and brought back a bag of potato chips and a couple of cans of sausages. It was the best she could come up with until she or her dad went to the store.

After putting everything, including napkins, on the coffee table, she walked over to Nick. He'd pulled a book from the shelf and seemed engrossed in it.

"What have you got there?"

"*The Sea Hawk.* I've seen the film with Errol Flynn but never read it."

"Sabatini's a fabulous writer. He wrote *Scaramouche* and *Captain Blood,* too, one of my favorites. Errol Flynn was my father's favorite actor."

"I like those old movies, too," Nick said. "I used to pretend I was Robin Hood when I was a kid. Then I saw him in *Dive Bomber* and it changed my life."

"I never saw that."

"We'll have to hope it shows up on TV one day so you can improve your education."

"What's the plot? Besides bombing, of course."

One corner of his mouth lifted. "Flynn did a brilliant portrayal of a pilot in the navy just before the U.S. entered World War II. The air sequences include shots of Vindicators and Curtiss Hawks."

"Like the one we saw."

He nodded. "The carrier scenes are set on the *Enterprise* the year before the ship fought in Midway."

Without hesitation she plucked both Sabatini books from the shelf. "Take all three of these. But let me give you fair warning—you won't get your homework done."

"What homework?"

Their eyes met. She'd never seen his full smile before. It had to be the rarest of occurrences.

"Well, in that case, Nick, there's one more book I have in mind. Maybe you'll read it out loud to me."

"You'd like me to read to you?"

"Yes," she said over her shoulder. "You probably have it memorized, anyway. Sit on the couch and I'll bring it to you."

After she'd found *The Spirit of St. Louis,* she handed it to him.

He stared at the cover, then raised his head. "I may not have memorized it, but there are passages…"

"That's what my mom used to say. If she loved a book, she'd find her favorite lines for me so I'd get excited to read it even if I didn't think I wanted to. It worked every time." Stefanie sank down next to him. After urging him to eat, she sat back. "Go on, Charles. Enchant me."

Nick put his arm around her and read to her for a while, making Lindbergh's solo flight across the Atlantic come alive. But at one point he closed the book and began kissing her. She'd been waiting for it.

With Nick, nothing felt awkward. They gravitated to each other in a natural progression of need. His mouth drew her into a maelstrom of increasing ecstasy. This level of communication changed her perceptions of everything she'd originally thought about the relationship between a man and a woman.

She was beginning to understand the meaning of rapture, a rapture so powerful she wanted to be swept away and never return to the place she'd been before. Her enchantment was so great she didn't realize her father had entered the house until she heard him call from the foyer.

"Stefanie?"

To have to put an end to this kind of passion brought her actual physical pain. "I can't believe he's home already," she muttered.

Nick's reluctance to let go of her gave evidence of his own entrancement. He checked his watch. "It's going on six," he whispered.

She'd lost track of the time. "I'm in the library, Dad! Nick's with me."

While she was gathering up the half-empty sack of chips and the sausage cans, her father appeared in the doorway.

"Hello, Nick."

"Mr. Larkin." He'd gotten to his feet.

"I wondered who belonged to that truck. I didn't know you were back in Mackenzie."

"He's made arrangements to stay with his boss for the rest of the school year, Dad. We were just doing our homework. He has a couple of days to catch up on."

"I hope you got lots of work done," he said with a deadpan face. "In case you forgot, Stefanie, your grandmother's invited us for dinner."

Stefanie *had* forgotten; she'd forgotten everything. She turned to Nick, who by now had put on his coat. "Here." She placed her loose-leaf binder on top of the books she'd given him. "I'll get it back from you in the morning."

"You're sure?"

"Positive." There was no way she'd be able to concentrate on her studies tonight.

The three of them walked to the front door.

"See you tomorrow," he whispered. She nodded. "Good night, Mr. Larkin."

"Good night, Nick."

The door opened and closed.

Her father stared at her. "So… He's back."

"Yes."

"I guess I don't have to ask if you're happy about it. Do me one favor, though."

"What?"

"Be careful."

Sara had said that, too, although Stefanie knew her motive wasn't the same. "We were just reading and eating."

"And other things," he drawled. "I wasn't born yesterday. Yes, I'm concerned to find you alone in the house with him, but it's more than that."

"More?"

"You wear your heart on your sleeve. I can see exactly how you feel, sweetie, because you're a giver. You don't hold back your emotions."

"You make that sound like something bad."

"On the contrary, it's the greatest gift in the world. You remind me so much of your mother it hurts. But you're too young to get this involved."

"Involved?" she cried. "I've hardly ever been with Nick outside of our first-period class."

"I'm talking emotional involvement. That's different. *Nick* is different. There's no one around here like him. I can see that. But I can see something else."

"You don't like him."

"That's not it. He's mature in some ways, but he's still young and needy. Without his grandparents, he's going to depend on you more and more. Bringing you home from school today is a case in point." He paused. "That was all about what Nick wanted, not about doing *you* a favor."

"But—"

"You're missing your mother, so you're extremely vulnerable. I want you to promise me you won't accept rides home with him anymore. When he wants to be with you, he should make a date for a weekend night, preferably a group date."

"He doesn't have a lot of friends here."

"If you want to be with him, then you need to suggest that some of your friends go along. That's always been the rule at our house. Until you met Nick, it's never been a problem."

"It's not his fault!"

"I didn't say it was. *You* have to be the one to set the boundaries. Think about it while we drive over to your grandmother's."

"I'm not hungry. I'd rather you went without me."

She raced up the staircase to her room.

January 9, 1974

For the first time in my life, Dad doesn't understand. He simply doesn't understand. No one does. I don't want to be with other people. Nick is my joy. He knows me better than I know myself.

Mother once told me she and Dad complemented each other. I didn't know what she meant. Now I do. It's a matter of being together without having to explain anything. You just exist for the other person without any striving. With him I feel whole, even when we're not physically together.

Nick completes me. Things other people say and do no longer hurt because he heals me.

How odd to think there are millions and millions of people who don't realize there's a huge part still missing. Many of them live a whole lifetime and die without ever knowing that.

I'm the luckiest woman ever to have happened on this discovery. Nick's my missing part. Like solving for X, Y or Z, the solution's always been out there. But the chance of finding it is as serendipitous as Nick being seated behind me the first day of class.

At school the next morning Nick put the loose-leaf binder on her desk before walking to his seat. While Mr. Detweiler was writing an assignment on the board, she opened the cover. Nick had written her a message.

Thanks for the notes and the books. I've asked Dries for time off on Valentine's. It'll be a Friday, but school gets out early that day. How would you like to drive to Eureka with me right after class so I can check on my grandparents? It's only an hour-and-a-half trip. You can read to me. I promise I'll have you home by midnight. Give me your answer in the cafeteria at lunch. N.M.

Stefanie had never imagined that the school cafeteria would become her favorite place. But from then on those stolen twenty-five minutes with Nick five days a week made it possible for them to be together without her father knowing it. Sometimes Frank sat with them.

While mayhem exploded all around them, Stefanie sat there oblivious and talked to Nick across the table. She treasured this time alone with him, time when she didn't have to share him with flying lessons or his job. Pretty soon she'd be going on a little trip with him.

On Friday the fourteenth, five weeks later, Stefanie got up early to make breakfast. "Happy Valentine's Day, Dad." She leaned over her father's shoulder and handed him a gift with a card.

He kissed her cheek. "Well, this is a nice surprise." He opened her valentine first. "I love it."

"You'll like your present more."

With a laugh he tore open the wrapping on the square box. "Golf balls!"

"I know you're waiting for golf season with bated breath, Dad. I sent some to Richard, too. Put these on your desk at work and dream. Maybe we'll have an early spring this year."

"Maybe we'll go to Mars this year, too! I have to admit I can't wait to tee off. Thanks, sweetie. So what are your plans for tonight?"

"Nick asked me out."

Her father sobered. "I expected as much."

"There's just one problem. He promised to visit his grandparents, so he asked me to drive to Eureka with him after school. We'll be back before midnight." She bit her lip. "Before you say no, Nick checked with the highway patrol. The roads are clear and there's no storm forecast.

He has tools in the truck in case anything goes wrong and he keeps a container of gas in the back."

He finished eating his bacon and eggs without saying a word.

"School's out at twelve-thirty. We'll be in Eureka by two, two-fifteen. I'll call you from his house so you'll know we got there safely. Nick wants me to meet his grandparents. You can even speak to them if you'd like."

When he still didn't answer, she said, "I told Nick you wouldn't give your permission. He said he wouldn't take me if I didn't have it. So I guess that's that."

She pushed herself away from the table.

"Stefanie, wait."

"I know what you're going to say, Dad."

"No, you don't. I want to thank you for being honest with me. It's all right with me if you go."

"Oh, Dad—thank you!" She threw her arms around his neck.

"You're welcome. Grab your stuff and I'll drive you to school. All I ask is that you call me when you're ready to start home from Eureka."

"I promise! And if by any chance you need to get in touch with me, call Van Langeveld's Air Cargo. D.V.L. will know the Marsdens' number."

"D.V.L.?"

"He's the owner, the man Nick lives with. I guess I never told you his name."

"What does the D stand for?"

"Dries. He's Dutch."

"I couldn't tell," he said drily.

"*Dad!*" They grinned at each other. She felt a new appreciation for his sometimes sarcastic humor—and for him.

Nick didn't have money except enough for the necessities, so she packed enough lunch for both of them to eat on the way. She put it in an airline bag, along with a Jack London novel and a camera. So far, she didn't have a picture of Nick, but on this trip she was determined to get one, as well as some with his grandparents and Fred.

When he walked into class that morning, she gave him the victory sign. He didn't react, but that was his way. She knew he'd seen it. At the end of class, as she walked out the door, he was standing on the other side of it and squeezed her arm. "See you in the parking lot after our last class."

Excitement exploded inside her body.

Three hours later they drove away from the school. He darted her a glance. "Are you hungry?"

"Yes, and I know you are, too." She reached inside the bag and passed him a cheese-and-bologna sandwich, then took one herself. "I have sodas for when you get thirsty."

He kissed her cheek, then her mouth, before taking a bite.

By the time they'd finished eating, Mackenzie lay far behind them. Stefanie felt inside the bag and pulled out the book.

Nick leaned closer to see the title. *"White Fang."*

"Have you read it?"

"No."

"Neither have I. My brother says it's his all-time favorite. He always loved animal stories."

"Not you?"

"No. They make me cry."

"Why?"

"Well, Dumbo's mother was kidnapped, and Bambi's mother was shot by a hunter."

"So you read *War and Peace* instead, where thousands of mothers got killed," he said with a straight face.

She chuckled. "I know it doesn't make sense."

"It doesn't have to." He stole another kiss from her parted lips. Only then did she remember that his mother had abandoned him. She wished she hadn't touched on the subject.

"Let's hear this story that makes your big brother tick."

He was so good at hiding his feelings you didn't dare blink or you'd miss a vital piece of information about his personality.

Stefanie settled back and started to read. From the first page they were both caught up in the story. Surrounded by the wintry landscape, she felt transported to a world of permanent ice and snow.

"'Running at the forefront of the pack was a large gray wolf—one of its several leaders. It was he who directed the pack's course on the heels of the she-wolf. It was he who snarled warningly at the younger members of the pack or slashed at them with his fangs when they ambitiously tried to pass him. And it was he who increased the pace when he sighted the she-wolf, now trotting slowly across the snow.

"'She dropped in alongside by him, as though it were her appointed position, and took the pace of the pack. He did not snarl at her, nor show his teeth when—'"

Suddenly Stefanie noticed that the truck wasn't moving anymore. He'd pulled into the driveway of a house that looked similar to his uncle Walt's rental house back in Mackenzie. She turned to Nick, who was smiling.

"Luckily all good things don't have to come to an end. You can read some more on the way home."

"We'll need a flashlight."

"No problem." He motioned to the house. "My grandparents are waiting for us."

The elderly couple stood at the front door while Fred dashed down the porch steps to rub his head against Nick's legs. He made low moaning sounds that reminded her of White Fang. Weren't dogs descended from wolves?

"Come in," Nick's grandmother said. She was shorter than Stefanie's five foot seven, but her husband topped Nick by several inches. His grandfather could hardly walk, though, and leaned on a cane for support.

Nick removed her parka and hung it in the hall closet with his. The living room appeared comfortable but colorless, except for one painting of a Biblical scene with a lot of blue in it. Maybe it was colorless to Stefanie because she'd grown up in a technicolor house. Anyone visiting the Larkin home for the first time exclaimed upon entering it.

"You seem well," the frail-looking woman said to Nick.

He nodded in response.

Stefanie noted at once that neither of them reached out to hug their grandson, nor he them. They seemed happy to see him, but the lack of any physical affection troubled her for Nick's sake.

She didn't understand it. Not when Nick was such a physical person with her. Whenever they were fortunate enough to find themselves alone, he always touched— holding her hand, sliding his arm around her shoulders, stroking her hair.

In her family everyone hugged and kissed upon arriving

or leaving or for no reason at all except that they felt like it. Her friends' families were pretty much the same.

"This is Stefanie Larkin. These are my grandparents, Vera and Ralph Marsden."

"I remember talking to you on the phone, Mrs. Marsden. It's very nice to meet you."

His grandmother managed only a faint smile.

"So, young lady, you're the girl who gave Nick the coconut," his grandfather said.

"Yes. Considering you ran a grocery store and probably sold them from time to time, it seems silly to have brought a coconut all the way from Hawaii. But they're such a strange fruit I wanted him to have one."

"Did you hear that?" Nick asked his grandfather. "She thinks I'm strange."

The old man quietly smiled.

"Dinner will be ready in a half hour," his grandmother announced.

Nick's grandparents spoke in statements—*when* they spoke. Their manner was so flat and unemotional. Stefanie didn't know people like them. She couldn't imagine growing up in a world where you didn't do a lot of talking with your family, yet this was Nick's world.

He turned to her. "That'll give me enough time to chop some wood. Then I'll make a fire."

Nick had already told her there were a few things he'd have to do when they arrived. How much guilt he suffered for not being with them, Stefanie didn't know. He probably needed to do a dozen different chores for them. She understood the importance of that. When he'd chosen to stay in Mackenzie, any happiness must have gone out of their existence.

"I'll help your grandmother, Nick. Maybe I can set the table or something." She could smell a roast in the oven and felt a pang remembering when her mom was still alive to cook for them.

After he'd disappeared with his grandfather shuffling slowly behind him, his grandmother eyed Stefanie. "Sit down."

"Thank you."

"Nick has told us you're a brilliant girl."

Stefanie was surprised he'd told his grandmother anything about her. "He would say that, wouldn't he? Even if it's not true. I know he loves the two of you very much."

Without acknowledging her comment Mrs. Marsden said, "I guess Nick told you about his mother."

Stefanie stirred in the overstuffed chair. "Only that she left to find a job when he was eight."

"Nick hasn't seen her since."

"That's what I understand."

"Our son shouldn't have married her." Her tone, her body language, exuded such sadness Stefanie was shaken by it.

"But then you wouldn't have Nick," she blurted. She couldn't comprehend life without him.

"He's a good boy."

Good could mean many things. It covered a whole range of possibilities. Without the words having to be said, Stefanie knew that she meant he gave them a reason for living.

"Do you have any idea where his mother is living now?"

"No."

It was such a clipped and final answer. The kind Nick had given Stefanie the first day of school.

The older woman handed her a framed picture from the end table. "This is the three of them before our son died."

In the photograph, Nick was just a toddler held by his father, also a tall man. Stefanie saw similarities in the eyes and the hairline with its defining widow's peak.

"He was very attractive. What was his name?"

"Matthew."

The lower half of Nick's face resembled the beautiful young blond woman who'd been his absent mother all these years. Now that he'd grown up, she could see he'd inherited her strong nose and wide mouth. Both features added character to his face.

She returned the picture. "What happened to him?"

"Nick didn't tell you?"

"No."

The older woman shook her head and got up from the chair. "It's time to take the roast out of the oven and make the gravy."

"Let me do something, too." Stefanie followed her into the kitchen. She couldn't help wondering what was so terrible that Nick's grandmother wouldn't even talk about it.

In the little nook by the window there was a table. It had already been set. Outside, Stefanie could hear the sound of Nick wielding an ax.

"Almost two years ago," she said, "my mother died of an aneurysm. I know how hard it is to lose a family member, Mrs. Marsden. I miss her dreadfully, and my father's still grieving."

"Nick told us."

She handed Stefanie some paper napkins without looking at her. "If you want to put these on the table…"

End of discussion.

Before long, the men came in with Fred and they all sat down to eat. His grandmother was an excellent cook, and Stefanie was moved to see all the trouble she'd gone to for his arrival. Probably Nick's favorite foods. He must've eaten half a dozen of her homemade rolls.

Living with D.V.L. had to be a shock in comparison. She wondered if he made Nick cook all the meals since he was letting him live in his house near the airfield. He worked Nick hard.

But Nick had chosen it and he went about his jobs without complaint, whether here or at the airfield. Perhaps the thing Stefanie admired most about Nick was his willingness to do whatever had to be done. She saw no anger in him. He didn't kick against the pricks. Not ever. It was a remarkable trait, one she'd like to develop. To her chagrin, she wasn't as strong as Nick.

During the meal, his grandfather did what little talking there was. After a delicious dessert of apple pie with rich cream, Nick pushed away from the table and started filling the sink with hot water. Over his shoulder he looked at his grandmother. "We're going to have to get going soon. Stefanie's father will be expecting her."

His grandparents nodded.

"I told him I'd phone when we were ready to leave," Stefanie said. "I'll call collect."

"That's all right. I'll pay for it." Nick had his pride. She didn't fight him. "The phone's over there at the end of the counter."

"Thank you."

She made it quick. "Dad? We're just about to do the

dishes, then Nick and I will be leaving to come home. Everything went fine on the drive here. The roads are plowed, so you don't have to worry."

"Are you having a good time?"

Stefanie gripped the receiver a little tighter. There was that word again. *Good.* A word with a multitude of meanings. At the moment it meant this trip had been a revelation she'd needed to experience in order to understand Nick better.

"I'm having a wonderful time." She looked at the two old people clearing the table. "His grandmother's food tastes like Mom's."

"You're a lucky girl." She heard the catch in her father's voice. "Hurry home, honey, but not too fast."

"We'll be careful, Dad. Bye."

While his grandfather went in the other room to sit down, Stefanie dried the dishes, then took some pictures of his grandparents and the dog and more with Nick. Maybe he had a lot of family photos he'd taken to D.V.L.'s. In case he didn't, she'd order double prints so he could have his own set.

Ten minutes later they said goodbye. She thanked Nick's grandparents for dinner, urging them to stay inside the house, where it was warm. Fred followed them out to the truck, trying to herd them back so they wouldn't leave. Like the sad faces at the door, it tugged at her heart.

As Nick helped her into the truck, she chanced a look at him and saw that he was staring back at her with a question in his eyes. Was he worried she hadn't had a good time?

He couldn't believe that. Good didn't enter into it. This was his family! Yet something was obviously bothering him.

Once they'd left Eureka, he surprised her by pulling into a lay-by and stopping the truck. Actually it didn't surprise her. His tension had been too heavy.

"She told you about my father, didn't she?"

There was no mistaking what he meant. "No. I was trying to make conversation with her. When I asked what happened to him, she realized you hadn't told me so she changed the subject and we went into the kitchen."

"He took his own life."

Chapter 5

Stefanie gasped, horrified by the revelation.

"If you think I'm going to kill myself, you can think again."

"I would never think that!"

"The hell you wouldn't. But just because *he* committed suicide doesn't mean it runs in the family."

Aghast, she cried, "Of course not!" His pain was so real she was in agony for him.

He studied her for a minute. "Let's get out of the truck. I want to show you something."

She had a hard time keeping up with his mercurial moods but did as he asked. What he'd just told her would have blighted his life. There was no question that it had devastated his grandparents. Their only son...

She was starting to understand so much she couldn't

have possibly understood before tonight. Stefanie wanted to comfort Nick but didn't know how. If her mother had chosen to end her life, Stefanie couldn't imagine how she would've been able to go on living.

It was one of those imponderables no one wanted to contemplate, yet it had been Nick's reality all these years.

"Look to the northwest."

The truck was facing south. When she turned, she let out another gasp, this time in awe.

"They say Eureka is one of the best places in the U.S. besides Alaska to see the northern lights."

She raised her eyes to the heavens. "Oh, Nick…" Irregular billowy bands of red, deep blue and green spread across the northern sky above the horizon. "It's glorious," she cried softly. "I wish I could take a picture."

"Why can't you?"

"My little camera's meant for snaps. It could never pick up an image that far away. I didn't even realize you could see it from here."

"The weather has to be right. We picked the perfect night to come."

The perfect night.

Being with him made it perfect.

"Thank you for the most beautiful Valentine gift I've ever been given."

"Have you ever noticed the best gifts can't be bought?" he said.

Nick had already learned something most people never found out until it was too late—if then.

The two of them watched in reverence for a while before she turned to him again. "I wouldn't have missed this trip for anything. I love you, Nick." Like exhaling air, the words left her lips just as naturally.

He caught her face between his hands. It was too dark to see into his eyes, but there was no mistaking the force that was driving him when his mouth came down hard on hers. She was ready, eager to show him how she felt.

They didn't talk on the way home. Stefanie would have curled up next to Nick with her head against his shoulder, but he insisted she fasten the lap belt.

A few days later, her grandfather brought her home from the office. Before getting out of the car, she talked to him about suicide.

He looked at her soulfully. "Do you have a friend who's threatened it?"

"No." She decided to be truthful. "The father of the boy I've been dating killed himself when Nick was four."

"I see."

"He said I didn't need to worry about him doing the same thing. Why would he say that?"

Her grandfather took a deep breath. "Because the incidence is higher with suicide survivors. Not much but a little."

"Why?" she asked again.

"Because it was his father. You don't just get over suicide. The loss is felt forever, even if Nick was a child at the time. Personal values and beliefs are shattered, and the individual is changed emotionally. Every victim of suicide needs support at the time of the loss. Do you believe Nick ever got this help?"

She bowed her head. "No." Not his grandparents, either.

She was shocked at how their grief continued to affect them, more than a dozen years later.

"Most people don't, and that complicates their bereavement. Nick requires long-term support best given by others affected by similar losses. I'd say he needs individualized counseling to understand what it's done to his life."

"I think he's too proud to ask for it."

"Or too afraid."

"How can I help him, Grandpa?"

"Let Nick be who he's become. Just try to be there. Support whatever form his grief takes. In Nick's case, you know he's frightened."

Stefanie nodded. She'd heard his fear. "Do you think that's why he wants to be a pilot?"

"You mean to prove he's not afraid?" her grandfather asked.

"Yes."

"Maybe, maybe not. It's hard to tell. The thing is, you can't relate to what he's experienced, but you don't have to. Expect some anger and conflicting expressions toward his father."

"He doesn't act angry about it."

"I'm sure there's anger in there somewhere. At some point it'll probably come out. Don't try to set a timetable for recovery, because there isn't any. We'll never get over missing your mother, will we?"

"No. Never!" She threw herself into his arms. "Did you know Nick's mother abandoned him when he was eight? His grandparents raised him."

Her grandfather held her tighter. "That's tragic, honey. It doesn't seem fair, does it?"

"No."

* * *

February 17, 1974

Yesterday I went to Mother's grave after school. I had a long talk with her about Nick. I don't understand why she has to be gone when I need her so much. I'm sure Nick feels the same way about both his parents. But his pain is worse. He can't resolve anything if his mother never comes back and he'll have to wait for the next life to talk things over with his father.

After I left the cemetery, I bought some gifts for Nick's grandparents. I found a French country tablecloth with a border of lemons in blue and yellow I think she'll like. It'll look pretty in their dining nook.

At the bookstore I came across a fabulous art book that showed all the photographs of Hillary's ascent of Everest. I'm hoping his grandfather will be able to enjoy it for hours.

On my way home I stopped at a pet store and bought Fred a box of doggie treats. I'll never forget the look in his eyes as he watched Nick get in the truck. I saw the same look in the eyes of his grandparents. I wrapped everything and I'm mailing the package this afternoon.

Today at lunch I asked Nick if his grandparents had enough money to move back to Mackenzie if they wanted. He said yes, but they're too set in their ways to pull up stakes at their age. Apparently D.V.L.'s going to let him fly there on Sunday mornings so he can help out.

I have to take back what I said about D.V.L. He may drive a hard bargain where Nick's concerned, but he's allowing him to achieve his dream of being a pilot. Letting Nick take the plane to see his grand-parents makes him a very special man. Though I've never met him, I think he's wonderful. If he hadn't offered to help Nick, we'd be apart now.

What would my life be like without Nick? I already love him so much. Nothing must ever happen to him. The thought of Nick crashing is unfathomable to me.

Stefanie found herself sobbing as she read those words. Then the phone rang.

The phone!

Galvanized into motion, she hurried to the end table next to the overstuffed chair and grabbed the receiver. Caller ID indicated it was Nick's office. Thank God!

"Dena?"

"I'm sorry to say it's not good news."

The journal Stefanie had been reading for the last hour slipped to the chair cushion.

"I've called every airport I can think of where he might've had to put down because of a problem. There's no sign of him."

Her heart leaped to her throat. "This has gone on long enough. I'm leaving for the office right now so we can decide what to do. See you in a few minutes."

After hanging up, she shut off the gas log and ran to the kitchen to turn off the oven. On the way down the hall to get her hooded parka and purse she heard the clock chime seven. Three hours and still no word.

I love you, Nick. Come home to me.

She repeated the mantra all the way to the airport.

The Present—Nick

I'm waiting for help to come.
No one's here yet.

He decided to ask the lady at the front desk.
"You'll have to share a room tonight. Here's your key. Number twenty. Now go on and don't bother me again."
Barracks don't have doors or keys, but this one did. Nick passed down a long, wide hall with white Dutch doors evenly spaced on both sides. The floor was clean enough for a baby to crawl on.
He found number twenty at the end and curled up in front of the door, unable to tell if it was morning or night. He needed to get someplace else but couldn't remember where.
"Nicholas?"
He rolled onto his back and saw a man in a bathrobe standing in the doorway.
"I didn't know you were in there."
"I've been waiting for you," the man said. "What are you doing on the floor?"
"I couldn't get in."
"All you had to do was push."
"I thought whoever was in here wanted everyone to keep out."
"I did, but I've made an exception for you."
"Thanks." Nick got to his feet. "I haven't seen you for a while."
"Ditto. You in trouble?"
"Is that what you think? That I'm always in trouble?"
"Take it easy, son."

"Maybe if you'd stuck around, you wouldn't have to ask that question."

"Well, I'm here now."

"For how long?"

"Not long."

Nick winced. *"That's what I thought."*

"What do you need?"

"Nothing. Absolutely nothing."

"You must've wanted something or you wouldn't be here."

"I made a mistake."

He smiled. *"Lie to anyone but me."*

"If I'm a liar, it's your fault."

"The sins of the father, hmm?"

"How come you left?"

"That wasn't my fault."

Nick clutched the key so tightly it dug into his palm and drew blood. *"Then whose?"*

"You're smart enough to figure it out." He started to close the door, filling Nick with panic.

"Where are you going?"

"Not far." The door clicked shut.

Nick pushed on the door, but it didn't budge. *"Come on, damn you. Let me in!"*

"Get some sleep, son."

A sob tore from Nick's throat. *"Don't leave—"*

He tried to run down the hall for help, but he sank with every step. It took forever. He pounded on the front-desk bell. Now both his hands were bleeding.

"What do you want?" the lady called from behind a partition.

"Open the door! I've got to get in."

"Get in where?"

"Door twenty."

"There is no door twenty. Anyway, I'm leaving now."

"If you go, I'll be alone."

"You're a big boy now."

"It's raining."

"You're a damn crybaby. Get over it."

"Let me come with you."

"I said no! Stop your hollering!"

"Please—" He sobbed.

"Don't start that again. Nobody wants a kid who cries all the time."

"I'll stop!"

"Stay in your room or I won't come back!"

"Don't go!" he screamed, scrambling to find her.

The walls surrounded him. He pounded against them until he came to another door. He couldn't get in. The only thing left to do was write a message on the door.

I shall wait for night, and if I'm still alive, I'll walk alone on the highway that runs through my town till I find my tropical bird with her piercing green eyes. Alone and safely isolated in my beloved's arms, I'll ask her why is it I ought to die.

The Present—Stefanie

Snow fell steadily, sticking to the ground. If the storm kept up all night, this part of Montana would waken tomorrow under a heavy blanket of white.

But a nightmarish scene if Nick was out in it somewhere. Stefanie couldn't afford to think like that. She turned on the radio and listened to the local news, afraid to listen yet afraid not to.

After so many years of coming and going to the airfield, she could find her way blindfolded. It was a good thing. The windshield wipers had difficulty keeping up with the falling snow.

Outside the office, Dena's car sat parked near Nick's, both of them already shrouded in fresh white powder. Even with the lights on, the place looked lonely. Stefanie shuddered involuntarily before she got out of her car and hurried inside.

Her eyes sought Dena's. The auburn-haired woman shook her head.

Dear God.

Stefanie removed her parka and shook it out on the mat, then tossed it on one of the chairs. "Give me another number to phone."

"I've exhausted the list. It's time to call the Montana State Aeronautics Division in Helena. Maybe they know something we don't."

She glanced at her watch. Twenty-five after seven.

Three and a half hours. There should've been some news. Because of the nature of Nick's job, it was their unwritten law that he'd phone her if it was humanly possible.

And if it wasn't?

Hardly able to breathe, she sat down at the other desk and asked Dena for the number. This was the one call she'd hoped never to make.

After listening to the voice-mail menu, she connected with the air search-and-rescue emergency service. A man answered.

"Hello? This is Stefanie Marsden calling from North

Country Flying Service in Mackenzie, Montana, airport ID
S55. My husband, Nick Marsden, left Spokane for Mackenzie at two-thirty this afternoon in his Cessna 182 blue-and-
white Skylane. There weren't any passengers with him.

"He called the office at quarter to four saying he'd arrive
in fifteen minutes, but there's been no word from him
since. We've checked out every possible airport where he
might've put down for mechanical problems."

Maybe he'd become ill and blacked out. Or suffered a
heart attack. But he'd gone to the doctor for a physical
before Thanksgiving and was given a clean bill of health.

Stefanie broke out in perspiration. "So far we've had no
news." Her voice shook.

"Let me have your number and I'll call you back,
Mrs. Marsden."

"Thank you." She recited it, then hung up.

The two women looked at each other while streams of
unspoken thoughts—unspeakable thoughts—flowed between them.

Dena made coffee. As she handed Stefanie a mug, Grant
Livsey, Dena's husband, walked through the door and
made a beeline for Stefanie. He'd been outside with the
snow-removal machine, trying to keep their runway clear.

"I called him." Dena mouthed the words to Stefanie.

Uncaring of the snow dusting his jacket and hat, he
pulled her out of the chair and gave her a hug. "This isn't
the first time, remember?"

The fact that Dena had told her husband to stop what
he was doing and come in meant she was really frightened, too. A sob broke through the tightness banding

Stefanie's throat. She clung to Grant. "This time it's different, and you know it."

"Nick can handle anything."

She nodded and eased away from him.

"The weather was good. He still had daylight when he contacted Dena. That plays in his favor."

Against what odds?

May, 1974

"I won't paint a rosy picture for you, Stefanie. It's what you Americans call a crap shoot. Nicholas could be wiped out at any time. He doesn't worry about it. *You* do."

D.V.L. pushed his index finger into her forearm. "Until you're all grown up, you'd be wise to run along and get your homework done. Stop hanging around here—and don't park this close to my runway!"

The rangy Dutchman went back into the office, leaving Stefanie rigid with anger. Ever since he'd allowed Nick to live in his house for the rest of the school year, he'd been acting more like a possessive father.

Using her hand to shield her eyes, she watched the two-seater plane circle the field before coming in. Though she was no judge, the landing looked pretty flawless to her. Nick jumped down from the wing still wearing the jeans and shirt he'd had on at school that morning.

He'd arranged his schedule so he could work every day and weekend in exchange for flying lessons. He'd been able to fly solo for months now and already had his license. The end of their senior year was coming up in a week. She could feel the onset of change and it made her jittery.

He moved quickly toward her with a kind of lope that distinguished his walk. "Hi. I saw you talking to Dries. Where'd he go?" he asked, running a hand through mussed hair. He wanted his mentor's approval.

No female could put that light in his eyes. She had to control her jealousy. "Where do you think?"

He squinted at her. "What's the matter?"

"Did you tell him to warn me off?"

Nick flashed her a curious glance. "No, but it doesn't surprise me."

"He was mean to me." She knew she sounded childish but couldn't help it. Since meeting D.V.L. in March, Stefanie had only talked to him a few times. On each occasion he seemed to grow more hostile toward her.

"I guess I never told you about him."

"What?"

"When he wouldn't give up flying, his wife couldn't take it and asked for a divorce."

"No. You didn't happen to mention that." There were a lot of things he never talked about—including the seasoned pilot who still spoke English with a heavy accent.

"He married an American woman who changed on him and demanded he get a different job. She refused to have kids if he didn't quit. So they divorced."

"That's awful."

"She knew he lived for flying. He never lied about it or told her he'd give it up for her sake. When they first met he was honest with her up front. She went along with it and he believed everything was fine, so they got married.

"That's when the fighting started. If he got home later

than she thought he should have, she was afraid he'd crashed and she'd fall apart. He finally couldn't take it anymore."

Stefanie could understand how his wife had felt. Every time Stefanie saw Nick go up in the air, her heart seemed to stop beating until he came safely back to earth.

She drew in a shaky breath. "I'm sorry for him, but it still doesn't give him the right to be rude. He shouldn't compare every woman to his wife."

Nick stared into her eyes. "Most women don't want their husbands to fly for a living."

"If I loved my husband and that's what he chose to do, then I'd learn to deal with it."

"Like hell."

Stung by his remark—because deep down she knew he was right—she started to walk toward her dad's car. She could feel Nick behind her.

"Are we still on for Saturday night?" he asked.

She'd been anticipating it every minute of every day. Today was only Thursday. Yet, to her own disbelief, she wheeled around and cried, "Wouldn't you love it if I said we weren't?"

His eyes darkened. "No."

Every once in a while his features would take on a haunted expression that communicated pain. She could never resist trying to comfort him. Attractive, inscrutable Nick. She was a slave to the emotions he evoked through no conscious effort on his part.

He lifted his hands to her face. "No," he murmured again before giving her a rough kiss. Nick had never kissed her in anger before. Stefanie remembered what her grandfather had said. One day Nick's anger would manifest itself. Was that what this was all about?

If so, she could get angry, too. Angry and hurt that he didn't even attempt to explain the particular demon driving him today. She pulled away from him.

"I have to get the car home." She climbed in the driver's seat and drove off, for once just leaving him there wondering what was going on. Or so she thought. But when she looked in the rearview mirror, he'd already disappeared inside the office, his mind somewhere else. These days it was often somewhere else.

Stefanie worried that she had more in common with D.V.L.'s ex-wife than she wanted to admit. If she ever met the other woman, she told herself wryly, they'd probably become best friends.

When she pulled into the driveway at home, she discovered her father out in front fertilizing the rose bushes. He always worked in a denim shirt and an old Stetson that covered his dark blond hair, now streaked with gray.

She got out to join him. "Hi, Dad."

He glanced at her with a smile. "Do you know you look more like Liz every day? And both of you look like your mom."

She considered that a compliment. Growing up, people had frequently remarked what a beauty her mother was. "Thanks."

"Got to get this place in good shape for her wedding reception."

Twenty-three-year-old Liz was getting married in June to Donald Winegar, a fellow pharmacy student. Only three weeks away until the wedding.

Don was from Miles City, Montana, and had a lot of relatives. Richard and his wife, Colleen, would be coming home shortly. It was going to be a big affair.

"I'll change clothes and help you."

"How come?" he asked with his signature deadpan expression.

"Dad!" A twinge of guilt assailed her.

He stood up and leaned on the handle of his shovel. "I guess I don't have to ask where you've been."

No. Her comings and goings presented no mystery to her father. But she had to admit that since the day she'd gone to Eureka with Nick her father hadn't given her any grief about him. As long as she obeyed the rules, her dad seemed to accept it.

"Why the long face?"

"It isn't anything."

"Just your whole life." His gaze probed hers. "I hate seeing you like this. Your mother's death has contributed, certainly, but there's more to it than that."

She bit her lip. "Did Grandpa talk to you about Nick?"

"No. Why do you ask?"

Stefanie couldn't remember a time her father had lied to her, so she had to believe him.

"I thought maybe you were going to say you didn't approve of my seeing Nick anymore."

"If I were going to say anything, it would be more along the lines of I wish you'd date other boys, too. That didn't happen, did it? Not after you met Nick."

What other boys? She'd never been able to see anyone but Nick.

"So you still don't approve of him."

"My reservations have nothing to do with approval."

Her father was being cryptic. "Then what?"

He cocked his head. "Until you met him, you were my sunshine girl. Where's she gone?"

Her hands formed fists. "Why do you always talk about me changing?"

"Because you have. Every time I see shadows in your eyes, I know you've been with him. He's not good for you."

She flinched. "It's cruel of you to say that."

"But it's true," he persisted. "I've seen single-minded types like him before. He's into flying. It's already taken over his life and dominates it to the exclusion of every other consideration, including you."

"That's not fair!"

"I agree. It's a shame he didn't stay in Eureka. Since he came back, you've been like a moth to his flame."

His words really hurt. "I've never heard you talk like this before." Still reeling from what had happened with Nick at the airfield, she couldn't handle this conversation and started to go into the house.

"If I don't, Stefanie, who will? No one else loves you the way I do."

Chapter 6

Stefanie recognized the love in his voice. It stopped her from walking off. She turned back to him. "I love you, too."

"Sweetie? Can you give me one instance where Nick put your interests ahead of his own? Has he asked what you're going to do with your life? What *you* want out of life?"

"Not exactly."

"In other words, he hasn't."

She stiffened. "Nick's not like other guys."

"That's an understatement."

"He didn't get the same start in life. There's been a lot of sadness he can't talk about." She hadn't mentioned Nick's dad to her father. It would only give him another reason to be worried about her. "With no money, he's been forced to work for every single dime. I don't know another guy at Clark who's so dedicated."

"I'm sure you're right. It's because he was born with a fire in the belly, the kind that will always burn hot. A vital quality if he's going to be a top-notch pilot. But it's lethal for you. Everyone who wants to get close to him he'll leave in the contrails."

Her father could have brought up Nick's grandparents, who lived several hours away and needed his help; despite that, he'd chosen to room with D.V.L. because Nick's wants came first. His argument would've seemed logical, but there was another side to that story.

"Then how do you account for the pilots around the world who fly for a living *and* have wives and children?"

"Good heavens, Stefanie. Surely you're not thinking of marriage! You're too young to have any concept of a real relationship yet. He's going in a different direction from you. I hate to tell you this, but he doesn't feel about you the way you feel about him. There's no place for you in his plans. Surely you can see that by the way *you* always run to *him*."

If her father had brought up any of the usual arguments, she could have accused him of being a snob. But everything he'd said made a gut-twisting kind of sense. He'd painted a picture of her that was pathetic. Humiliating. Especially coming from her own father.

"My question to you is, what about *your* plans? Have you decided if you want to attend the university in Bozeman?"

Stefanie had just learned that she'd won the high school scholarship in English, which gave her an entrée to Montana State.

"I haven't decided anything, Dad."

"Then how about the University of Colorado at Boulder? Richard and Colleen love it there. Or you could attend Colorado State at Fort Collins, where your mom and I met."

She shook her head. "Right now I don't know what I want to do."

After a silence, he murmured, "Because of Nick, you mean."

Tears burned her throat. She burrowed her face against his shoulder, shaking with sobs.

"How can I help?" he asked quietly.

"Nobody can help me."

"Except yourself. What I'd like you to do is go overseas on one of those summer-abroad programs through a university. Travel a little, then start classes in the fall and have some normal dating experiences. Find out who you are, what you want out of life."

The idea of leaving Nick to go anywhere was out of the question. Why couldn't her father understand that? She eased out of his arms.

"Why do you look so surprised?" he asked. "Your grandfather's hoping you'll eventually go to Rush Medical School in Chicago and become a doctor. You'll have an in with him writing a referral for you."

She wiped her eyes. "Dad, when Liz decided to go to pharmacy school in Missoula, I may have said something about becoming a doctor, but that no longer appeals to me. Neither does being an English teacher like Mom."

"With Nick in the picture, I don't suppose anything does. That's why you need to get away and gain some perspective. I want my daughters to have careers. It's important, because you have no idea what the future will bring.

"I'm also hoping you'll end up with a man who'll support you emotionally—instead of you supporting him all the time and getting nothing in return."

"You make Nick out to be so unfeeling. Knowing his background, why can't you cut him some slack?"

"Listen to you defending him," her father said. "It will always be thus."

"You don't know that!"

He put his hands on his hips. "You remember Rex Hollinger?"

"All of Montana remembers him, Dad. One of the state's most famous sons."

Rex and her dad had been best friends growing up. After Rex married Barbara Linford, he'd ended up singing at the Met and at other major opera companies around the world. Eventually he became the lead tenor at the Vienna State Opera. Their family still lived there.

"But you haven't heard the whole story."

"What?"

"Barbara was so crazy about him she didn't go on to college. Instead she followed him wherever he went."

"I don't understand why that's so terrible. They've been happily married and have raised a nice family."

"Is that so?"

"It's what I thought, anyway."

Her father sobered. "Just before your mother died, Barbara dropped by to see us while she was visiting family here. When your mom asked her if it was exciting to be married to a world-famous opera singer, she said she'd never really thought about it. She'd been too busy doing his business for him, taking care of the children he rarely saw, being there to pick up the pieces when he'd had a bad night or strained vocal cords. He could be moody and difficult to the point that she didn't like to be around him.

She said even though everyone caters to him, nothing makes him happy until he has a new project. It never occurred to him that she might have needs or would like him to share something of her world. He never reaches out to her. They lead two separate lives. If it weren't for the children, she would've left him years ago."

Stefanie cringed.

"You could have knocked your mother over, she was so surprised to hear that. But I saw it coming. The truth is, when one person's the brightest star in the firmament, someone else has to supply the backup."

She bowed her head. "You're saying Nick will always be the star."

"What else? To make matters worse, with Nick there's the added stress of his physical safety taking its toll on those who worry and care about him most."

Stop, Dad. I don't want to hear any more.

"It requires a mental toughness not many have. Can you blame me for wanting my daughter to avoid that kind of suffering?"

"No."

"Has he made plans with you for graduation?"

"No. He has to work."

"Nick told you that or are you assuming?"

"He told me."

"Nobody has to work on his own graduation day. He *wants* to. There's a world of difference. The sooner you understand that distinction, the sooner I hope you'll decide to invest your feelings elsewhere."

There was a pause before he said, "If you've already made love, then you probably haven't listened to anything I've been saying. Has he told you he loves you?"

"No to both," she whispered in a broken voice.

"Good for him," he said ironically. "He's even more obsessed with his career than I'd supposed."

A pan of scalding water thrown in her face couldn't have hurt her more.

In the next instant her father had lowered the shovel and put his arms around her. "I really laid it on thick, didn't I? Don't you know I've only said these things because I'm your dad and I want you to be happy?"

Of course she knew. In fact, she hated to admit her father was right about Nick.

Halfway through their first picnic last Saturday afternoon—the one Stefanie had talked him into—Nick had suddenly stopped kissing her. He was always the one in control.

When she asked what was wrong, he'd said it was time to go home. No explanation. She hadn't seen or talked to him again until this afternoon. That was why she'd gone out to the airfield. The fear that his feelings for her had changed in some way was intolerable to her. She had to find out what he felt, what he thought, what he wanted.

Well, she'd found out when she'd driven to the airport to see him today. His mind was on flying and nothing else. It was galling to realize her father understood the situation and had seen this coming.

"If I wasn't aware you've lost your appetite, I'd take you out for Mexican. We need to spend more time together."

Much as the idea of food revolted her, it suddenly dawned on Stefanie that he must miss going out with her mom for their favorite bean dip and chili *rellenos*. All this talk of emotional support reminded her that she hadn't been there for her dad in a long time.

Despite the pain she couldn't relieve, she said, "I'm ready to go when you are."

His face lit up. "I need ten minutes to finish here, okay?"

What she'd give for Nick to respond like that just once without her having to plan everything out weeks in advance. She kept remembering what her father had said. Nick *wants* to work on graduation day.

Her dad was right. Nick had never told her he loved her. When she'd said those words to him the night they'd seen the aurora borealis, he hadn't said them back. Since then, she'd been waiting and waiting to hear them returned.

Three months had passed. He could have told her on his birthday, when they'd gone ice-skating, or on Easter Sunday or on their picnic. Or even in a note at school. They sent each other a lot of messages, but all he ever put was his initials. Nothing like "Love, Nick."

No way was she going to throw herself at him again. She was through with driving out to his job and being rebuffed by him and D.V.L., who obviously had no use for women.

She needed to forget how it felt to be with Nick. Stop remembering the pleasure of just looking at him. Stop reliving the excitement he engendered with a touch of his finger or the pressure of his mouth when he deigned to give her his attention. It happened far too infrequently.

Yesterday in the cafeteria Joey Johnson had invited her to go to the graduation dance and a party afterward with him and his friends. She'd told him she already had plans because she intended to spend graduation day with Nick. Not dancing, of course. Not partying with the others, either. Something unique, because being with him was enough.

Except that it wasn't! She didn't want to be any man's afterthought.

Unlike Nick, Joey *was* thinking about her. According to the girls, he'd been thinking about her for years. He'd gone to the trouble of asking her out. She'd go and phone him right now. If he hadn't found anyone else to take, she'd tell him her plans had changed and she'd go with him.

He was very cute and entertaining. She knew she'd have a good time with him. Joey didn't have Nick's baggage or a dream that drove him night and day. For one evening, at least, she'd be the brightest star in Joey's firmament. What would *that* feel like?

Before she could change her mind, Stefanie went to her room and looked up his number in the school directory. His mom answered and told her he was working at the filling station over on Juniper Drive and gave her the number.

After thanking her, Stefanie dialed it and asked to speak to Joey.

"Just a minute."

In the background she could hear the person who'd answered say there was a girl on the phone for him.

"This is Joey."

"Hi, Joey. It's Stefanie."

"Hey, Stef—what's up?"

"Have you asked anyone else to the dance?"

"Not yet."

"Would you still like to take me? I'd really like to go with you if it's not too late."

She could hear the question he wanted to ask. Nick and she had never acted like a couple at school, but most of the kids knew there was something between them. Or thought they knew, she amended. According to Stefanie's father, it was all in her mind, not Nick's. Well, as of now, she intended to forget him.

"This is your lucky day, Stef." She chuckled at his response. "But can I call you later? I'm changing a tire on a car and they're getting impatient."

"Of course. Thanks for inviting me, Joey. It's going to be fun."

"It is now. I always did want to take you to a dance but was afraid to ask."

"I'm glad you finally did!" She meant it.

"So am I. I'll see you at school tomorrow and we'll talk."

"Great."

No sooner had she hung up than her father rapped on her bedroom door.

"Be right with you, Dad."

He remained standing in the doorway. "You've got a visitor downstairs."

"Who?" she asked in a dull voice.

"Nick."

Stefanie's heart started to thud painfully. She slid off the bed.

Nick had come here out of the blue?

"I'll be happy to take a rain check on dinner," her father said, walking to his bedroom.

Trying to compose herself, she went downstairs and entered the living room as calmly as she could.

He stood next to the mantel studying some photos of her family. She could tell he'd gone home to shower and change clothes. No one wore a T-shirt and jeans the way he did, and despite everything, she admired the way he looked. His head turned in her direction.

"I took off work early to talk to you."

Following their argument and then the talk with her father, Stefanie was in a precarious frame of mind. "Why?"

"Why do you think?"

"I don't know, do I, Nick?"

He moved toward her. "I was going to give you this on Saturday, but after you left so angry a little while ago, I changed my mind."

Before she could respond, he reached for her hand and pressed a little black box into her palm.

She opened it and stared at the plain gold band, uncomprehending.

"That's the wedding ring. I know the diamond engagement ring should come first, but I can't afford it yet. I need four years before I can financially support you. You need that long to decide if you want to be married to a pilot."

She raised her eyes to his, unable to speak.

"Keep the ring," he said. "If or when the day comes that you meet someone else, send it back to me. That's all you have to do. I'll understand."

Send it back?

Stefanie couldn't think, let alone take it all in. "Where will you be?"

"In the Montana Air National Guard."

Air Guard?

"I'm leaving for basic training on Monday morning. That's why I can't be here to take you to graduation. In September, I'll be in Prescott, Arizona."

She shook her head, totally bewildered. "What's in Prescott, Arizona?"

"Embry Riddle University, where I'll study professional aeronautics."

"Does that mean you're going into the reserves?"

"Only until I graduate. The Guard will help pay for my college tuition. Dries and I talked it over, and after I receive my degree, he's going to take me on as a partner."

Stefanie could feel his jubilation. He couldn't wait to leave!

"Will you have to go to Vietnam?" she asked fearfully.

"No. The war's winding down. Dries thinks another year and the U.S. will be out of Cambodia—and Laos, too."

Dries didn't know everything. Something might happen to prolong the war. Four years of Nick being in Arizona flashed before her eyes. Endless years when anything could happen to him—like an accident…or another woman.

Not one word about *her* plans. Not a thought for what *she'd* be doing in the meantime. He didn't care.

How simple for him just to drive over here and tell her he was making an exit out of her life. And by the way, here's a ring if you want it. And one more thing—while you're pining for me during the next four years, you'd better decide if you hate my flying, because that's what I do. It's who I am. If you don't like it, you know what you can do about it. So long, babe.

Remembering her father's words, she began to understand the importance of emotional investment. If it wasn't there on both their parts…

Heat scorched her cheeks. "I don't want the ring." She kept her voice impassive, hiding the agony she felt inside.

His expression grew bleak. "Then I don't want it either."

"Wait!" she cried, rushing after him because he'd deprived her of the chance to throw it back at him. But he was out the door too fast for her to catch up and tell him in so many words that their relationship was over.

Frantic, she reached the bottom of the porch steps in time to hear his truck engine rev up. Then he was gone.

Her body shook as she stared down at the ring. The gold glinted up at her. He'd bought this at great personal sacrifice, denying himself the things other guys saved for, like cars, skis, stereos. "Boy's toys," her brother called them.

Nick didn't have toys. He didn't own any. He was interested in bigger things that flew…and could explode or crash.

Unable to help herself, she slid the ring onto her finger. A perfect fit. It seemed to burn where it touched her skin. Scalding tears dripped onto her hand. She pressed her lips to the shiny surface.

"Stefanie? The phone's for you."

The phone?

She moved the back of her left hand away from her lips. That voice wasn't her father's.

Her drenched gaze swerved past Grant to Dena, who read Stefanie's mind and answered the unspoken question with a shake of her head. No news of Nick yet. Covering the mouthpiece, she said, "It's your son. He wants to talk to Nick. I told him that he wasn't back yet but you were here."

The children. They didn't know.

Her heartbeat was erratic as she took the receiver from Dena.

"David, honey?"

"Hey, Mom. What are you doing at the office? I just tried to get Dad on his cell, but I guess he turned it off."

Nick rarely turned it off. She could count the times on one hand.

A shudder ran through her body. David worshipped his father. She didn't know how to tell him his hero was missing in action. This wasn't just her pain. It was her children's, too.

"Mom?" He sensed her hesitation. "Is everything okay?"

Stefanie smoothed the hair off her damp forehead. The protective instinct of a mother had taken over. "I'm fine. I'm waiting for your dad. His flight's…a little late."

"What else is new?" Sometimes he projected a tone of irony that sounded exactly like Nick. She closed her eyes for a second.

She could hear David's nine-month-old, Jack, fussing in the background. Nick was crazy about their grandson. He'd already started a college fund for him.

David had received his MBA in August.

He and Amanda were settled in Kalispell, where he was managing one of his grandfather's bank branches.

Their beautiful world was intact with a promising future ahead of them. Learning that his father was in serious trouble would shake his world to its foundations the way it had Stefanie's.

Fear stabbed at her heart. "Listen, honey. Could I call you back? Grant just walked in. I need to talk to him."

"Sure. Give me a jingle as soon as Dad shows up."

"I will."

Feeling out of breath, Stefanie put down the receiver wondering what to do next. Both of her children deserved to know the truth, but there was no point in alarming them until there was something definite. Otherwise, whatever she said would only make them as frantic as she was. Anything to spare them agony if it wasn't absolutely necessary.

"Why doesn't the man in Helena call back?" Her cry resounded in the room. "Nick couldn't just have disappeared off the map without a trace."

"It can happen if the ELT failed to operate properly."

At the sound of Dries's gravelly voice, Stefanie swung around. The eighty-seven-year-old looked like a hunched-over snowman as he shuffled toward her on the arm of Nick's other mechanic, Wes Holbrook.

That old warhorse coming out in this storm was the very worst sign. His presence meant he was afraid for Nick, who was as close to him as a son. The son he'd never had...

The widow maker's nightmare had begun.

He poked his finger into her upper arm. "Now is not the time to fall apart, Stefanie. Nicholas was trained to prepare for the worst. He'll know what to do with what he has on hand. He'll survive."

Housebound these days, Dries was still the tough old fighter pilot who had liquid steel running through his veins. She caught back the fresh tears that threatened. "Sure he will." Over the years Stefanie had fought to think only positive thoughts about her husband's safety in the air.

Sensing that the ornery Dutchman was in need of comfort, too, she helped him off with his coat. "Sit down,

Dries. I'll get you a hot drink." She needed to keep busy or she'd go mad with fear.

After pouring coffee into two clean mugs, she handed them to him and Wes, who removed his hooded jacket before taking it from her. "I checked with the weather bureau. This isn't a major storm. It's already letting up, which is a blessing and will aid in the search."

"I can stand to hear that kind of news about now," she said, her voice wobbling. She looked at the wall clock. Nine o'clock and no word yet.

When her cell phone rang, her first thought was that it was Nick. Maybe he'd made an emergency landing in a field or on a road and his cell phone didn't work so he'd had to walk out to find a phone.

She grabbed it from the purse she'd set on the desk. Not bothering to check the caller ID, she said hello. Every anxious eye was fastened on her.

"Mom? Dave just called me. I found out it's snowing there. How late *is* Dad?" Nan demanded.

The panic in her voice made Stefanie shiver. She might've known she hadn't fooled her son earlier. She'd been wrong to keep the news from him. Now she'd really upset her daughter, too.

"Five hours."

"And you didn't tell me?" Stefanie could hear her daughter's frightened anger all the way from Seattle.

"Honey, your dad's been late before."

"Not *that* late, Mom. When's the last anyone heard from him?"

She let out a ragged breath. "He spoke to Dena at quarter to four."

"So he should've been home by four-fifteen at the latest!" Nan was the one who loved flying with her dad. "What have you heard from search and rescue?"

She gripped the phone tighter. "Nothing yet."

"What do you mean *nothing?*" she cried.

"Listen to me, Nan. We don't know what happened or where he is. I'm still waiting for word from Helena."

"You mean no one's out there looking for him?"

"They will as soon as they get a fix on his location. The snow's letting up."

"I'm coming, Mom. Ben and I will be on the next flight to Salt Lake. Then we'll fly to Kalispell. It'll be faster. Dave and Amanda will drive us from there. Don't fall apart, okay? Dad's tough."

You don't need to tell me about tough, darling girl. Nick invented the word and taught it to a lovesick seventeen-year-old destined to be tortured by it every second of her life.

"The moment I have any news, I'll call you. I'm glad you're coming, Nan. Forgive me for not calling you sooner."

"There's nothing to forgive, Mom. We know how much you and Dad love each other. If it were Ben, I'd be in denial, too. It's like if you don't say it, it hasn't happened, right?"

She could always count on her daughter to be blunt and to the point; Nan had that much of her dad in her. "Right, my darling girl. Please hurry. I need you."

Without hesitation she clicked off, then phoned the number for search and rescue again. "This is Stefanie Marsden. Isn't there anything you can tell me yet?"

"Hang in there, Mrs. Marsden. We're doing everything

we can to find your husband. As soon as we learn anything, we'll notify you immediately."

"I know you will." She could hardly swallow for the pain. "Thank you."

When she turned to the others, they were huddled around the desk, where Dries had spread out a well-worn U.S. geological survey map.

"Since he didn't run into a storm, it means something happened to the plane. He would've cut his speed, so I figure he went down somewhere here." His index finger pointed to a spot. "Get them on the phone again, Stefanie."

She was still holding her cell. She quickly pressed the redial button and handed it to him.

"Is this Marty?" he asked in a gruff voice. "This is D.V.L. Now listen to me. Nicholas has gone down in the northeast sector of the Cabinet Mountains."

After a silence, he muttered, "How do I know? Because of his trajectory and the time configuration! He couldn't be anywhere else. The snow's easing up, so I want you to start a search around the Grambauer Mountain area. Work your way to the northeast edge of the Cabinet Wilderness. He might've caught a tailwind and reached Scenery Mountain, so check it all!"

Thank God for Dries.

"No, no! Dome Mountain is too far south! You do that search where I told you and you'll find him! He'll have built a fire. Now get going, dammit!"

There was more conversation from the other end. By the time Dries hung up, his face had turned a dark red. She knew that angry look.

"What's wrong? Tell me!"

He slapped his thigh—another telling gesture. "They can't start any kind of a search without having a more precise location."

"But we can't just sit here and not do something to help him! What if they never get a fix on where he went down?"

"Then they'll start an air search tomorrow."

"At dawn, you mean."

He shook his gray head. "No. I suspect the earliest they can go out will be around ten in the morning or even later, depending on the density of the clouds and the ceiling. There's a lot of fog this time of year. They'll have to wait till it lifts."

"But that's twelve hours from now. He'll freeze to death," she agonized aloud.

"It'll be in the low twenties up there, but if he gets a fire going, he'll be all right. Since this is going to take a while, go home and get some rest. Grant and Dena will help me hold down the fort." His gnarly hand placed the cell phone back in hers.

"But, Dries—"

"Didn't you hear me?" His voice boomed.

He'd reverted to the Dries of thirty-four years ago, but this time Stefanie knew why and understood. He loved her husband as much as she did.

"There's nothing you can do for Nicholas here, Stefanie. If you stay, you won't be any good to him when he needs you."

"Dries is right," Dena murmured. "Would you like me to come with you?"

"Thank you, Dena, but I'd prefer to be alone right now. My children are on their way. If I want company, I can always go over to Dad's."

Except she wouldn't do that yet. Instead she made a phone call to her father, alerting him that something was wrong. The memory of a warning he'd given her in the garden years ago was difficult enough. She couldn't bear to see the compassion in those hazel eyes now.

After giving Dries a long hug, which he reciprocated, she put on her parka and went outside. Dries and Wes had been right. The storm had blown itself out here, leaving a serene white landscape in its wake. Everyone's vehicle had accumulated a good four to five inches. But it wasn't a full-scale Montana blizzard, and she was grateful for its short duration. Nick needed every possible break in order to survive.

At the sight of his four-wheel drive still parked where he'd left it that morning, a sob rose in her throat.

By the time she reached her Toyota, Wes had removed the snow from both their cars. "Follow me to your house," he called.

"You don't have to do that. I'll be fine."

"Just do it!" the forty-year-old mechanic insisted. Fear for Nick had made him short with her. That was okay. She was grateful to have an escort home through the fresh powder. Few people were out in it.

Was it still snowing on Nick? She couldn't stop shivering.

Once they arrived at the house, Wes started the snow-blower and cleared the drive and paths before heading for the airfield again. That was his way. He just did what needed doing.

Nick was like that, too. If there was something to be taken care of, he applied himself without discussion. Everything had a place, and everything needed to be in its place.

Life had been an adjustment their first few months of marriage. Stefanie kept a clean house but, like her mom, she tended to be messy, which didn't bother her because she had more important things to do.

If a book didn't get put back on the shelf for a week, no problem. If newspapers cluttered the house, she'd get around to stacking them on the back porch in her own sweet time. To her it wasn't a big deal. If she left the mail on the kitchen counter for a few days, it didn't cause her to lose sleep.

But she soon found out that Nick noticed everything and couldn't relax until their home was tidy. Maybe it came from the necessity of keeping any plane he was flying in perfect shape. An admirable trait, but he'd annoyed her when he'd walked through the door of their apartment in the old Liston mansion and done little jobs on his way to finding her—sorting mail, putting away dishes, straightening up shelves.

Of course, she'd had no complaints once he would taxi to a stop and draw her into his arms. They'd make love until late, often enjoying midnight suppers in bed.

He might belong to the skies during the day. At night he gave his body up to her. Her husband was brilliant in anything he pursued, but to Stefanie, he did his best work between dusk and dawn.

Now, on leaden legs, she walked over to the oven and pulled out the baked potatoes. They'd turned into cool, hardened lumps.

She needed to call her father. But in doing so, she was admitting that the brightest star in the firmament might have been extinguished tonight.

The clock started chiming. She clung to the counter, waiting for the sound to end.

Nick, darling, it's ten o'clock. Are you alive? Are you awake? My silent, brave husband.

She sank down, burying her face in her hands, tears pouring down her cheeks. Her cell phone rang, and her pulse raced as she pulled it from her pocket.

"Hello?" she cried. *Oh, please, let it be Nick. Please let it be a miracle.*

Chapter 7

"It's your father."

"Dad…"

"Both David and Nan phoned me with the news. Are you at the airport or home?"

"I just came from the office. Dries insisted. Now I'm at home. I was just going to call you."

"I'll be over in a few minutes. You shouldn't be alone."

"Please don't try to come here." These days, her eighty-three-year-old father still drove to the bank almost every day. He'd bought a new four-wheel drive, which got him around town without trouble. But this was no night for anyone to be out if they didn't have to be. "I'm all right." Tears continued to gush down her cheeks.

"Of course you're not."

She stood up. "How did you do it, Dad?"

"What do you mean?"

"How did you handle it when you knew Mom might not wake up from that coma?"

He waited before speaking.

"We do what we have to do. In your case, you don't know what's happened to Nick, so we're all assuming he's alive and expecting to be rescued as soon as possible. Renae and I will be there shortly."

There was no stopping him. Thanks to Wes, her father wouldn't have problems pulling into the driveway.

After saying goodbye, she put her phone on the charger, then hurried around the island to turn on the gas log and warm the place up. Before she forgot, she switched on the front porch light.

Needing to keep busy, she made a fresh pot of coffee and sandwiches, trying to act as normal as possible. Inside she was dying while she waited for the phone to ring with the news that they'd found Nick's location.

Soon she heard footsteps on the porch and ran to the front door to let her father in. "You poor thing," Renae said the second she saw Stefanie's tear-ravaged face. They hugged. Small and trim, Renae had a lot of energy for a woman eighty years old. Her stylish silver hair gleamed in the hall light.

"Sweetie," was all her father said before enfolding her in his arms. So much love conveyed in that one endearment choked her up all over again. "I've called Liz and Richard. They're making arrangements to come, too."

She sobbed against his shoulder as she'd done so many times in her life. He'd seen her through every joy and sorrow growing up. They'd grieved together for her mother. But this was different.

"I don't know what I'll do if I lose him, Dad."

"I've been praying you won't have to find out."

"No word yet?" Renae asked.

"No. And they won't be able to start an air search until ten tomorrow." The tears kept falling. She broke away from her father. "I'm such a mess. Forgive me."

She helped him remove his parka. Renae had already taken hers off. "Hand me your coat and I'll hang them both up."

While she went to the hall closet, they walked into the great room. She followed in time to see Renae pick up something from the floor near the overstuffed chair. The older woman handed it to Stefanie. "At first glance I thought this was David, but now I can see it's Nick. He looks too young to be flying a plane."

"That must have fallen out of my journal." It felt like centuries instead of hours since Stefanie had looked up the recipe for Janet.

Her father reached for the two-by-three-inch picture and nodded. "This was when you were both in high school."

Stefanie could hardly breathe. "I took that on his eighteenth birthday. He had to work first, so I drove to the airfield. While I waited, I shot a whole roll of him inside and out of the cockpit. That's one of my favorites."

She took it from her father, unconsciously pressing it against her heart. There was a blown-up framed copy of the same photograph in their bedroom.

It was two weeks after Liz's wedding that a heartbroken Stefanie had first shown the photos to her Grandmother Dixon. The older woman had studied them for a long time....

* * *

"I know Nick's gone out of your life, and you haven't figured out what to do with yourself yet. But I have to tell you, these photos are good. You're a very artistic girl, and it shows in the way you've set these pictures up."

"You're just saying that."

"No. I never say what I don't mean."

That was true enough. Stefanie lifted her head from the throw pillow on her grandmother's bed. "Mom said the same thing about the pictures I took of their flower garden."

"That's because my daughter could see you have a definite flair. Have you ever heard of Brooks Institute?"

Stefanie shook her head.

"It's one of the best places in the country to get a degree in professional photography."

A degree in photography? Stefanie would never have thought of such a thing. Not in a million years.

"Where is it?" she asked in a dull voice.

"Santa Barbara, California, where my sister Loretta lives."

Loretta had been a favorite aunt of Stefanie's mom.

"I think it's one of the most beautiful places on the West Coast. What do you say you and I take a short trip? Your grandfather can do without me at the office for a few days. We'll spend a little time with Loretta. Because of her broken foot, she couldn't come to your sister's wedding so she'll be glad to see us. And while we're there, we can check out Brooks. If you're not interested, at least we'll be able to have a visit with family."

Santa Barbara was far away from Mackenzie. Good reason for Stefanie to tell her grandmother she'd like to go.

It had been six weeks since Nick had fled the house

without his ring. Stefanie knew this because she'd kept count of every minute without him. There'd been no phone call, no word. She didn't expect a letter. It was over.

"How soon could we go?"

"How about the day after tomorrow? That'll give me time to make flight arrangements and clear up a few things at the office. I'll ask Joyce Emery to fill in for me." Joyce was another retired nurse, like her grandmother.

"Dad'll be pleased."

"I'm sure he will. He's concerned about your depression."

"You think I've lost it? Penny said I have."

"Penny hasn't fallen in love yet."

That brought an unexpected smile to Stefanie's face.

"First love is very powerful. You'll never forget Nick. But until you make an effort to meet someone else, he'll stay alive in your heart. Doing something constructive with your life is the first step to opening your heart to someone else. Your grandfather wasn't my first love—or the second or even the third."

"I know. It was Raymond Carlisle."

Her grandmother chuckled. "Yes. If there hadn't been a war, we would've been married. The day he left, I wanted to go to bed and never wake up, but my father wouldn't let me. Being the manager of the phone company, he put me to work as a comptometer operator. That's where I met Arnie Miller and then Perry Watkins.

"When Ray came back three years later, he brought an Italian wife with him. If I'd just stayed home waiting for him, I can't imagine how I would've coped. But, as you know, I'd already started nursing school.

"One day at the hospital this handsome resident and I

literally bumped into each other. 'I'm Dr. Bradford Dixon from Montana. Who are you?' The time was right, we fell in love, married—and that's how a Chicago girl ended up in Mackenzie."

Stefanie had heard the story so often she had it memorized.

"Honey, I realize you've listened to all this before, but I'm hoping you'll understand a little better. No one can make us happy. We have to do that for ourselves. And there isn't just *one* right person for us in this world."

That was what Anne Morrow Lindbergh had said.

"Do you remember Dr. Scobey?"

"Yes. Grandpa's friend."

"He's a wonderful psychiatrist who happens to believe there are many people in the world who could truly enrich our lives. All we have to do is put ourselves out there and find them. Nick was your first but certainly not your last."

Her grandmother meant well, but she was wrong. Nick was the only person for her.

In *The Nun's Story,* one of the books Stefanie loved, she'd scoffed at the rules of the order forbidding postulants like Gabrielle to keep anything that reminded them of their past lives.

"A nun's world is one of detachment."

Stefanie no longer found the rule ridiculous. A day hadn't gone by that she hadn't put the ring on her finger and fantasized about a future with Nick. It was fast becoming her obsession. She needed to give it back while she still could.

But even if she dared send it by mail, she didn't know

his address. Much as she hated the thought, she could drive out to D.V.L.'s tomorrow and leave it with him. The Dutchman despised her. She could guarantee that he'd relieve her of the ring with the greatest pleasure.

Aware that her father and Renae were watching her, Stefanie wiped the moisture from her face. She and Dries had come a long way since that painful time. Taking a shuddering breath, she went over to the chair to pick up her journal and put the picture back inside it.

She eyed the two of them. "I've made some food, if you're hungry."

"Why don't you sit down on the couch with your father. I'll bring it in."

A moment later Renae put everything on top of the large, square pecan-wood coffee table, where Stefanie had arranged some art books and a fat, transparent crystal jug. It held a mass of lifelike silk buds in yellow and white that brought the essence of spring into the room.

Please, God, let Nick see spring again....

Stefanie cleared her throat. "Thank you, Renae."

She really was a wonderful woman—a woman who'd lost her spouse around the same time Stefanie's mother had died. Renae's husband had been a board member at the bank. That was how she and Stefanie's father had met. It took Stefanie several years to warm up to her.

He'd remarried when Stefanie was twenty-two. She'd had a struggle seeing him with anyone but her mother. But by then she'd married Nick. Only time and maturity had helped her accept the fact that her father deserved to find happiness again.

* * *

"I know it's hard to see your father with someone else," Nick whispered into her hair during her father's wedding brunch. "But it was bound to happen. He's still relatively young."

"I thought he loved Mother. He vowed to love her forever."

"She's gone, Stefanie. Did you expect him to go through the rest of his life alone?"

"Yes. If anything happened to you, I'd never marry again."

Nick heaved a sigh. "You say that now, but none of us knows what we'd do until the moment is upon us."

She pulled away far enough to look into his eyes. "Meaning you'd marry again?" she cried.

"Let's talk about this later."

"You *would!*" she persisted, feeling a new kind of pain.

"Don't you think Dries would have been better off if he'd found another woman to marry? He could've had a family."

"He wasn't a widower. It's not the same thing."

"Might as well have been."

"No. There's a huge difference. Dad and Mom adored each other to the very end. How could Dad forget all that?"

"Could we talk about this back at the apartment?"

"There's nothing more to say."

Suddenly a conversation she'd had with her father four years earlier came back to her.

Nick's still young and needy. Without his grandparents, he's going to depend more and more on you.

That was what her father had done after her mother died—he'd started depending on Renae for comfort. It made Stefanie wonder how long it had taken him to transfer his feelings.

Maybe the evening he'd walked in on her and Nick in the library he'd been trying to tell Stefanie he was interested in another woman. But she'd been so involved with Nick she hadn't been able to see beyond the blue of his eyes.

"I think we're having our first fight," Nick whispered.

Oh, Nick…

Why hadn't they heard anything yet?

The question had barely formed in her mind when she heard her phone ring. She grabbed for it. "Hello?"

"Stefanie? It's Dries."

"They've located him?" Her cry resounded through the house.

"Not yet, but there's been a promising development."

"Tell me!"

"Although the signal was weak, the pilot of a Cessna 414 Twin happened to be on the same frequency when he overheard another pilot's Mayday around four this afternoon."

"That had to be Nick!"

"It's a strong possibility. This pilot relayed it to the crew of a Montana Air National Guard C-130 Hercules operating in the area that was at altitude and on center frequency. Unfortunately they didn't have direction-finding equipment. When they returned to base, they notified SAR with the coordinates of the location. We should hear back soon."

"Oh, Dries…"

"I'm counting on this as much as you are, Stefanie."

"It would mean he was conscious when he realized he was in trouble and activated the ELT."

"All this time you've been worried he suffered a heart attack and passed out?"

"It could happen."

"Not to Nicholas. He's healthy and strong."

"But—"

"No buts. It's a waste of energy."

Her eyes closed tightly. "You're right."

"Your children phoned here and are keeping in touch with me. I'll call you when I know anything else."

"Bless you, Dries."

"There's only one thing he loves more than flying—that's you. He'll do whatever it takes to come home to you."

Stefanie had never dreamed she'd hear words like that from Dries. "You think so?" She could hardly talk.

"You should've been in the office the day you and Nicholas had that argument just before your graduation—when you told him it was over. It was my fault for hurting your feelings. He charged inside, defending you like a she-wolf protecting her cub. He told me he'd bought you a ring. I'm afraid I underestimated both of you, and he's never let me forget it."

She couldn't swallow. "Thank you for telling me that. Oh, Dries, he's *got* to be alive!"

His eyelids felt heavy. He opened them but couldn't see anything. *I'm blind,* Nick thought. *I'm freezing.*

The next breath he took made him cough. Something was suffocating him. He brushed frantically at his face and connected with snow.

"What the hell?" he muttered when he found he was half lying in the pilot's seat. It was jammed crosswise against the two rear seats. The front passenger seat was still on its rails.

He stared through the cracked windscreen of the cockpit. The nose of his plane was buried in snow up against a stand of pines. Its altitude on the downward slope was probably at a thirty-degree angle. The left-side door was no longer there.

His head ached. When he put his hand to his forehead, there was a whopping goose egg. No wonder. The left grip of the pilot's yoke had broken off.

With teeth chattering, Nick craned his head to look around, surprised he could move. He made another discovery: his harness had been unfastened, not ripped apart.

When had he done that?

The fuselage had split open at the rear window. At least a foot of snow had blown in, but it wasn't snowing anymore. Everything was quiet except for the occasional low gust of wind. White darkness surrounded him.

What time was it?

When he looked down, he saw blood on his hands and sweatshirt. There was more blood on his knee pad, where he kept his notepaper handy. Several sheets with scribbling on them lay at the side of his leg. He couldn't remember writing anything. Snow had cauterized his wounds.

His left arm hurt like the devil. No doubt it was broken.

He glanced at the face of the watch he wore on the inside of his wrist. Dries had given it to him when he'd received his degree. It was the old-fashioned kind with Roman numerals. This watch had made it through the Second World War with Dries. "To bring you luck, Nicholas," he'd said.

The crystal had cracked on impact. He couldn't read the dials. Using his right hand, he slipped off the band and raised it. After a lot of squinting, he made out three fifty-two.

How many hours had he been unconscious? It couldn't have been days or he wouldn't be alive. Not at twenty above zero.

When he didn't return on time, Stefanie and everyone else at the airport would alert SAR to start looking for him.

His wife had always feared this day. She'd put up a great front, but Nick knew. Today the law of averages had caught up with him. Nick was no more exempt than the next man, but the families always suffered.

He was comforted by the knowledge that Stefanie and the children had each other. They were a close-knit family. They'd be there for Dries, who'd stay formidable to the end, but as Nan once said, "He's just a marshmallow inside, Dad."

The remembrances were sweet as he struggled to work the watch onto his right wrist so he wouldn't lose it. It was an almost insurmountable task, but he finally succeeded.

Was his emergency locator transmitter still putting out a signal?

He rolled onto his knees and discovered that his left hip was on fire. Gritting his teeth, he reached behind the seats with his right hand and felt around for the ELT box. The snow driven through the rear window had covered everything. His hand was so numb from the cold he doubted he'd be able to feel anything, but he kept digging.

When all he produced was the end of the coaxial cable, his heart almost failed. It had become separated from the box, which was buried under the snow somewhere. Unless the signal had been detected before impact, he was on his own.

Dear Lord.

The first thing he had to do was get warm. He'd be damned if some hiker found his remains in the summer and the coroner told Stefanie he'd died of hypothermia. She was his wife, the woman he adored. The woman who'd loved him with the steadiness and warmth of a furnace that never went out.

Except for the time he'd had to leave for the Air Guard, there'd been no bitterness between them, no harsh words they couldn't take back. How blessed could a man be?

He began another search for his stash of emergency winter clothing. He kept a sheepskin-lined parka and other items rolled up beneath the backseat.

After a desperate attempt that made him cry out in pain, his fingers touched a plastic-covered bundle. Thank God it hadn't become dislodged! He tugged at it and blacked out for a few seconds. When he came to, excruciating pain was radiating through his left arm.

Nauseous, he broke out in a cold sweat and had to stop and catch his breath before he could finish the job.

Lying back, he felt inside the roll for his ski hat. Stefanie had knitted it for him last Christmas in a navy-and-white design of her own making. He found it and pressed it against his nose in a compulsive gesture.

Despite the cold, it smelled of home. Her scent. In his mind's eye he could see her sitting on the couch with her legs tucked beneath her while she knit. She was a born artist. It was reflected in everything she did, not just her photography.

She was a natural beauty, too. He'd sell his soul to draw the curving heat of her body into himself once more. He envisioned burying his face in her fragrant tumbled mass of dark satin. Every time they made love he experienced a renewal of life.

Life.

Nothing was more precious, yet it could be snuffed out as simply as blowing a piston. But not if he had anything to say about it.

The plane wasn't that old. There must've been a weakness in the metal no mechanic could have detected. He hoped Wes and Grant wouldn't blame themselves when the findings of the investigation came out. Both men were perfectionists.

He groaned. The effort of getting the hat on his head with one hand taxed his strength. He had to rest before he reached in his right trouser pocket for something to eat. He needed calories. Because of his body warmth, his Snickers bar hadn't turned to brick quite yet.

Nan always kept him supplied with them. Her brother Dave preferred Milky Ways. No way of knowing what Jack was going to like. They'd have to wait a few more years.

Stefanie loved Hershey's Kisses. So did Nick. He particularly liked to feed them to her before they did other things. Over the years he'd heard guys complain that their sex life with their wives didn't have that zing anymore.

Nick knew when to be quiet, and it was during conversations like that. He couldn't relate to their problems. Stefanie was a sensual woman. He had a wife who met him all the way, all the time. He wasn't sure if she had any idea how much power she had over him, because she never used it to hurt him. He knew he was a lucky man to be loved by a woman like Stefanie. He prayed to God he hadn't waited too long to tell her that—and to tell her how much he loved her in return.

After devouring his candy, he slowly rolled onto his other

side to pull the cell phone out of his pocket. Another nightmare, because he had to use his left hand. Unbearable pain swept through him. His fingers came in contact with the phone. He realized immediately that it had been smashed.

He lay back once more to get his second wind, then sat up with difficulty. Even contemplating the prospect of putting on the parka exhausted him. He could only accomplish it by climbing out of the plane. But he needed to do that anyway to get his bearings.

Inch by inch he worked his body toward the opening where the door used to be and groaned his way into the snow, boots first. He dragged his parka after him. His gloves fell out.

While he staggered in place, he started to pull the sleeve over his left arm, which hung limply at his side. His fingers were swollen, tightening beneath his wedding ring. The whole left side of his body was in pain. It took ten minutes before he managed to get the coat on and could zip it up.

He leaned over to get the gloves and noticed the plane door several yards off. If the wind increased, the door could serve as a screen while he made a fire.

After another exercise in agony, he got both gloves on. Then he lifted his head and looked around. There was a low ceiling of clouds but no sign of more storms for the time being. That was the second blessing he could count. The first was that he was still alive....

He'd come down on a mountain ridge. If he remembered right, there'd been a fire east of Scenery Mountain in '94. He couldn't see the point of impact, but he could tell his plane had slid a long way. He recalled heading for a patch of clear ground. The plane's trail had uncovered stumps.

This area had been logged. Since there was no logging

in the Cabinet Wilderness, he'd crashed just outside it. That meant a road was nearby. If nobody came for him tomorrow, he'd have to walk out. But only if his hip hadn't been injured too severely.

At this altitude he couldn't plan to live off the land, but he had water all around him. If he rationed the few snacks he'd brought, he could last for some time, provided he stayed warm enough and the weather cooperated.

The best place to build a fire was behind the plane, where the belly had plowed the snow, exposing parts of the ground. It would have to be away from the spilled fuel. But pain shafted through his body with every breath, hampering any movement he tried to make.

Quickly before he passed out again and never woke up, he needed to forage for wood. He had matches and packets of kindling in the other pockets of his parka to get one going.

Once Dries heard the news and found out Nick had been flying home from Spokane, he'd know where to tell SAR to begin the search. The two of them had done this particular flight many times.

Stefanie would be terrified, but Dries would keep her from falling apart. Thinking back to the past, Nick could hardly believe those two had struggled through such a rocky history in the beginning.

Chapter 8

July 2, 1974

"**D**on't look now, but we've got company, Nicholas." Nick jerked around in time to see the Larkins' car driving toward the office parking area. His heart knocked against his ribs. How did Stefanie know he'd finished basic training? Who'd spoiled his surprise? He'd stopped here on his day off expressly to see her.

"I thought you said she hadn't been by the office since I left."

"She hasn't, and there's no way she could know you're in Mackenzie. Whatever bad wind has blown her here, if you're smart, you'll go back to the kitchen while I deal with her."

Dries hadn't approved of Stefanie from the outset. After learning she'd rejected Nick's ring, he'd congratulated him on his lucky escape and warned him to have nothing more to do with her.

But Dries didn't understand that his own marriage had failed because he and his ex-wife hadn't been soul mates. Stefanie hadn't rejected Nick; otherwise she would've followed him to Dries's house that afternoon and thrown the ring at him.

"I came back to see her, Dries. Can I take the plane up?" Nick had already been on a short run with him earlier that morning to show him what he'd learned so far.

The older man squinted. "With Stefanie?"

"I think it's time she found out it's safer than driving a car. I'll take her around the field once or twice and bring her back."

Nick had planned to take her flying for a graduation present on Saturday, but things had gotten in the way. He could have written ahead of time to tell her he was coming home for a day, but he didn't want her running away from him. This was better.

Dries gave him a fierce scowl, but the scowl meant yes.

"Thanks," he murmured, then vaulted over the counter and out the front door to Stefanie's car.

"Nick!"

Surprise had its virtues. Sitting behind the steering wheel, she was all eyes. They were as brilliant in color as a new growth of pine needles, fresh and lush. They shone with the look of that special place still reserved for him. She could hide a lot of things, but she couldn't hide that.

"Hi. You're just in time to go for a ride with me."

She didn't make a move to get out. "I had no idea you were here."

Stefanie behaved like a woman with a guilty secret. He knew she'd driven over to get his address from Dries so she could send him back the ring. In his gut he was positive she wouldn't have gone through with it.

"The Guard flew us in late last night. You've saved me the trouble of driving to your house to get you."

Her gaze traveled over his green fatigues. He liked the fact that she was staring at him with her heart in her eyes, even if she didn't realize she was doing it. Perhaps Stefanie's greatest gift was her lack of self-consciousness. It was one of the unique qualities that made her completely desirable to him.

"I thought you'd still be in training."

He'd been right. She was trying to end something that had no ending. She just didn't know it yet.

"I'll be flying back out at dawn tomorrow. Come on." He opened her door. She'd dressed in a wispy skirt and blouse in an apricot color. The picture of summer with those shapely bare legs and sandals. "Let's not waste time."

"I'd rather stay here, if you don't mind."

"What's the matter, Vampira? Are you afraid to be alone with me?" he asked in his Bela Lugosi voice.

He saw the pulse in her throat speed up. Her reaction pleased him.

"No. I came to leave this with D.V.L because I knew he'd give it to you with great delight." She pulled the little box with the ring out of her purse and tried to hand it to him.

Nick didn't lift a finger to take it. "That wouldn't be a good idea. Dries isn't in the best mood right now. Tell you what—why don't you return it to me on our ride."

She bowed her head. "If D.V.L.'s so unapproachable, what makes you think he'd let you take his truck?"

"I had something much better in mind. You and I are about to leave the bonds of Earth."

When comprehension dawned, her head reared back, causing the glistening brown strands to swish against her shoulders. She stared at him, disbelieving.

"This morning I took Dries up for a test run. He told me I'm getting to be a pretty good pilot, but I'd like your opinion. You've only watched me from the ground."

Stefanie shook her head. "I can't."

"You're afraid I'll crash?"

"That isn't what I meant."

"Then what did you mean?"

"I'm leaving for California tomorrow morning and I have to get back home to finish packing."

If he'd flown into Mackenzie a day later…

"Are you going on a trip with your family?" They had the means to travel where they wanted and often did.

"Actually I'm checking out schools."

His hand tightened on the door handle. "You have a scholarship to the U of M at Bozeman—to get your degree in English." He was counting on her being there when he flew home on leave over the next four years. A couple of the guys lived there and had agreed to let him stay with them.

"Why did you automatically assume I'd use it?"

"Because it's free tuition—not that you need it. Mainly because you're well-read enough to be a professor of English already. It would be a natural for you. Frank Willis told me he couldn't have gotten through English last year without your help."

"He hates to read."

"Reading's everything."

Stefanie's eyes darkened with emotion. "Did you tell Frank that?"

"Yes."

"What did he say?"

"He told me I was a weirdo."

Frank had told Nick a lot of other things, including the fact that Joey Johnson had been in love with her forever. Nick could understand that. But she'd been destined for *him,* not Joey. The poor devil could live in hope, but he'd be deluding himself.

"Teaching English was my mother's profession. I'm interested in doing something different."

"With your grades you could choose anything."

"That's what I plan to do."

"*Anything* covers a lot of territory."

She averted her eyes. "I'm leaving my options open."

For me, you mean. "Then you should experience everything life has to offer." Nick took her left hand and pulled her out of the car.

"No, Nick…"

He held her against him. She was all woman, soft and feminine.

"Just once around Mackenzie," he whispered against her sweet-smelling neck. "Pretend you're Saint-Exupery, the only mail courier between France and North Africa. The battery's charged. She's all tanked and ready to go. Don't you want to feel what it's like from the cockpit of a two-seater?"

He led her toward the plane sitting outside the hangar. With every step he felt her resistance waning.

He opened the door and helped her inside, then climbed in behind her. The second she sat down in the passenger seat, he leaned around her left shoulder and kissed her.

Her lips parted and spontaneous combustion took over. She gave with a warmth and honesty he'd never known from another soul. Only Stefanie.

No words were necessary. As the kiss went on, he forgot the time—but not the place. She'd ventured into his world at great risk and now she was going to share it with him. He could feel her muscles strain toward him.

Every line and curve of her filled his hands. Each little moan of surrender thrilled him. This was flying in a whole new dimension, and they hadn't even left the ground yet.

When Nick heard a distinct rapping sound, he was slow to understand until Dries opened the plane door.

"Sorry to interrupt, Nicholas, but there's an emergency. We have to deliver some blood to Libby pronto. A Red Cross truck just brought it over."

No matter how much Dries decried Nick's association with Stefanie, he wouldn't have broken in on them like that unless time was critical. There must have been a disaster and the hospital in Libby had run out of blood. Unfortunately Stefanie would only see it as more of Dries's cruelty, but this wasn't the moment to explain.

"We'll take that ride over the Mediterranean another time," he promised against her swollen lips before removing the upper half of his body so she could get to her feet. She was so unsteady he had to help her out of the plane. He watched her turn a flushed face away from Dries, who'd started to load the boxes.

Nick grasped her hand with the intention of walking her to the car, but she pulled away.

"It's okay, Nick." She sounded out of breath. "You have your work to do, and I need to get home." She ran from him on those long, elegant legs.

She could keep running. That was fine with him. Stefanie still had his wedding ring, but she wouldn't realize it until she got in the car and discovered it lying on the seat next to her purse.

He hurried back to the plane, knowing she wouldn't try to approach him with Dries hovering.

The testy Dutchman had loaded the last of the blood and was waiting. Once he'd joined him, they both remained quiet during takeoff. Nick followed her car's progress out the passenger window until they were out of range. Then he turned to Dries.

The older man's blotchy red face revealed an anger barely leashed—because of his own bitterness and because he resented Stefanie for complicating Nick's life.

"One day I'm going to marry her, Dries. Just thought you should know."

The plane went into a stall. If Dries weren't such a damn good pilot, he might not have recovered in time.

The present—Nick

Even after the wedding four years later, Dries hadn't believed Nick's marriage would last six months. The first few times his flight was late delivering cargo, Stefanie had become hysterical, and Dries had said to Nick, "I told you so."

Yet she'd hung in there. When they'd lost Matthew, Dries had been convinced Stefanie would somehow blame Nick because of his dangerous profession and ask for a divorce.

Instead, in front of the church congregation in June of 1981, she'd insisted they name their second son David Dries Marsden.

Nick had caught Dries in the hangar the next morning crying like a baby. He'd been to the christening and had heard every word. From then on, he never again talked about the state of Nick's marriage. Stefanie had won over the feisty pilot who'd suffered one too many losses in his life when his wife had left him. Beneath his gruff exterior beat the softest of hearts. Their children called him Uncle Dries.

Nan adored him. Soon after she met Ben at college, she brought him home to meet the family. She made sure he got to know Dries. Her uncle's opinion meant a great deal to Nick's daughter.

The fact that Dries flew Ben around the area proved how much he loved Nan. For years Nick had suffered for Dries because he'd never found another woman to marry. But at least he'd experienced happiness with Nick's family.

By now everyone at home would be frantic with worry. The only thing he could do for his family right now—for little Jack whose growing up he intended to watch and, above all, for his wife—was to stay alive until SAR rescued him.

He *had* to stay alive. But he was cold. So cold…

Keep working, Marsden. Forget the pain. You need a lot more wood than this.

I need to tell Stefanie something. It has to be in person while my lips can still move.

Chapter 9

Stefanie's sandwich tasted like sawdust. As she was putting it back on the plate, her cell phone rang. Her dad's eyes met hers before she answered.

"Hello?"

"Are you ready for some good news, Stefanie?" The happiness in Dries's voice brought her back to life.

She sprang to her feet. "Tell me!"

"That weak Mayday signal came from the Scenery Mountain area."

"You said he might be there. Oh, Dries!" Her cry of joy caused her father to stand, too.

"The Lincoln County sheriff, Bill Farriday, will be co-ordinating the rescue effort. He's organizing the county snowmobile club to help SAR. It's possible a couple of them can start looking for Nick tonight."

"I've needed to hear this."

"He'll call you when the command post has been put together."

The second she'd hung up, Stefanie hugged her father. "They know where to begin the search for Nick. He's somewhere in the vicinity of Scenery Mountain."

His eyes teared. "That's wonderful news, sweetie."

"It is, and they're going to look for him tonight! I've got to phone the children."

Her next two calls ended on a note of tearful optimism. "I *know* he's alive. Keep saying your prayers, David, and don't stop."

The clock chimed eleven times.

"Dad?" Stefanie turned to her father. "Why don't you and Renae go into the guest room and lie down? Just knowing you're in the house helps me. As soon as I hear something, I'll tell you."

He studied her features. "What about you, Stefanie?"

"I couldn't possibly sleep. Sheriff Farriday will be calling soon. The only thing I want to do is stay right here by the fire and wait for his call."

"All right." He patted her cheek. "Come on, Renae."

Stefanie walked them down the hall and flipped on the light. "There are clean towels in the bathroom. If you need anything, just ask."

When she returned to the great room, she put the journal back in the bookcase and pulled out the next one. Reading the entries made her feel the connection to Nick she needed to get through this excruciatingly painful night.

She sat in the chair near the fireplace. For thirty-six years she'd been writing on these pages. Except for looking up a name or a date she'd forgotten—or a recipe—she'd never read the contents.

They were like a precious gift that had been waiting for her all this time, yet she'd only stumbled on it tonight.

With trembling hands she opened the cover.

July 12, 1978

I've been on Webb Mountain outside Eureka for the last two nights, photographing the northern lights. There's been a spectacular display in the heavens. Long swirly chutes of green, pink, purple and red filling half the sky.

In March I made arrangements with the forest service to rent this cabin. It's twenty-five miles outside Eureka and totally dark up here at six thousand feet. There is no one else around. This is my final project before graduating from Brooks in August.

Neither Joey nor Dad wanted me coming up here alone, but I told them I work better this way. I've needed this time, not only for the pictures but for me.

It was in Eureka that I told Nick I loved him. I never thought I'd say those words to another man. But sweet, smart, communicative Joey has never given up on me. He followed me to California and proposed to me out there.

I've learned to love him. Not the way I love Nick, of course. That would be impossible.

I haven't seen or heard from Nick since the day I drove out to D.V.L.'s to return his ring. I still have it. On my way back through Eureka, I'll leave it with his grandparents. It's time.

I'm trying to be strong like Anne Morrow Lindbergh. Tonight I've been reading her book again. She talks about acceptance and said, "But—and this is a big but—we also know, if we are honest with ourselves, that we are not completely in charge.

"Terrible things happen to us no matter how good we are and how well we choose. We all experience loss, disappointment, we are hurt by other people and we hurt others. Genetics and environment have their way with us well before our minds have developed sufficiently to even be aware of it.

"There are some things we simply have to accept, some things that we cannot change. If we want to experience some semblance of emotional and spiritual peace, we have to learn to be accepting, to surrender to the fact that the world does not revolve around us; in fact, there are days when the world takes precious little notice of us."

Stefanie stared blindly into space, remembering the jolt she'd suffered the next morning in Eureka to see an attractive blond woman, probably in her mid-twenties, open the door of the Marsden home. A girlfriend of Nick's? His wife?

So much for learning acceptance!

"Hi. Can I help you?"

"Hello. My name's Stefanie Larkin. Are the Marsdens home?"

"I don't know any Marsdens. My husband and I bought this house a couple of weeks ago from someone named Twitchell."

When had Nick's grandparents moved?

"Do you have any idea how I could get in touch with the Twitchells?"

"Sorry. I think they went to Nebraska. My husband's company arranged our move here. That's all I know. I wish I could be more help. Try one of the neighbors."

"I will. Thank you."

After three houses down the street she found an old woman home. Surely she would know what had happened.

"My memory isn't what it should be." She laughed at herself. "Ralph died quite a while ago, maybe in '76. I think Vera passed away a year later."

Stefanie groaned. "What about their grandson, Nick?" By now adrenaline was spurting through her body.

"I haven't seen him. He was such a good boy. Serious. Whenever he came for a visit, he used to shovel the walks along here without being asked." That sounded like Nick. "I always made him a batch of gumdrop cookies. He was a real help to me and everyone around. I never got married, you see, so I had no grandchildren. They were lucky."

That was true, because Nick was all those things and more....

"Thank you for the information. Bye."

She barely remembered the drive back to Mackenzie. There was one person who'd know, and that was D.V.L. Stefanie had sworn she'd never go to the airfield again, but that was before she'd learned this news, which would have brought more sadness to Nick's life. Wherever Nick was today, she had to know he was all right.

Once back in town, she took the turnoff for the airport. But when she drove down the road leading to D.V.L.'s, she saw something so disturbing she thought she was in the middle of a bad dream.

The old wooden structure had been added to and remodeled. Light blue paint and a new slightly pitched roof made it look like a different place. A new sign in large letters spanned the width of the building. North Country Flying Service. Beyond the old hangar she saw a brand-new one.

No more D.V.L? Had something happened to him? How would Nick handle all these losses?

She pulled her rental car into the parking area next to half a dozen other cars and hurried inside the newly refurbished office. The clock on the wall said ten after eleven.

"Hi," said an unfamiliar male voice from the hallway. "Be with you in a minute."

Before long a thirtyish-looking blond guy in overalls came out to the counter. She saw male interest in his eyes. "Can I help you?"

"Are you the new owner?"

"Don't I wish." He smiled. "Are you new in town?"

Stefanie didn't mind when an attractive guy tried to flirt with her, but this was one time she couldn't make small talk. "No, but I've been away for four years."

"Well, this must be my lucky day. I'm Stewart Henley, one of the mechanics. If there's no one else here, I run the office. What can I do for you? Besides booking you a flight, I mean." He winked.

"That isn't why I'm here. I came to see the person who used to own this place."

"If you mean D.V.L., he still owns it," the other man said. "He just changed the name."

"Oh, I'm glad." Despite the animosity between her and the Dutchman, she was reassured by that for Nick's sake.

"At the moment he's flying some freight to Cut Bank. He'll be back around four. If you want to leave your name and number, I'll make sure he phones you."

Stefanie could do as he suggested, but she didn't want this man calling her for personal reasons.

"He wouldn't be able to reach me."

"Why not come back this afternoon?"

"I'm afraid I can't."

"Would it help to talk to his partner?"

She stared at him. "D.V.L. has a partner?"

"Yes. He's the one who hired me as a mechanic."

"When did this happen?"

"A couple of months ago."

"It wouldn't be Nick Marsden, would it?" Her voice shook as she said his name. Was it possible?

"Yeah. You know him?"

Yes, I knew him....

"Yes." She couldn't breathe. Nick had done exactly what he'd said he was going to do. Had he moved back in with D.V.L.? "The last I heard, he was in the Montana Air Guard."

"Not anymore."

"I-is he married?" she asked, her voice faltering.

"Not yet." He grinned. "I'm not married either. Not even close."

Meaning Nick *was?*

She glanced at her watch. "I have to go," she said abruptly. "Thank you for your time."

"Wait," he called as she reached the door. "He's at the new hangar checking over the plane. You're welcome to walk out there. He'll be happy to pass on anything you want to say to D.V.L."

Nick was so close? Suddenly she was afraid.

If he'd been back in Mackenzie for several months and hadn't tried to get in touch with her through her father, then he really had moved on emotionally.

It appeared *she* hadn't.

"Thank you, but no thanks."

Stefanie rushed outside to the car, anxious to get away before Nick came back to the office. They'd been apart more than four years. Anything could've happened in that length of time.

He was already making his dreams a reality—as a pilot and as D.V.L.'s partner.

This was her moment of truth.

She could tell herself a dozen lies, but when it came down to it, she hadn't been able to resist seeking him out one last time. The ring had provided an excuse. A ring he no longer cared about.

She wasn't a heroine in one of her favorite novels. She wasn't Katherine Swynford who dared to intrude on the Duke of Lancaster by virtue of the ring he'd given her when they'd been lovers years earlier.

Nick wasn't John of Gaunt, who'd told Katherine, "You're my heart's blood. My life. I want nothing but you." Stefanie would never hear those words from Nick's lips. They wouldn't go on to have children and be the forebears of the Stuart and Tudor dynasties, let alone continue the line of Larkins and Marsdens.

No more fantasies. She was Stefanie Dixon Larkin, soon-to-be college graduate with a marriage to Joey in her future and a promising photographic career in Los Angeles. It was time to end the life she'd left four years ago and begin a new one.

She'd already visited with her father and grandparents a few days ago, when she'd first flown in. They'd said their goodbyes this morning before she'd driven to Eureka. But she hadn't counted on finding out Nick was back. It had come as such a huge shock she needed to talk to her father about it. He'd help her to keep the past in the past and focus on her future.

If she stopped by the bank, she'd have time to treat him to a quick lunch before her three o'clock flight to Kalispell. Mackenzie was a town of only fifteen thousand, so the small airport at the south end wasn't far away. A connecting flight would take her to Seattle. From there it was back to Santa Barbara.

When she reached his office, one of the loan officers said he'd already gone to eat at Chez Marcel. How curious. The French restaurant across town wasn't a place he'd go for one of his typical business lunches.

She drove over there and parked the car, then rushed inside, anxious to talk to him. But she stopped in mid-stride when she saw him seated at a corner table, enjoying wine with an attractive sandy-haired woman of his age, both of them intent on each other.

Stefanie was staggered to see her father with another woman. There was no mistaking what it was. By no stretch of the imagination was he talking shop with some bank manager or meeting with an important client.

He had every right to do what he wanted in his personal life, of course. But it proved to Stefanie that a man couldn't live without a woman, even if he'd had the best possible marriage.

What did it mean where Nick was concerned?

Stefanie knew exactly what it meant. She hadn't heard from Nick because he'd had four years to be with any woman he chose. And according to Stewart Henley, Nick *was* involved with someone else.

Take it easy, Stefanie. You have Joey. He's wonderful. He's waiting for you in California.

She left the restaurant, making the decision to drive to Kalispell and return the car rental there. The thought of sitting at the Mackenzie airport for hours, waiting for her flight, was intolerable. She had to get away from Nick and her father. If she drove fast, she wouldn't miss the flight to Seattle.

She stopped by the Mackenzie rental-car office and made arrangements to drop the car at the Kalispell airport. Two hours later, as she walked in with her luggage and camera case, she heard herself being paged.

"Stefanie Larkin? Please come to the Big Sky Airlines ticket counter. Stefanie Larkin."

Emotionally spent, she was barely aware of her surroundings and more or less collided with a man coming the other way.

"I'm sorry!" she cried.

"Don't be. It was my fault."

At the sound of that male voice, she lifted her head and found herself staring into a pair of unforgettable blue eyes.

"Nick!"

She couldn't say anything else. She'd lost her breath. Somehow he'd caught up to her. No, no, no. This wasn't how it was supposed to happen. *Nothing* was supposed to happen. She was supposed to be boarding her flight to Seattle.

"Aloha, Stefanie."

Her whole body was trembling. "How did you know I was here?"

"Stewart's a typical interested male who wrote down the name of the rental car company and your license plate number. Then he came running out to the hangar to tell me about your conversation.

"When he described you to me, I made a phone call to the company and learned that you'd changed your plans and intended to drop your car off in Kalispell."

Her heart rate had skittered off the charts. "I can't understand why you flew all the way here."

"Can't you?"

"Your mechanic told me you're involved with someone."

"I am."

"Then I don't think she'd appreciate you following me this far, whatever the reason. I know for a fact that D.V.L. wouldn't condone it."

"She'll understand when I tell her."

"Then she must be a remarkable woman."

"She is. As for Dries, he can say what he wants about my personal life, but it's mine to live, not his."

Four-plus years had turned him into a striking man.

He wore his dark hair shorter. There was a new network of lines at the corners of his eyes. The smile lines were a little more pronounced. He was tanned and fit.

His chest rose and fell visibly beneath his pale blue button-down shirt. The sleeves were rolled up to the elbows, showing his hard muscles as he gripped her upper arms. "It's been a long time," he murmured before his mouth closed over hers.

At a disadvantage because her hands were full, she stood helpless while he drew her close and coaxed her lips apart.

She could pretend she'd been caught off guard and that was why she couldn't resist him. She could damn him for exposing her in front of dozens of passengers milling around. But she couldn't lie to herself. The old magic was still there, more electrifying than before.

What was it about Nick? Where was her spine, the spine her father had talked about? The one she should have developed to ward off the Marsden effect.

His hands slid to her shoulders as if he had the right to touch her at will. For someone who was interested in another woman, he was being far too familiar with her. If Joey could see what was going on, he'd be devastated.

"Let's go for a ride, Miss Larkin."

Her heart was going to pound right out of her chest. "Go where? I have a plane to catch."

"I know. I'm flying it."

"Be serious."

He took her suitcase from her. "We never got off the ground before. Now we're going to take that trip I promised you so I can impress you with what I've learned."

She shook her head. "It's too late. That was years ago, Nick."

He didn't respond.

More forceful than ever, he strode away on his long legs. He still had that lope, but he moved fast, forcing her to keep up with him.

Nick hailed a taxi and loaded her things in the trunk,

then opened the rear door. "After you." As she climbed in, he squeezed her hip, sending an unmistakable message that needed no explanation.

After following her inside, he directed the chauffeur to the small airfield. Stefanie was in a daze. When they arrived, they stopped at a gleaming white one-engine plane with a broad red stripe.

"This looks brand-new," she murmured.

"It is. Dries and I went in on it together. He only had the one place before—remember? Now we can fly cargo in his two-seater and passengers in this. Our business has started to take off. By the end of the year it'll be thriving."

He paid the driver and loaded her bags in the outside storage compartment at the rear of the plane. Next he helped her inside the four-seater before taking his place in the pilot's seat. This was his world. She would never forget the night he'd told her he was going to be a pilot.

"I'm flying you back to Mackenzie. We need to talk and we can do it better at my apartment. Strap yourself in."

She would've argued with him, but he'd already put on his headgear and was talking to the tower in Kalispell. Maybe this was for the best. A final goodbye to finish all the unfinished business.

Before long they taxied out to the runway. He waited for the go-ahead, then rose into the great blue sky. They soared higher and higher, in perfect harmony with the elements. His expertise at the controls spoke for itself.

Stefanie turned her head and stared at him. Nick had always been confident, but there was a new assurance in the way he handled himself. Instead of the restlessness and that constant striving, he seemed…grounded. What an irony to be thinking that while they were thousands of feet in the air.

What was she doing here with him? Somehow it was as if no time had passed at all. But instead of his grandfather's car or his uncle's truck, she was with him in his own plane and he'd become a man. A very handsome man.

Chapter 10

Nick noticed her looking at him, his eyes smiling as he did. "Do you like what you see?"

Heat rushed to Stefanie's cheeks, but she didn't turn away. "You seem happy, Nick."

"Almost."

She thought she understood the cryptic response. "I stopped by your grandparents' house this morning. I had no idea they'd passed away. It really shocked me when a stranger answered the door. I—I'm sorry I didn't know. Otherwise I would've sent flowers."

"It was better that you didn't. Less painful for me not to be reminded of you."

But I'm in pain, Nick. I'm in pain now. "They were very kind to me when we visited them that Valentine's Day." She bowed her head. "Being in the Guard so far away, I can't imagine how you managed. It must've been hard for you to lose both of them."

"It was their time to go."

That was the Marsdens' answer for everything.

"Do you have Fred with you?"

"No. He died before my grandmother did."

"He seemed devoted to your grandfather. Poor dog. I'm sure his heart was broken."

"That happened when Uncle Walt died."

She felt his sorrow. It echoed her own sorrow for him. "I talked to one of your neighbors down the street who was able to answer my questions. She was probably in her nineties. She said she'd never married."

"Lulabelle."

"She sang your praises and told me your grandparents were lucky to have a grandson like you. She said she used to make you cookies for being so kind to her."

"They were for Fred."

Oh, no, they weren't.

"H-how's D.V.L. these days?" She stumbled over the question because the mere thought of the older pilot made her uncomfortable.

"Grumpy as ever."

That was honest, at least. Somehow Nick got past the Dutchman's abrasive nature and made their relationship work. D.V.L. would probably be a lot grumpier when he found out Nick had flown to Kalispell looking for her with the intention of bringing her back. Stefanie hoped they wouldn't bump into him.

"When I drove over there, I hardly recognized the place. I guess it's your place now, too. How does it feel?"

"Good."

What an absurd question, when she knew it had been his dream from childhood.

"I gather you're the one who hired that mechanic. He seemed nice, eager to help me out."

"I had to set him straight on a few things."

Nick's comment surprised her. "What do you mean? He's the perfect kind of person to deal with the public." Unlike D.V.L.

"He didn't see a ring on your finger and figured all was fair. I had to tell him you were taken."

She swallowed hard. "By whom?"

"Who do you think?"

"Nick—there's something you need to know. A lot of time has gone by since we saw each other. I've been seeing Joey Johnson. He's asked me to marry him."

"That's too bad. He'll have to find someone else while he's at Stanford getting his law degree."

She blinked. "How did you hear about Joey?"

"Frank Willis is my friend, too. We've stayed in touch while he's been away at college in Missoula. Last year he flew down to Arizona with his fiancée, Ellen Tate, so I could meet her. He's kept me posted about you and Joey."

And I haven't known one thing about you *all these years?*

"The last time I saw Frank was at high school graduation."

"He and Ellen got married in Missoula, where her family lives. I was his best man. I saw Joey at the reception."

"H-he didn't tell me he saw you." She moistened her lips nervously. "Nick, about Joey—"

"If you were going to marry him, it would've happened by now. Is he aware you still have my ring?"

They'd been dancing around the subject. She could no longer avoid it, yet the ring was the reason she'd stopped in Eureka to see his grandparents, so she could ask them to return it.

"He never knew," she confessed. "I didn't tell him because I always intended to give it back to you."

"Somehow it never happened." She heard the satisfaction in his voice.

That was true. She still had tangible evidence of the bond between them. She knew she'd been right not to send it to him. It was much too personal to mail off. Nick was such a private person; it would've hurt him, and he'd had enough hurt to last several lifetimes.

"As you've gathered, I'm ready to return it now."

"You can give it back to me later."

She stirred restlessly in her seat. "Nick—"

"I understand you're quite the photographer now. Ever done underwater filming?"

"Obviously you know that's what Brooks is famous for."

"So how did you like taking below-the-sea pictures?"

"It's a whole other world."

"That's not what I asked."

Stefanie knew what he was driving at. "If you mean, have I found my raison d'être photographing squids and marine life among the coral reefs? The answer is no. I prefer being aboveground."

"So do I," he murmured.

She took a shaky breath. "Did you enjoy your time in the Guard?" It was a loaded question. She suspected he'd never answer or satisfy her curiosity—who's the other woman? When did you meet her? But she had to ask.

"The flying part."

"And the rest?"

"Like you, I treaded water waiting for it to be over so I could get out and do what I've always wanted to do."

"You mean fly where you want, when you want?"

He shot her a keen glance. "Isn't that how you feel about photography? Instead of being told what pictures you're going to film every class, every day, you choose what speaks to you."

She could hardly deny it, not with the film she was carrying of the northern lights. That'd been her most exciting project to date. If Nick ever found out, he'd know exactly what her last four years had been like without him.

"Something like that."

Stefanie wasn't sure he'd even heard her response, because he was communicating with the tower at Mackenzie. Before she knew it, they were landing with flawless technique on D.V.L.'s airfield. Except now it was Nick's airfield, too.

He taxied them over to the new hangar. While she struggled with the seat belt, he jumped down from the plane to get her luggage and camera case. Without waiting for her, he headed for one of the cars parked in front of the office and stowed everything in the backseat.

"I bought it used, but it gets me around," he said as he opened the passenger door. "I traded the truck for it."

They left the airport and drove into town. She had a hard time believing this wasn't a dream, that she was actually sitting next to Nick again after all these years.

He flashed her a glance. "Do you remember the old Liston mansion?"

"Yes. I used to walk past it on my way home from school."

"Things have changed while you've been gone. The family sold it to an investor who had it turned into six apartments. I've rented one on the main floor. After my grandparents died, I sold the house in Eureka and moved their furniture here. With the money, I bought half an airplane."

Stefanie was so proud of Nick she could hardly contain her emotions. Barely twenty-three, and already he had a degree and was running a business with D.V.L. He'd worked hard for everything. Harder than almost anyone she'd ever known.

They pulled up to the side of the Victorian mansion, where tall chestnut trees shaded the three-story house. "We'll go in through the back door." He walked up the steps and unlocked it.

The kitchen had been added and looked brand-new. He urged her to keep going. The apartment was big, with tall ceilings and hardwood floors. There were two bedrooms, a bathroom, good-size dining area and a living room with a wicker bookcase full of reading material. She loved the rounded windows.

"It's beautiful, Nick." The mahogany moldings gave the rooms an added elegance. She recognized some of the furniture. He'd hung the painting she'd admired in the dining room. "You can't imagine how happy I am to see you realizing your dream."

His expression grew sober, reminding her of a younger, sadder Nick. "Where's the ring?"

Her chest tightened. Now that they were alone, he was ready to get this over with.

"In my purse." She reached inside for the little box and handed it to him.

He removed the lid to examine it. Then he put it on the table and felt in his khakis pocket, pulling out a gold ring with a modest square-cut dark emerald. Before she could react, he'd grasped her left hand and pushed it onto her ring finger.

His eyes blazed into hers. "It's taken long enough, but I can support you now. If you want to work, there's enough scenery around here for you to take pictures and freelance indefinitely. I can fly you anywhere you need for special photo shoots. You can come with me when I'm delivering people or cargo. We'll find remote spots no one else has photographed. You'll dazzle any editor with your expertise and credentials."

"Nick—"

"If you didn't approve of me being a pilot, you wouldn't have flown with me today."

"But—"

"I don't want to talk anymore, Stefanie."

He picked her up in his arms and carried her into his bedroom. He placed her gently on the bed, then followed her down with his body.

He threaded his hands through her hair, kissing her forehead, her ears, eyes and nose. She heard a primitive cry— was it her own voice or Nick's?—before his mouth locked onto hers, drawing the very essence from her.

They'd never been able to keep their hands off each other. This was her Nick, making her feel things she hadn't known were possible. She'd never wanted to be with anyone else.

The long separation had only increased their passion until she was dizzy with it. "These have been the hardest four years of my life, Nick," she whispered. "They've been endless."

In response he kissed her neck and shoulders. Everywhere his lips grazed, fire shot through her body. "You're going to have to call Joey and tell him you can't marry him because we're getting married as soon as you graduate next month."

She would never have guessed how well Frank had kept Nick informed about her life in California.

Poor Joey.

Nick gathered her body against him, as if he was saying, *Don't feel sorry for Joey. You were never his and he knows it.*

Carried away by ecstasy, Stefanie found herself loving him, responding to him with no thought of holding anything back. But at the last minute he rolled away from her.

His eyes were burning as he got to his feet and looked down at her. "I want our wedding night to be our first time. I want everything perfect, Stefanie. After you make that phone call to Joey, let's go talk to your father."

July 13, 1978

I can't sleep tonight. I'm sitting in the middle of my bed at home while I write. I'm wide-awake. So much has happened since Nick found me in Kalispell I can't believe I'm the same person.

He brought me home last evening to talk to Dad. My father's in shock, Joey's in pain, and I've never been happier in my life.

Nick is so grown up, such a *man,* Dad couldn't help respecting him tonight. I know my father. He hasn't changed his mind about Nick. He's afraid his future son-in-law will always be the star and he doesn't like the inequality of it.

But I love Nick Marsden with the whole of my body and soul. I love everything about him, his single-mindedness, his strength. His character. His will. He is who he is. There's no pretense. Every time he takes me in his arms I know he loves me.

I knew it in our senior year when he came back from Eureka after New Year's. The look in his eyes spoke to my heart. I knew it when he came to find me at the Kalispell airport. It didn't matter that four years had gone by.

Oh, Mom. I wish you could be here. You'd love him, too. We're going to have the most wonderful life!

Maybe you already know Dad was with a woman today. It just about killed me. I haven't mentioned that I saw him with her, and he hasn't said a word to me about it. I have no idea how long it's been going on. When I call Richard and Liz to tell them I'm getting married, I'll ask them what they know. I wonder if it'll hurt them the way it hurts me. But I can't dwell on that right now. I'm too happy. I feel complete. Nick complements me. Do you hear what I'm saying?

I'm flying back to Santa Barbara tomorrow. Literally speaking, today. Joey's going to meet me at the airport. He knows it's over, but he wants to talk to me in person. I'm not looking forward to it. I should never have let Joey get close to me. Deep down it was always Nick, but Grandma told me I had to reach out for new experiences. For Joey's sake, I wish I hadn't. I have no doubt he'll meet someone else, but the last thing I ever wanted to do was hurt him.

The trouble was, I always loved Nick. I didn't want to be with anyone else. With every guy I dated I was looking for Nick. Because Joey did all the work in our relationship, that made it easy for me to fall in with what he wanted to do. He should never have attended college in California. I'm the reason he went to Stanford. He's a brilliant guy and could've gone to Harvard or Yale or anywhere he chose.

I realize it was his own choice. I warned him he could be hurt, but he said it was worth the risk. Joey's not feeling that way now.

My only consolation is that I know his soul mate is out there somewhere. He just has to find her. I found mine years ago. Anne Morrow Lindbergh had a lot of wisdom, but she was wrong about one thing. Nick *is* my one and only.

He's going to drive me to the airport. After that, I won't be seeing him until graduation. Four more weeks of separation, but it's the only way to handle it. We barely have any control left and he wants our wedding night to be the first time. Though it's killing me now, so do I.

I'm sure Nick has been with other women. If he's made love to them, I don't want to know about it. I never slept with Joey. He wanted to. He begged me. He said that if we slept together, it would change everything. But I couldn't do it.

Nick and I have planned August twentieth for our wedding. Dad says I can have the reception here at the house.

Before Nick left tonight, he told me he's going to

fly down for my commencement on the fifteenth of August, then bring me back. That'll give us a few days before we say our vows to move some of my things into the apartment. We can't wait any longer than the twentieth. I don't want to wait. I wish I was Mrs. Nicholas Marsden right this minute.

He's going to ask D.V.L. to be his best man.

D.V.L. doesn't like me. He never did. His failed marriage ruined him. When he learns we're getting married, he'll probably refuse to come to the wedding. I hope that doesn't happen. Nick loves and reveres him. Now that they're business partners, I couldn't bear to be the reason for any problems between them.

I'll have to get in touch with Sara and Penny right away to plan bridesmaids' outfits. I'm pretty sure Sara had a crush on Joey back then. Yet neither of them had a serious boyfriend when I left to go to school in California, yet both of them are now married. Penny's husband is from Libby. He works for the forest service. They eloped. I was a bridesmaid at Sara's wedding. She and Mike Hillstead, a guy she met at junior college, are expecting their first baby.

Grandma Dixon's going to help me find the perfect wedding dress. One that will "knock Nick's socks off," she says. There's a lot to do in becoming Nick's wife. All this time he's been preparing to be my husband. What woman ever had more proof? No one could possibly be as happy as I am.

The present—Stefanie

Stefanie heard the clock and lowered the journal to her lap. It was midnight. Each chime felt like a sledgehammer blow to her heart.

How much longer before the sheriff phoned to tell her what they were doing about finding her husband?

You have to hold on, Nick, darling. You have to be all the things you've always been to me. Reach deep down and find a way to survive. Like you did when your mother left you, when you found out your father took his own life. Be that strong man with a will of iron. Be my Charles and my Saint-Exupery.

The present—Nick

That's the last of the apple chips. Got to save the jerky for later. Got to get more wood or the fire will go out. Can't let it—

My hip is shot. There's no way I can walk out of here.

My left hand's numb. If help doesn't come soon, I'm going to lose my whole arm—

Jack'll be terrified of me. The kids will pretend it doesn't matter.

Stefanie won't want half a man making love to her. She'll just feel sorry for me. I'd rather die here than be one of her mercy projects. She should've married the Stanford man with the big law practice down in Newport Beach.

There are things she's got to know!

Where's the damn pencil? I can hardly feel it. Ah, here it is.

Stefanie, all that ever mattered to me was you. I knew what it was going to be like when we saw each other after four years. That's why I stayed away and never tried to call or write you. It would've been too hard on both of us. Dries told me I had to let you go. If you came back of your own free will, then that was a different matter. He was wasting his breath, because I knew you'd be there.

But I've brought you pain. Our first baby died because of me. It didn't matter what the doctor told me about stillborns. I knew I was to blame. Mother told me my father wasn't his parents' first or second baby. He was their third. The first two were still-born.

The Marsden genes. The Marsden curse. Mother put the fear in me that I'd go off the deep end like my father. I've been haunted by that ever since she came to Mackenzie two years after our wedding, but I couldn't tell you.

All I seem to do is bring you pain. Because of me you didn't stay in California. Without me you could've had a Hollywood career.

I want you to know I've loved you more than any man has ever loved a woman. If I get out of this alive, I vow never to let a day or night go by without talking everything over with you, without telling you how much I love you and always will.

My gorgeous, sweet wife. You're the Little Princess whose tender heart wouldn't let you walk away from a noxious weed growing on your planet. You saw beyond the spikes and thorns and tamed me.

Oh, Lord—the fire's dying. I can barely see to write.
Get up, Marsden. You've got to find wood.
What if I freeze to death? I'm halfway there.
Got to finish this first.

If this is my last flight, don't worry. I'm all right. I will never leave you, my beloved soul mate. Exupery said it so much better. "In one of the stars I shall be living. In one of them I shall be laughing. And so it will be as if all the stars are laughing when you look at the sky at night. You, and only you, will have the stars that can laugh.

August 20, 1978

"You may kiss your bride."

Nick was already kissing her before the minister had given him the directive. Since that first day in Mr. Detweiler's class four years and eleven months ago he'd been waiting. Now the long wait was over.

"Alone at last, Mrs. Marsden," he said hours later in their very private one-bedroom villa on the west end of Tortola. The living room opened onto a spacious terrace and pool. A spectacular view of turquoise water and white sands lay beyond it.

Blessed by balmy trade winds, the British Virgin Islands provided the setting he wanted for them to start their married life. Since the first time he'd flown over this tropical paradise on a weekend pass with some Guard buddies Nick had dreamed of bringing her here.

They'd arrived in time to watch the sun sink into the deep blue waters farther off in the distance. Evening had come to their own desert island with its luxurious oasis. He pulled her close, bringing her back to rest against him while his hands explored her curving waist and hips.

"How do you like being marooned with me?" he whispered into her hair. She smelled of her own fragrant scent and the gardenias from the wedding.

She turned in his arms. In contrast to the scenery, her dark-fringed eyes glowed a brilliant green. He'd heard the term *love light* before. Now she defined it.

"It feels like I've been waiting forever."

Her heart-shaped mouth beckoned him closer. Minus any artifice, her breathlessness and that slight trembling made her unspeakably erotic to him. He was too filled with the need to love her to talk.

They bestowed on each other the beauty of their bodies. In all other ways they might be different, but in passion they were equal. For six days and nights they experienced ecstasy. His wife was such a generous, exciting lover he didn't want to sleep. He was afraid to miss a single second of the rapture she brought to their bed, whether it was inside the villa or out on the sand.

Nick needed to be in her arms. That was when the dark places in his soul grew light and he felt whole. Safe. She made his world golden. Anything became possible. He felt *loved*.

On their last evening, he could hardly tolerate the thought of going back to civilization soon. Refusing to let the world intrude, he embraced her with primitive need, making love to her over and over. She was with him every second in an effort to hold on to the night.

Morning came anyway.

It brought those inevitable separations of daily life. Back at home, he craved their nightly reunions after the days spent apart. But he needn't have worried that anything had changed. Her body welcomed him every time with an eagerness that took his breath. The whole marvelous ritual would begin again.

Until they buried little Matthew in the city cemetery.

Nick experienced sorrow as profound as their joy had been while they'd waited for their baby. Now when he raced home every night from the airport, he knew he'd find his wife sobbing.

He would take her to bed and hold her, but he couldn't comfort her. She'd gone away from him to a place he couldn't reach. It terrified him.

One day, two months later, he came home at lunch to surprise her with flowers, but her car was gone. He went inside wondering where she might be. Normally they discussed their plans at breakfast.

When he passed the bedroom they'd turned into a nursery, he stopped in his tracks.

She'd dismantled it. Every vestige of baby clothing and blankets was gone. The drawers in the little dresser she'd painted stood empty. He'd bought a wolf cub with a winsome face; it had disappeared, along with all the family gifts from her baby showers.

With the crib denuded, Mathew's death became a reality for him.

Sobs racked his body.

Once they were spent, he left the mansion and went for an hour's workout at the gym. Being in the Guard had gotten him in the habit. He'd been meaning to do it on a regular basis right after work but hadn't gone lately because he knew Stefanie needed him.

Obviously she didn't. At least not at the moment.

When he returned, he saw that her car was parked in its usual place and was relieved.

As he walked in the back door, she seemed startled. Her face looked wan. "I saw the roses in the living room. They're beautiful. Thank you."

He nodded. "Where have you been?"

"At Grandma's. She said I could leave the baby things in her storage room."

"If you'd asked me, I would have helped."

"I know. It was something I wanted to do myself."

In other words, you don't want me. *Is that what you're saying, Stefanie?*

"How come you didn't tell me you'd be home early today?"

He grimaced. "I wanted to surprise you." *But the feeling isn't returned.* "I should take a shower."

Nick left the kitchen abruptly.

Later, while he was dressing in clean jeans and a T-shirt, she came into their bedroom.

"I have something to tell you."

Did she want a divorce? His heart couldn't take it. "What?"

"I got my portfolio together and went job hunting today. I—I've been offered one," she stammered.

On the same day she'd applied?

His temper flared. "I earn enough money to support us."

"This isn't about money. Without the baby, I'd like something to fill my time."

He put on his socks and shoes. "Before you got pregnant, you seemed happy enough."

"Please try to understand, Nick. Being in the apartment all day is too painful right now. I need something to distract me."

"So—what kind of work is it?"

"The local newspaper's hired me to do some photography. When one of their reporters goes out on a story, I'll take pictures."

He averted his eyes. "What are the hours?"

"Between nine and five. It's part-time and it'll depend on when they need me. Since you leave for the airport at eight and rarely get home before six, you won't even know I'm gone."

You've already left me....

Chapter 11

July 18, 1980

"When does your job start?"

"They want me to come in on Monday and get acquainted with the staff. I don't know which editor I'll be working under yet. I'm one in a pool of photographers."

That gave them the weekend. "If it's what you really want."

"I have to do *something,* Nick, and I'm trained for this. I think I'll enjoy it. But it would be nice to know you're happy for me. If you have serious reservations, I'd like to hear what they are."

Yes, I have reservations. But they're about you and me. What's happened to us, Stefanie? Do you hate me now because I got you pregnant? Is that why you haven't touched me since you came home from the hospital? If I don't hold you, *there's no contact.*

He inhaled sharply. "As you say, you went to college to become a photographer. How could I possibly have any objections?"

There was a moment of silence. "Thank you, Nick," she finally said.

"For stating the obvious?"

Her face fell. Hell, what was he doing going at her like that? He hit his fist into his palm.

She lowered her head. "You have every right to be upset. I should've told you I wanted to clean out the baby's room. It wasn't something I planned. After you left this morning, I went in there. I always end up in there during the day."

He didn't know that. Between her friends and family, shopping, cooking, her books—he'd assumed she was managing. The revelation ripped him apart.

"Today I found myself smelling the baby powder and playing with the little stretchy suits. That's when I realized I'm going crazy. It frightened me, so I started boxing everything up. Before I knew it, I'd loaded them in the car. Forgive me for acting without your knowledge."

Nick had been hoping they could try for another baby, but it was probably better for her not to have any reminders just now.

"There's nothing to forgive. I'll dismantle the crib and put it and the dresser in the storage shed around back."

"Thank you. I'll start dinner."

"Let's go out instead. You pick the place."

"I'm not very hungry. Maybe a hamburger?"

"That sounds good to me."

Within twenty minutes he'd completed the job. While he was washing his hands at the kitchen sink, he said, "Would you like to make the extra bedroom into a darkroom?"

She shook her head. "That's very generous of you, but no. I was thinking of a den for you. You could bring in your grandfather's oak desk from the storage shed. It's a beautiful old piece, but it needs work. I could refinish it."

It was the first thing she'd volunteered to do with any enthusiasm in the last twelve weeks, and he nodded vigorously. "Let's make that our project for tomorrow. After we eat, I'll drive us over to the hardware store. We'll rent a sander."

"Shall we use the same stain or a darker one?"

She was trying. He would try, too.

"Why don't we look at all the colors first?"

A trace of a smile curved her lips. He'd been worried that it had disappeared permanently.

Hopeful that this could be a new beginning, he took her for a quick meal, then to the hardware store. She was a natural at decorating and decided on a light oak stain that would modernize it. Nick admired her taste in everything.

On their way out, he paused to buy a paper. When they were back in the car with their purchases, he opened it to the movie section.

"We've still got time to take in a film. Here's what's on—*Every Which Way But Loose, Rocky II, Aliens, The Amityville Horror, Star Trek, Moonraker* and *The Deer Hunter.*" He deliberately didn't mention *The Muppet Movie.*

"I'm not dressed for one."

Refusing to be thwarted, he said, "We'll go to the drive-in. *Moonraker*'s playing there." He gave her a covert glance. "I know you like Roger Moore."

He had to wait a while before he heard, "Okay."

"Good."

He headed in the direction of the drive-in. She was doing this for him, and "okay" was better than "no."

To his relief, she sat through the whole movie without suggesting they leave. He was the one who found it difficult. During the entire two hours he vacillated: should he put his arm around her or not?

Never could he have envisioned a time when physical intimacy would be a problem for them. That part of their marriage had always been more than satisfactory.

Deciding to stay on the safer path, he kept his hands to himself and ate too much popcorn. Once they arrived back at their apartment, she thanked him for the lovely evening—as if they were strangers on a first date. The next thing he knew, she'd gone to bed.

He drank a soda before turning off the lights and joining her. She stayed on her side. He stayed on his. Nick knew it wasn't deliberate on her part. She was grieving. The hell of it was he couldn't figure out how to break through that barrier she'd erected. It might as well be an impenetrable wall of ice. He could claw and claw at it without making a dent.

The sanding of the desk took up most of the next day. He spread a tarp in the space where they usually parked their cars. Doing their project outside kept the dust and fumes from entering the house.

He liked working with her. As they applied the stain, she described her ideas for fixing up the den. Midafternoon her dad dropped by without Renae, who was apparently at the beauty salon.

Stefanie felt more at ease with her father when he came

alone. Nick told her he'd clean up if she wanted to go inside and fix John a sandwich. All in all, it was a pleasant day and evening.

After her dad left, Nick showered and got ready for bed. Once he'd climbed under the covers, he put a Peppermint Pattie on top of her pillow, then turned off the light.

He'd bought it at the drive-in the night before and hidden it until now. Of course, it wasn't the same as the thin chocolate mints put on their pillows by the management in Tortola every night. Yet he hoped to convey the message that he missed his wife and their closeness.

Soon he could hear the shower running. The second the mattress dipped, he knew she'd washed her hair. The scent of her shampoo overwhelmed him. He gripped his pillow like a life preserver thrown to a drowning victim.

"What's this?" She turned on her bedside light.

He rolled in her direction in time to see her remove the wrapper and take a bite.

"I haven't had one of these in ages. Between the mint and our toothpaste it reminds me of that drink at Naylor's Drugstore back in high school. Try it."

As she offered him a bite, his heart began a swift tattoo. This time there was a definite smile on her lips. "What do you think?"

With her hair still damp and her skin freshly scrubbed, he was suffocating with desire for her. "It's…interesting."

She finished the rest, taking her time. She was so alluring, so beautiful. She was his wife. Did he dare take her in his arms? He couldn't stand being rejected again. Not tonight.

Out went her light. She settled under the covers.

He turned and faced the other way to avoid temptation.

"Nick?" she whispered.

The blood thundered in his ears. "Yes?"

"Thank you."

"For what?"

"For being such a wonderful husband."

His body tensed. "I guess I should give you candy bars more often."

She made an odd sound in her throat. "Don't you know what I'm saying? Or don't you care anymore?"

Nick jackknifed into a sitting position. "What do you mean?"

"I mean this." She got to her knees and slid her arms around his neck. "And this." She kissed his eyes. "And this." She kissed his jaw. "And this." She kissed his mouth.

Dear Lord, her mouth—

He could feel the ice cracking, uncovering the tender shoots buried during the long, bitter winter. Spring was breaking out, warming him to his very bones, healing him. Healing them both.

One night, three months later, about the time Nick thought they'd put the worst of their grief behind them, Stefanie emerged from the bathroom with a worried look on her face.

"Nick? I just did the test. We're pregnant." She didn't give him even a second to react before she said, "Don't plan to turn the den back into a nursery. Doing everything right the first time didn't save Matthew, so I want to wait. And I'm not going to quit work."

Her fear of losing this baby masked the joy Nick felt that they were on their way to being parents again. Another baby wouldn't replace their son, but it would bring new joy to their lives. He refused to believe lightning would strike twice at the Liston mansion. The trick was getting her through the next seven months.

Don't talk about the baby, Marsden. Pretend it isn't happening. That's what she wants. Carry on as normal. Keep up the same routine. Don't grill her every time she comes home from an appointment with her OB. Let her broach the subject when she wants. Listen to her. Otherwise leave it alone.

Over the next months Nick played that game. He was still playing it when her contractions came five minutes apart and he drove her to the hospital. He'd talked privately to her OB and arranged to be in the delivery room. Whatever they had to face, Nick planned to be there with her.

Dr. Milton did a final check. "Let's go have a baby, Mrs. Marsden."

Sheer terror gave her beautiful face a gaunt, chiseled look. As the orderlies wheeled her out of the labor room, she said a panicked goodbye to Nick.

He followed her across the hall to the delivery room, where one of the nurses gowned and masked him.

"Put him in rubber gloves," the OB directed her. Above his mask, the doctor's eyes smiled mysteriously at Nick.

"I don't want my husband here!" Stefanie cried in alarm.

"Who has a better right?" The doctor spoke in kindly tones while they put her feet in the stirrups and draped her. "You stand at her head, Nick."

"You don't understand, Doctor. He's lost everyone he loves. I don't want him to see another dead baby."

Nick's eyes squeezed shut. *Stefanie, darling—*

Her delivery went fast. She only had to bear down hard

twice before he heard a burbling sound, then an infant cry that crescendoed with every lusty repeat.

"We've got a lively one here. He's mad and he's hungry," the doctor said.

Our May baby.

Pure unabashed laughter burst out of Nick. He felt just like he did every time he achieved cruising speed. The tug of the earth's gravity suddenly let him go and he was set free to float.

The doctor placed their wiggling, red-faced baby on her stomach so she could see him. "It's a boy. He's got all the right equipment. He looks good."

Stefanie's cry of joy was one Nick would remember all his life.

"Since Daddy's responsible for half of this miracle, we'll let him do the honors."

After the doctor showed Nick what to do, he cut the cord. A minute later the pediatrician took over.

By this time Stefanie's Grandpa Dixon had slipped into the room wearing a gown. The older doctor had been worried sick about her, but no longer. He nodded at Nick, literally beaming.

Their OB smiled, too, before addressing Stefanie. "What have you decided to name him?"

Nick was anxious to hear her answer. He hadn't dared bring it up. When they'd considered names for their first baby, the choices had been narrowed down to Matthew for Nick's father or David for Stefanie's paternal grandfather, who'd died when she was a child.

He didn't know what was going through her mind. She'd just given birth for the second time. He was in awe of her strength and courage.

"David Dries Marsden."

Dries?

In front of everyone, Nick lowered his mask and leaned over to kiss her lips. "It's a perfect name," he whispered.

Tears streamed from his eyes as well as hers. "We have a little boy, Nick. Our own little boy!"

And I have my wife back.

While she was in the recovery room, he slipped out to phone his friend Frank and tell him the news.

"Couldn't be happier for you, Nick. Ellen and I know what to do. You stay with your wife. By the time you bring her and the baby home from the hospital your nursery will be put back together. Ellen's going to prepare some food and take care of your plants."

"I can't thank you enough, Frank."

"You were there for us when Scott was born. It's the least we can do."

After they hung up, he phoned Dries.

"Are you ready for some good news?"

"Well, go on."

He could tell that Dries was nervous as a cat. "There's a new aviator in the family."

The quiet at the other end could only mean Dries was too choked up to talk.

"I'm counting on you to live long enough to give him his first flying lessons. He weighed in at eight pounds three ounces and he's twenty-two and a half inches long."

Nick heard a whistle come through the wires. "A big boy."

"He shot out like a torpedo, wailing his head off. The doc let me cut the cord."

"Uh-oh."

"It was a breeze. Nothing like the first time you put me in control of the two-seater."

"All right, all right. Give me a description."

"Well, he has brown hair. Lots of it. And his eyes will probably go blue, but I hope they're green. He's got all his fingers and toes—and a great-looking antenna, if I say so myself."

The Dutchman chuckled in glee.

"You've got to come over to the hospital and check him out. He needs his uncle's seal of approval."

"I think you're drunk."

"I'm so happy I refuse to take offense at that remark. We'll celebrate later."

"*Ja, ja.* So how's Stefanie?"

"I'm sure you already know the answer to that. You should've seen her. The pain didn't seem to touch her. How do women do it? All I can say is I thank God I was born a man."

"Amen to that. Does this noisy little firecracker have a name yet, like maybe Nicholas Jr.?"

"Try David *Dries* Marsden."

Silence was golden.

"Say that again?" The crusty pilot croaked out the words.

Nick grinned. "You heard me the first time. I swear on your mother's Bible that his middle name was Stefanie's idea. I wouldn't be surprised if she ends up calling him D.V.L. Jr. That is, when she's mad at him."

"Ha!" he barked.

"I told you she likes you. It was just a matter of time." *My wife doesn't have a mean bone in her body.*

"When should I come to the hospital?"

"The pediatrician said the nursery's always open. Let me know and I'll wheel Stefanie down. We'll all look at him together."

"You're sure she won't mind?"

"After what I just told you? Are you crazy?"

"Crazy with happiness for you, Nicholas. Congratulations."

"Thanks, Dries. See you soon."

I've got to hang up now. I've got to go back to her.

I have to see Stefanie again. I need to explain so many things. I have to tell her what she means to me. I can't die yet. I need more wood. Got to get more wood.

It's so damn cold.

"…so Nan and Ben are in the air, on their way from Salt Lake," David was saying. "They should arrive in Kalispell in about an hour and a half. We'll pick them up and drive straight to Mackenzie."

Stefanie's eyes darted to the clock. It was already twelve-thirty, which meant the four of them wouldn't be home for at least four hours, depending on road conditions.

"Call me when they land, honey. By then I should have talked to the sheriff and we'll know a lot more."

"Phone me the second you hear."

"I promise."

"Dad's going to be all right, Mom. Nothing gets him down. He's the ace, remember?"

She smiled through the tears she'd been holding back for his sake. "I know. I love you."

"Love you, too. I'm glad Grandpa's there."

"So am I. He phoned Richard and Liz. They're on their way."

"When Dad sees a crowd, he'll give us that Clint Eastwood stare and say, 'What's all the fuss?'"

David could always make her laugh. "You're right. That's exactly what he'll say." And nothing else...

But she didn't care about that anymore. Nothing mattered except that he be found alive.

"Bye for now, Mom."

She hung up and went into the kitchen. She took two aspirin with a glass of water. The throbbing in her temples was growing worse. Maybe the pills would dull it.

When she heard the front doorbell ring, she jumped. By the time she'd hurried through the house to answer it her father had come into the foyer.

A deputy around forty years of age stood on the porch in his winter gear.

Nooo...

He wouldn't be here unless he had the worst kind of news.

Her ears were ringing. As her legs started to buckle, she clung to the doorjamb. Her father put his arm around her waist to steady her.

"I'm sorry if I frightened you, Mrs. Marsden. I'm Deputy Posner. The sheriff asked me to come by and give you an update. He thought you'd appreciate it in person."

"Then—then you don't know anything about my husband yet?" she cried.

"No."

Her dad gave her an encouraging squeeze. "Come in, Deputy."

Fortunately her father had the presence of mind to invite

the officer inside. Stefanie felt as if she was enveloped in a layer of cellophane, disconnected from her surroundings. They walked into the great room and sat down on the couch. Renae appeared from the hallway and joined them.

The deputy removed his hat but remained standing.

"I'm sorry to hear your husband's missing. Let me say first off that all the people involved are doing everything possible to find him. After a lot of discussion and input from various sources, the sheriff has decided to set up the SAR unit command post where the Cedar Creek Road meets Highway 2. That's just outside the Cabinet Wilderness, a forty-five-minute drive from here."

Stefanie nodded. "I know where that is. Over the years my husband and I have hiked to the trailhead many times."

"That's good news. His familiarity with the terrain will increase his chances for survival."

Unless he was knocked unconscious and never came to... She clutched her father's hand.

"From all accounts, his plane went down somewhere in that area. Using those logging roads, the snowmobilers can work their way up the mountain tonight and look for his fire or a flare. In case they see neither, maybe they'll be able to spot the crash scene before morning with the aid of headlights and flashlights."

Stefanie got to her feet, unable to stay still. "The sheriff said the helicopters might not be able to begin searching until after ten in the morning."

"That's right, so we're hoping the ground crew will be successful. If they find him, they'll build a fire and use their mobile unit radios to contact the command post. At that point, the EMTs will go up on Sno-Cats with a sled and bring him down. We'll have a Life Flight helicopter waiting to transport him to the hospital here."

She nodded. "Deputy? Are you going to the command post after you leave here?"

"I am."

"Can I ride with you?"

"Yes, but I have to tell you that once you get there it won't be very comfortable. It'll be cold, and you'll have little more to do than sit and drink coffee while you wait."

"That's all I'm doing here," she blurted. "I need to be where I can go with one of the EMTs when they rescue my husband."

"That'll be up to the sheriff. But if he says yes, you'll need warm clothes. It's twenty degrees up on the mountain. And bring something to eat."

"I've got everything. It'll only take me a moment to get ready."

"All right."

"Dad? You stay here with Renae. I'll keep you posted. Liz and Richard will be coming. I'll call David and tell him what's happening. Oh—will you call the magazine in the morning and tell them why I won't be in?"

"Leave everything to me. You go and be with your husband."

"Thanks, Dad. I don't know what I'd do without you."

Within five minutes she was packed. It was liberating to be able to take some real action at last. Renae had made her a lunch. Before Stefanie kissed the two of them goodbye, she grabbed her cell phone and the journal she'd been reading. If it was going to be a long wait, it would give her something to do—and keep her from going mad with fear.

The deputy helped load her things into his four-wheel drive. He called in on his radio with a progress report before backing out of the driveway.

Stefanie had been born a Montana girl, used to the fiercely cold winters of these mountains. She'd always loved the snow. Not anymore. It had become her enemy. If it took Nick from her, she'd move to a place where she never had to look upon it again.

"Are you feeling ill, Mrs. Marsden? Do you want to go back?" The deputy glanced at her with compassion.

"No, no. I'm fine."

"Say the word if there's anything I can do."

"You've already helped me by letting me come with you. You're very kind."

"The news has spread throughout the county. Your husband has a reputation for being the best pilot around. Those who know him well are convinced he's survived his ordeal."

She bit her lip to keep from breaking down. "I appreciate hearing that."

"I'll tell you something the sheriff, Shane Zabriskie, said to me. 'If I had to be stuck up there with anyone, I'd choose Nick Marsden. He just quietly goes about turning the odds in his favor.'"

"That's my husband."

Quietly loving me all these years.

Hot tears stung her eyes. "He's my life."

"I understand."

The deputy lapsed into silence. She reached in her purse for her cell phone to call the office.

"Stefanie?"

"Dries, I wanted to let you know I'm on my way to the command post with Deputy Posner. When Nick's been spotted, I'll ride up to the crash site with one of the snowmobilers."

"One glimpse of you will warm him in a hurry. Did I ever tell you what he said when we flew the blood to Libby that day?"

Remembering back to those early years, she felt her throat almost close with emotion. "No."

"He said, 'I'm going to marry her, Dries.'"

Her shoulders shook with suppressed sobs.

"I'll tell you something else you don't know. When he got back from the Guard, the very first thing he said to me was, 'I never slept with any of the women I met in Arizona. If I couldn't be with Stefanie, I didn't want anyone else, so not one word to me about her!'"

"You shouldn't have told me that." Her voice trembled as she spoke. Although Nick had confided this before their wedding, hearing it from Dries made it all the more significant.

"You need to hear it. The Great Sphinx has nothing on our boy."

The Great Sphinx of Giza, silent royal guardian of Egypt.

"Did I ever tell you I flew over it at sunset?"

"No." She wiped her eyes. "What else haven't you told me?"

"Only one more thing. Nothing else is important."

"What's that?"

"He'll stay alive because he loves you better than any-thing. Better than flying."

"As Nan would say, that's bull."

"Nan wasn't there the day I gave him another flying lesson after Halloween that first year. I asked him what had lit him up like a forest fire. He'd never looked like that before, not even when I offered him the job he'd been begging me for. Nicholas gave me this lopsided smile. 'There's flying, and then there's flying with Vampira.'"

Dear Dries. If anything happened to Nick, she knew the Dutchman would mourn the loss of his son to the grave.

Clearing her throat, she said, "I have a little secret for you, too. When we were planning our wedding, I asked who he'd like as his best man. He said, 'Dries, of course. Didn't you know I adopted him for my father?'"

For a minute the only sound she heard was the sobs he couldn't hold back.

"We both need him, Dries."

"*Ja.* Keep the faith, Stefanie."

Once they'd ended the call, she hugged the journal tighter to her chest, refusing to believe there wouldn't be another journal to fill with the life she and Nick still had ahead of them.

I promise I'm going to make every single second of it count, my darling.

Chapter 12

The deputy darted Stefanie a glance. "We're almost there, Mrs. Marsden, so let me explain a few things."

"Okay."

"Do you recall an incident in the news when it was reported that some trapped coal miners back east had been found alive? But then they had to change the story later on?"

"Yes. It was dreadful."

"I just want to warn you that when we do locate the crash site, all you're going to hear is that they have a find. For everyone's sake, especially yours, it's vital no one jumps to conclusions either way concerning your husband's status. In time you'll know."

She nodded. "Yes, but I want to go in with the snowmobilers. I've done a lot of it with my husband and our children. I *have* to be with him, Deputy."

"You'll have to convince the sheriff. He's a good man, but he's tough."

"So am I." Stefanie understood tough. She could do tough.

"If he agrees, you can ride with me."

"Thank you."

"How many children do you have?"

"A daughter and a son, both married. David has a nine-month-old son my husband's crazy about. They're on their way to Mackenzie right now."

"Your husband has every reason to live. In a case like this, the will to survive plays a paramount role."

"I know that's true." Yet her heart almost failed her as she looked up at those unforgiving snow-swept mountains, realizing Nick was out there alone. God only knew in what condition…

They rounded a curve and came upon a police roadblock. When Deputy Posner lowered his window to talk to them, she could hear water from the creek in the background.

After they were let through, they came upon a small uninhabited building. To the left of it she saw the yellow SAR truck and several police cars. Beyond the two-ton truck was a burn barrel, where several rescue people were warming themselves.

Further up Cedar Creek Road she noticed at least fifteen vehicles with snowmobile trailers parked alongside. One of them carried a sled to accommodate a victim.

Help is coming, my love.

Deputy Posner assisted her into the truck and made the introductions.

"Mrs. Marsden, this is Sheriff Shane Zabriskie. He's in charge of the operation from this end. That's Mike Cahill operating the radio. Deputy Pete Sanford heads the EMT team. Barney Robbins is the president of the Lincoln County Snowmobile Club."

They nodded to Stefanie and she shook hands with all of them. "I can't thank you enough for what you're doing to find my husband. He's been flying for thirty-five years. This is the first time he hasn't come home…"

The middle-aged sheriff tipped his hat. "I've met your husband. He's a hero to a lot of people around these parts who've called on him when they needed help with other air searches. We'll bring him home, Mrs. Marsden," he assured her. "Can you give us a description of what he was wearing?"

"Yes. When he left for work he'd dressed in a long-sleeved light blue sweatshirt, beige twill trousers and dark brown Sorrel boots."

"Good."

"He keeps a navy parka with a sheepskin lining on the plane, along with a navy wool ski hat I made for him with a white Scandinavian design. He also has a pair of heavy-duty navy gloves."

"Any jewelry?"

She swallowed hard. "His wedding ring. It's a plain gold band with an engraving that says 'Everlastingly Yours.' He also wears a gold watch with Roman numerals."

"Any identifying marks?"

She shuddered. Were they afraid they wouldn't be able to identify him any other way?

"Not really. Two chicken pox scars on his left shoulder blade. Oh, and a scar on his right ankle from a gash he got during parachute training."

"Thank you. That gives us plenty to go on. Why don't

you sit down back there. If you want coffee, help yourself. There's a Porta Potti around the other side."

"Thank you." When the time came, she'd prevail on him to let her go with the EMTs.

While the rest of them got back to business poring over maps and discussing strategies, she found a folding chair. It was all she needed. The interior of the truck was warm enough, and she had light so she could read. These were luxuries compared to what Nick faced up in the mountains with nothing but his wits and a couple of candy bars to keep him alive.

One by one the rescue people entered the truck to check in and receive instructions. At one point the sheriff walked over to her with a map.

"We have three sets of teams starting out now. One will follow the logging route to the trailhead here." With his index finger he showed her the place. "See this fork?"

Stefanie nodded.

"When they come to it, part of the group will go left and cross Cedar Creek, taking them up the eastern section. The third part will take the right fork to the western sector and on up."

She scanned the map. "That's a lot of steep terrain to cover."

"Yes, and it'll be slow going in order to make a thorough search."

She hated hearing that, but he had to say it.

"Of course. Thank you for explaining everything to me."

"You're welcome. Any questions you have right now?"

"Will you keep in touch with Dries Van Langeveld at the airfield? He's very anxious."

"Don't worry. He's been providing us with valuable information all the way along."

"I'm glad. If he wasn't eighty-seven years old, he'd be the first one up on that mountain."

The sheriff smiled. "I believe it. But because he's a pilot himself and has flown over this area so many times, he's more valuable to us on the ground. To be honest, his hunches are worth more than anyone else's."

"That's true."

Just then a state trooper entered the truck. The sheriff excused himself, leaving Stefanie staring at her watch. Quarter to two in the morning. Nick's plane had gone down around four. Almost ten hours ago.

The second she realized where her black thoughts were headed, she opened her journal to ward them off.

August 19, 1979

Tomorrow's our first wedding anniversary. Nick says he's made special plans for tomorrow night, but I have a surprise for him, too. He doesn't know that my photographs of the northern lights won first place in the graduating seniors' competition at Brooks—$3,500. When I received the check last October, Dad advised me to keep it for a nest egg because one day I'd want it for something important.

I think getting away with my hardworking husband constitutes one of those necessities of life. Grandma Dixon agrees with me. "The kind of thing you're planning needs to be done while you're young and healthy and have no children yet. With your grandfather's bad back and my arthritis, we can only be armchair adventurers."

After Christmas I broached the subject with D.V.L. He didn't look happy about it, but he agreed to go along with my scheme. I've learned you don't spring surprises on D.V.L. So far we've managed an uneasy truce. I stay out of his way as much as possible.

Hopefully he'll go fly-fishing with some of his friends, who are park rangers at Yellowstone Lake. Nick says fishing's D.V.L.'s favorite thing to do besides flying.

I don't care that much for flying myself unless Nick is at the controls. Then I can sit next to him and talk while we look for some special place that calls out to be photographed.

August 20, 1979

"Nick? I need the car to do some shopping so I'll drive you to work."

He swallowed the last of his coffee. "Let's go, then. Dries and I have to pick up a big shipment in Kalispell this morning. He wants to leave early."

When they reached the office, he leaned across the seat to kiss her. "I promise I'll be home in plenty of time for tonight."

"I've got a better idea," she said, kissing him back. "Maybe I'll come with you. I could shop in Kalispell while you're busy. Then it won't matter when we return because we'll be together."

This was the first time she'd ever suggested such a thing,

knowing D.V.L. would be on board with them. An astonished look crossed his face. "Sure," he said after a slight hesitation. "I'll tell Dries."

"*I'll* ask him, Nick. That way he'll bite my head off instead of yours."

They walked to the new hangar, where Stewart was towing the four-seater out onto the tarmac. Dries had already climbed into the cockpit.

She opened the plane's door. "Morning, D.V.L. Mind if I tag along?"

He looked over his shoulder and scowled at her. "Well, I guess if you're here, I don't have a choice."

"You always have a choice."

"Get in, Stefanie. I've got other things to worry about."

Nick remained curiously silent during the short flight. After D.V.L. set them down, he gave orders for Nick to unload the outside storage compartment. Stefanie followed him out of the plane.

"What the hell?" she heard him mutter as he retrieved two brand-new backpacks stuffed pretty full.

"That one's mine." She pointed to the dark green one. "Would you help me put it on?"

For a moment Nick acted like a man paralyzed by a stun gun.

"What's the problem, Nicholas?"

D.V.L. jumped down and held the pack for her so she could slip her arms beneath the straps. Then he picked up the navy pack. "You'd better hurry or your flight to Chicago's going to leave without you."

Suddenly Nick woke up from his daze. "What is going on?"

Stefanie smiled. "You have two weeks' vacation coming. This is the perfect time to take it."

Without hesitation she hugged D.V.L. and gave him a kiss on the cheek. "Thanks. I owe you. Stay well," she whispered.

His face went dark red. "Have fun, you two."

"Where?" Nick demanded.

"You'll find out soon enough," she teased. "Let's go." She started walking at a fast pace, leaving Nick in the dust. He didn't catch up until she'd entered the terminal of the main airport and handed both their tickets to the woman at the airline counter.

"No other luggage?" she asked.

"No. Just our packs."

"The plane's now boarding at Gate 3."

Stefanie put the tickets back in her purse with their passports and wouldn't let Nick see them until they'd taken off and reached cruising speed.

"Chicago-Paris? We don't have this kind of money, Stefanie."

"Yes, we do-o-o-o." After she explained where it had come from, he grasped her hand hard.

"Stefanie—"

"There's more." She reached in her purse and produced two first-class Eurail passes. "With these and this—" she pulled out the paperback *Europe on Five Dollars a Day* "—we can go wherever we want."

Nick was still speechless, so she continued. "I figure we can take a train ride to Amsterdam and bring our Dutchman back some souvenirs. We only have one deadline. We have to be in the South of France on the twenty-seventh. With D.V.L.'s help, I've arranged for us to fly in a single-engine plane from Toulouse to Rabat—Saint-Exupery's old mail run.

"We'll cross the Mediterranean, spend the night, then fly to Merzouga in the Algerian Sahara. A guide will take us to Erg Chebbi outside the town, where we'll ride camels. I'm going to take pictures of the dunes. I hear some of them are over a hundred and sixty feet high. Just like Exupery, we'll sleep out under the stars before returning to Toulouse the next day.

"We can make our way back to Paris via Switzerland if we want. With that part of the trip planned, I'm leaving the rest to you. Here's a Eurail map."

When he took it from her, his hands were trembling and his blue eyes looked as though they were about to explode with light. "I want to see the Victor Hugo Museum in Paris," he began, "and then I want to see Notre Dame Cathedral and the Normandy beaches." The excitement in his voice was tangible.

"So do I."

"And a little wine-tasting in Bordeaux, and a day on the beach at Cannes—"

"With a stop at Giverny to see where Monet paint—"

The rest was stifled because Nick's mouth had found hers. They forgot they were in flight until the Fasten Seat Belts sign flashed on and the pilot announced they'd be landing at O'Hare in a few minutes.

Twelve days into their trip, she looked up at her husband, who'd just entered their tent. "Nick? I'm so sick I can't bear the thought of getting on that camel for the ride back."

Everything had been idyllic until yesterday, when she'd

felt nauseous on the flight to Merzouga. It was a crushing blow to be camped here in the Sahara feeling like this. All she could do was lose her chicken dinner from last night and her breakfast this morning.

Her dream of a romantic night beneath the stars had turned out to be anything but. Nick took the pictures. She felt weak as a kitten.

"You must have food poisoning. I'll tell the guide we've got to get you to a doctor immediately." The alarm in his voice touched her beyond words.

"Don't panic. I'm sure it's not food poisoning."

"Then what?" He looked and sounded terrified. She'd never seen him as pale as that.

"It just dawned on me that I've missed my second period. I must be pregnant. We're going to have a baby. Our first baby. Can you believe it?"

His body went perfectly still.

"Stefanie…"

"Shocker, huh?"

He sucked in his breath. "What can I do for you?"

"Tell the guide we need to go back to town. When everything's packed, help me get on the camel. Please don't worry. I've never heard of anyone dying of morning sickness."

Although she was pretty sure she was going to make medical history and be the first. But this was one time she needed to be tough for Nick.

"Feeling better?" he asked when they were back on the train the next day, headed for Paris. He'd managed to get them a private sleeping compartment.

"Much," she lied. The swaying motion was almost as

bad as being on the camel, and it was hot. She tried to keep part of a roll down.

He watched her thrown up again. "We're catching the next flight back to Chicago," he insisted.

"No, Nick. We wanted to spend our last day at Versailles."

"We'll do it another time."

She agreed, feeling too sick to argue with him.

The next day, D.V.L. was there to pick them up in Kalispell. He took one look at her as she climbed inside the plane and said, "You've lost weight, Stefanie."

She gave him a wan smile. "Pretty soon you're going to tell me I've *gained* weight."

Nick got in after her and fastened her seat belt. "Better get used to being an uncle, because we're going to have a baby, Dries. You're the first to know. Let's get this show on the road. She needs to be checked out by the doctor pronto."

Once they'd reached altitude she heard D.V.L. ask, "How long has she been this green?"

Green was the perfect description.

When Nick explained about the camel, D.V.L. let out a bark of laughter. It was so contagious she found herself laughing along with them. Stefanie could never remember a time the three of them had laughed together.

Deathly ill though she felt, she suspected D.V.L. didn't dislike her quite as much as before. Probably because she'd brought his boy back safe and sound.

"After what I've been through the last few days, you're a sight for sore eyes, D.V.L. We've brought you some presents. They're in our backpacks.

"And we visited that brown pub on the canal you told

Nick about. The one you used to go to. It's tall and narrow and it's still leaning. We got some pictures of it. I had my first beer in your honor… I'll never drink beer again."

They all laughed again.

Back at the airfield, Nick wanted to drive her straight home. But she asked him to open their packs first.

They'd bought D.V.L. some blue hand-painted delftware. A beer stein, four mugs and a tile trivet to keep his coffeepot on.

He averted his eyes while he undid the insulated wrap around them. But his voice sounded husky when he said, "These are very nice, Stefanie. Thank you."

A big lump lodged in her throat. "Thank *you* for letting me steal Nick away when I did."

He clapped Nick on the shoulder. "Did you have a good time?"

Her husband's eyes met hers. "I don't even know where to begin."

Once they reached the apartment, Nick picked up the phone to call her grandfather and tell him he was bringing her in. Then he turned to her.

"Your grandfather wants you to see Dr. Milton, the OB on his floor. He's setting it up now. Their office will call us back in a few minutes."

"Okay."

"I know you want a shower. Let me help you."

"I'm fine, Nick. But maybe you could break up some ice for me."

"Do you want cola with it?"

"No, just a cup of ice chips to suck on."

He nodded and went straight to the refrigerator.

Two hours later the doctor confirmed her due date. April twenty-second.

"That's the same day as Nick's birthday, but the month before."

"What a wonderful gift. Well, you can tell him you're strong and healthy. Everything looks good. The nausea should pass soon. Start taking your prenatal vitamins and keep crackers by the bed. When you wake up in the morning, have a couple with some weak tea or cola and you'll find your whole day goes better."

"Thank you, Doctor."

"I want to see you in a month."

The waiting room was full of women, so she held back from saying anything to Nick until they'd walked out into the hall. He shut the door behind them.

"I'm definitely pregnant and due in April! Just think— our first child."

He still looked anxious. "But is everything all right?"

"Yes. I'm fine."

"Thank God."

"Guess which day the baby's supposed to come?"

"I have no idea."

"Would you believe the twenty-second?"

With those words, Nick wrapped his arms around her and pulled her against his shaking body. She could feel his joy—and his relief.

"Well, well," her grandfather said from clear down the hall. "I can see congratulations are in order."

One more match.

If I light the rest of my knee-pad paper and it doesn't ignite, that's it.

Got to make sure this end of the branch catches the flames.

Damn you, Mother, for telling me I'd probably kill myself. For twenty-eight years I've lived with the fear you planted in me—that maybe I was like my father underneath. It took landing in this mess to find out you had me figured all wrong. You never knew me. You never knew squat about me.

I want to live!

I've always wanted to live!

Hell, I'm glad I crashed. It's given me a wake-up call. I may have had perfect vision all my life, but I've been wandering around like a cowering blind man, afraid of everything. I don't know why you've put up with me, darling. I don't know how the hell I was lucky enough to meet the only woman for me.

When the good Lord breathed life into this frail clay, He must have put Stefanie there as part of His grand design for me. I would never have found her on my own otherwise.

He put Dries there, too. And my grandparents.

They loved my father the way I love David, the way he loves Jack. Whatever went wrong with my dad, I'm convinced he was in too severe a depression to know what he was doing. A mental sickness he couldn't help. The obituary in Grandma's cedar chest said he died from a gunshot wound while he was deer hunting. The self-inflicted part was left out.

No doubt they felt they'd failed him and were terrified I'd learn the truth. After my mother left, that must've been the time when they shut down. But they don't have to be terrified anymore. I'm not my dad or my mom. She's still a child looking for security. She'll never find it. But I'm me! And I'm going to make it out of here!

Grandma didn't say much except that God helps those who help themselves. I've got one good arm and leg. My lungs haven't given out. I'm still breathing.

If James Bond could do it riding on a cello, I can slide down to the logging road on the door of the plane. It should make a decent sled. If my fire goes out, I'll crawl over there and leave this place. Too bad I don't have Fred to do all the hard work.

I always wondered what went through Saint-Exupery's mind when he didn't return from his last mission. If he had some time before the lights went out, then I know exactly what he was thinking. It's what every man thinks about when facing his mortality.

I'm okay with everyone. I'm better than okay with my kids. My one regret is the way I've failed Stefanie all these years. I committed the worst sin a man can commit against his wife. She's so precious to me, I've always been too afraid of losing her. So I clammed up.

How could I have lived with her for thirty-five years without really talking to her, without telling her I love her?

You know how, Marsden. You were scared that once you opened up and bared your soul, she'd be snatched from you. So if you never confided your deepest fears, nothing could ever happen. But that was a bunch of superstitious crap.

Hey, bud—the joke's on you.

I'm the one who's been snatched away. I want her to know what I've held back all these years and realize how much she was loved.

But if I don't make it, if I don't get to tell her in person, she'll be able to read my messages...as long as they're not buried by wind and snow.

Without question, I have her forgiveness. The woman doesn't know the meaning of cruelty. It isn't in her. My wife's capacity for unqualified love doesn't leave room for anything else.

Maybe God gave me to her for her great test. I can tell Him she passed it the day my mother came to Mackenzie.

March 21, 1980

"What do you mean my mother's here?"

Nick hadn't forgotten he had a mother, but after sixteen years of silence, he'd assumed she never intended to show her face again. Or she'd died.

"I was at the apartment getting some photos ready to take to the post office when she called. I realize this is a shock for you, Nick. It is for me, too," Stefanie said in a tremulous voice. "She wanted to speak to you. When I asked her who was calling, she said, 'Tell Nicky it's his mother.'"

Nicky.

It *had* to be his mother. No one else ever called him that. She'd only used the nickname when she was in a good mood, which was rare. With hindsight he realized she'd had a drinking problem at a very young age.

"I told her you were flying some people to Cardston and wouldn't be home until dinnertime. She said she'd wait for you at our apartment and then she hung up."

Nick was incredulous. "How did she find me?"

"The Realtor in Eureka helped her trace you. I don't know all the details, but I'm glad you're back early. Please come home." He could hear the apprehension and concern for him in her voice.

"I'm on my way."

"What's going on?" Dries asked as Nick put down the receiver. "You don't look so good. Is it Stefanie? She's not due for another month."

The two men stared at each other. "Would you believe my mother's shown up?"

Dries squinted. "I can believe anything from a woman who walks away from all responsibility. Let me warn you now—she wants something, Nicholas, and I shouldn't have to spell out for you what it is."

"Money," he muttered.

"*Ja.* It isn't difficult to understand. She's down on her luck so she went back to Eureka for a handout. With the house sold, it didn't take her long to put two and two together and come looking for you."

"She's in for a big surprise," Nick snapped. "I just wish she'd called here instead of the apartment. Stefanie's been doing great, and I don't want anything to upset her before our child gets here."

"Then don't let it." Dries grunted the words.

He reached the mansion in record time. If his mother had come here, she hadn't driven in one of the cars parked in the areas designated for tenants. Nick recognized all of them, even the ones still covered in snow from the last storm.

"Hi," Stefanie said as he raced inside their apartment with his bomber jacket still on.

His wife wasn't alone. Seated across from her in their living room was his mother. She'd aged since the last time he'd seen her, but he had to admit she looked a lot better than he'd imagined. But then, she was only forty-two. She had short naturally blond hair and wore a pastel-blue sweater with a dark skirt.

She'd been eighteen when Nick was conceived.

His mother didn't stand. Instead she sat back in the overstuffed chair with her legs crossed, her hands palm down on the arms. Nick felt her scrutiny.

"Hello, Nicky. My, how you've grown."

Children do that, he wanted to mutter.

"You're even better-looking than your father was, and that's saying a lot. He was the local heartthrob in high school." She uncrossed her legs. "How old were you the last time we saw each other? Six?"

Stefanie bit her lip. Nick had wanted to spare her the pain of this confrontation, but it was too late. Rage consumed him.

"Eight."

She made a moue with her lips. "I wasn't in the best shape back then. Social services would've been down my neck if I'd taken you with me." She paused. "You were an unplanned pregnancy, preventing me from finishing high school."

Nick had figured as much. His parents had married at seventeen, and he'd been born soon after.

"I don't know how much Vera and Ralph told you, but my mother—your grandmother—never got married. She ran off after I was born."

He knew that, too.

"My great-aunt raised me. When she found out I was pregnant, she said I couldn't live with her anymore. That's when Matthew's parents insisted your father and I get married."

That sounded like them.

"They struck a bargain with me. If I went through with the pregnancy, they'd help tend you and give us some money."

My grandparents were saints.

"Marriage was hard enough, but after Matt did away with himself, four years in their gloomy house was four years too long. Something had to give. I guess it was me."

I guess it was.

"I left for Lincoln, Nebraska. When my sales job in the department store there didn't work out, I found another one in Atlanta and after that in New York. You could say I've been all over. Another job in a clothing store took me to Chicago, then Denver."

"I assume you're out of work right now."

"As a matter of fact, I am. The company lost too much business and had to close its doors."

"If you've come for money from the sale of my grandparents' house, everything I have is invested," he said without preamble.

She tilted her head to one side. "I must say you're blunt—and a lot tougher than the other Marsden men."

Nick was on the verge of telling her there was a reason for that, but Stefanie's moist eyes pleaded with him to hold back.

"Would you like to stay for dinner, Mrs. Marsden? It'll be ready in twenty minutes."

"Thank you. But I go by Mrs. Wallace now, even though I'm divorced. You can call me Leah."

"When did you get to Mackenzie…Leah?"

"About two hours ago. I came by Greyhound bus from Denver. That's where I've been living for the last couple of years."

"Did you check into a motel?"

"Not yet."

Stefanie was asking all the questions. For the life of him, Nick was afraid to open his mouth—afraid he'd blurt out something so damaging he'd shock his wife. Right now her well-being was the only thing that mattered to him. He couldn't relate to the brittle woman sitting in the chair. The fact that she was his mother seemed unbelievable.

"How long do you plan to be in Mackenzie?" Stefanie asked her.

"Long enough to get reacquainted with my son."

"You're welcome to stay with us if you don't mind sleeping on the sofa. I'm afraid the other bedroom has been transformed into a nursery."

His mother studied Stefanie for several minutes. "Are you for real?"

"Believe it or not, I always hoped to meet you one day, especially now that we're going to have our first baby next month. My mother died when I was sixteen. I'd give anything to see her again... I'm so glad you've come. I fell in love with your son in high school. When his grand-mother showed me your picture, I could see where he got some of his good looks."

Nick didn't know it was possible to love his wife more than he already did, but this evening she'd surprised him.

Slowly his mother turned her blond head in his direction. "Do you mind having a houseguest tonight?"

As long as it was just for tonight, Nick was prepared to tolerate it for Stefanie's sake.

"No." He expelled the breath he'd been holding. "Where's your suitcase?"

"In a locker at the bus station. I came over in a taxi."

"Then why don't we get it while my wife finishes making dinner." He didn't trust her to be alone with Stefanie.

"A very pregnant wife, by the looks of it. I remember what that's like."

Yet you managed to forget it all these years.

Chapter 13

March 21, 1980

Nick gave Stefanie a swift kiss before helping his mother on with her coat. Close to her now, he could see the map of lines on her face, testimony to a hard life. Damned if there wasn't a small part of him that could still feel something, even if it was only pity.

"Did I let the cat out of the bag about your father?" she asked as he drove them toward town.

"I told her a long time ago."

"That's good, because she deserves the truth. Vera and Ralph never wanted anyone to know."

"Can you blame them?"

"Yes. Because secrets have a way of coming out." She

paused. "Are you worried it might happen to you? Killing yourself, I mean?"

He refused to answer that. "Have you considered the harm you might've done if I *hadn't* told Stefanie?" he asked instead.

She eyed him curiously. "You seem to have found yourself a mother-earth kind of girl. My exact opposite. Does she know all the family secrets?"

Nick gripped the steering wheel tighter. "I'm not aware there are any."

"My great-aunt knew people who knew your grandparents. Apparently there were two other babies before your dad came along. Both were stillborn. Hope it doesn't happen to you and your wife."

That did it.

He wasn't about to let his mother anywhere near Stefanie, who didn't need comments like that. With their first baby almost here, he'd do whatever it took to keep them separated.

If Dries was correct about her wanting money, Nick would take care of that right now.

Once they'd retrieved her baggage and had gotten back in the car, he turned to her. "You say you wanted to make contact with me after all these years, but why did you really come?"

She shrugged her shoulders. "I need enough money to get to Australia."

Though Dries might have originally misread Stefanie, he was right about Nick's mother. She was contemptible— and yet he pitied her.

"How much is enough?" He didn't want to know why

she'd decided to go there. Probably a man, but once again she'd picked the wrong kind. The right one would have married her first and taken her with him.

"Fifteen hundred."

"Tell you what—I'll drive you to the airport and buy you a ticket from here to Sydney." He pulled out his wallet. Nick always carried a fair amount of cash when he flew. He never knew when he might need it and be unable to find a bank open. "I've got five hundred dollars on me. That's it."

He showed her the bills. "This is my only offer. It's non-negotiable. If you don't want it, then I'll drive you to a motel where you can spend the night until you figure out what you're going to do. The decision's yours."

She glanced at the money, then him. "I'll take it."

Nick handed it to her with his business card. "That's my office phone. If you want to get in touch with me again, call me there, not at home."

"What are you afraid of?"

"The same thing you are—that the blackness of our earlier lives will blight my happiness with Stefanie. Isn't that why you keep running?"

She lowered her eyes. "Well, I guess that says it all."

I guess it does. Telling the truth hurts, but it was liberating. Thank you for coming back long enough to let me say it to your face.

Twenty minutes later he'd charged the airfare to his credit card and she was booked on the next flight to Kalispell. From there to Salt Lake and on to Australia. He walked her to the small airport lounge with her suitcase.

She turned to him. "I don't know if I'll be seeing you again."

Once upon a time those words would have destroyed him.

"Who knows what the future holds?" His gaze traveled over her features. "Have you got everything you need?"

"Yes."

"Then if you don't mind, I have to go. Stefanie's waiting for me." He was too anxious to get back to his wife to linger. "If things don't work out, you can call me."

"I believe you mean that."

"Whatever went wrong, I *am* your son, and you'll always be my mother. I wish you well."

"Thank you, Nicky."

Facing the woman who'd given birth to him, he said, "Take care of yourself." He kissed her cheek before he wheeled away, haunted by the things she'd told him about his grandparents' babies.

They'd survived two stillbirths. Where did they find the courage to try a third time? A human being could only endure so much pain.

It didn't take long to return to the apartment. He found his wife in the dining room filling the water glasses. She'd put out their best china and crystal. His heart melted at the sight of her doing everything possible to honor his mother. Stefanie didn't know any other way.

She looked up when she saw him. "Where's your mom?"

He guided her into the living room and sat on the couch, pulling her onto his lap. While he gently rocked her, he said, "She's left for Australia."

Stefanie buried her face in his neck. "What happened?"

His hands roved over her back. He could feel their baby against his stomach.

"Without you there, we were able to talk frankly." He

could feel her shudder. "I promise we didn't fight. I simply got down to the bottom line. She admitted she needed money."

"How much did you give her? Don't tell me nothing, because I wouldn't believe you."

After he told her, she pressed her lips to his mouth. "No man had a greater right to turn her away, but you didn't, Nick."

"When her money runs out, we'll probably see her again."

"I don't mind. She needs it a lot more than we do. We'll always be fine because we have so much she'll never have. I love you for your goodness, Nick." She covered his face with kisses. "I can't even imagine all the emotions you must be feeling. I know you're in pain."

I am, but not for the reasons you're thinking. "Oddly enough, it wasn't that hard to see her. In many ways she's a stranger to me. When she abandoned me years ago, I felt powerless. To be honest, tonight it was a relief to be able to send her where she wanted to go. Her staying here for a night wouldn't have accomplished anything."

All it took was one hour in my mother's presence for her to darken my world in new, insidious ways.

"Maybe when she's figured her life out a little more, she'll be back to build a relationship with you."

"Maybe." His mother had a lot to learn. He didn't appreciate her taking advantage of Stefanie—showing up uninvited and expecting to be welcomed.

"You can tell she's lost, but no child is born that way, Nick. She was obviously damaged early in life. No matter what her failings, though, she married your father and they had *you*. I'll always love her for that, because I can't fathom my life without you."

Full of need for his wife, he covered her mouth with his own and carried her into the bedroom. "Let's forget everything." *All I want is to concentrate on you and our baby.*

When we're together, no fire burns hotter.

I need your fire, my love. Mine's gone out.

Got to drag myself over to the door. It's my only way off the mountain. Can't wait for first light.

Got to keep moving or I won't be able to.

Forget your body, Marsden. Think of Stefanie.

Think of all the things you're going to tell her when you see her again.

"What have you got there, Mrs. Marsden?"

Stefanie looked up at the head of the EMT team. "One of my journals. Reading it makes me feel connected to my husband."

"That's a good thing." He handed her a clipboard with a form. "Forgive me for interrupting, but it would help us if you could fill this out now."

"Of course." She studied the questions. What was Nick's blood type? Was he allergic to any medications? Did he have any medical conditions the doctors should be aware of? Had he been in a hospital recently for any medical procedures?

She filled it out quickly, not wanting to think about why this was necessary. After handing it back to the EMT, she returned to her reading.

May 18, 1985

Today we bought a house over by Frank and Ellen's. It needs a lot of work, and I miss the tall ceilings at the mansion. But it's ours. We all get together. They're a wonderful couple. David and their Scott are almost the same age. They have twin girls ten months older than Nan.

Since Nan's birth a year ago Nick has seemed happier. I know the flying service is doing better and better, but I think there's more to his good mood than that. Maybe one day he'll tell me. Probably not.

While the weather holds, we're anxious to get busy painting the outside. We've decided on pale yellow with white trim. Then we'll start on the interior.

I can't wait to plant flowers around the foundation. I remember helping Mom and Dad dig holes for the tulip bulbs. I want our children to have the same experience.

It's a cozy little bungalow with three bedrooms, a fenced yard and a basement, where the children can play during the winter months. Nick's going to put in another bedroom and a bathroom downstairs.

Nan toddles around after David. Her golden-blond curls and hazel eyes make her look like a cherub. Nick must have noticed that she resembles his mother, but he never remarks on it.

Nan imitates everything her brother does. David, who has Nick's coloring and bone structure, imitates everything his father does. No one imitates me, which is a good thing.

I'm afraid David's got a bit of a speech problem. Whenever he's around other four-year-olds, whether at church or at the park, he doesn't seem to get the words out right. Liz's boy, Thomas, who's only a year older, speaks in perfectly executed sentences. Richard's two girls don't have problems pronouncing words, either. I can understand everything my nieces and nephews say on the phone.

Not with David. I may understand him, but no one else does, so I have to be his translator. I'm positive Nick's aware of it, but I think he's hoping it'll just go away. When I mentioned it to Dad, he said I couldn't speak properly at that age, either, but I grew out of it with a lot of help from Mom, who read to me constantly so I could hear the sounds and try to imitate them.

I didn't know that.

Luckily I've been reading to the children since the day they were born. I could open a children's bookstore already, but Nick never complains about the money I spend. He reads to the children every night, all the books he missed out on as a little boy. Frankly I think he loves story time more than they do.

I hope all the attention is helping David. Just to be on the safe side, I talked to Grandpa. He suggested I take him to a children's speech therapist. I'm of two minds whether to tell Nick. He's so crazy about David he'll hate it if anything's wrong.

I hate it, too, but after losing Matthew, I'm so thankful to have another boy I'm determined to deal with whatever might be wrong. What if reading isn't enough and he still has problems when he starts school?

I think I'll take Grandpa's advice and make an appointment with a therapist. I'll decide how to tell Nick later, depending on what I find out.

May 23, 1985

The therapist came to the house and suggested they all sit on the floor. She talked to David for a while so he'd feel comfortable. When he'd settled down, she flashed various cards in front of him and he had to identify the pictures.

Stefanie was proud of her son. He knew every picture. The therapist praised him. While she was talking to him, Nick suddenly appeared in the living room. What had brought him back to the house this morning?

Her stomach tensed with guilt. This was the first thing she'd ever done that they hadn't talked over ahead of time.

David got up and ran over to hug his father's leg. Luckily Ellen had agreed to keep Nan with her until the appointment was finished.

Slowly Stefanie got to her feet. "Honey? This is Annette Barnes. She's a children's diagnostician from the speech therapy clinic. I asked her to come and test David."

Nick didn't meet her eyes. He leaned over to pick David up. The look on his face was hard to read. A nerve twitched at the corner of his mouth. He was obviously upset.

"Annette? This is my husband, Nick."

The woman smiled. "The resemblance to your son is hard to miss, Mr. Marsden."

He didn't move a muscle. "Did I interrupt the test?"

"No. We just finished."

"And?"

The air felt trapped in Stefanie's lungs. By not telling Nick, she'd put both him and Annette in a difficult position.

To her credit, the therapist behaved as if she didn't notice the tension. "On the intelligence segment, your son tested a hundred percent perfect. Very few children his age can identify everything.

"According to your wife, you both read to him consistently. If more parents did that, they'd see huge improvements in their children's integration with the world around them.

"What he has is an articulation problem. I was about to give your wife a set of cards that you or she can use with him several times a day to work on certain sounds. If you have a few minutes now, I'll go through them with David so you can see the result we're trying to achieve."

Nick nodded, but his expression remained wooden.

"Why don't you sit on the floor with us, Mr. Marsden. David will think we're playing a game."

"Come on, sport." He got down on the carpet and David sat next to him, crossing his legs just like his dad. Stefanie felt her eyelids prickle.

With every card, their son tried to imitate the therapist. Some sounds improved through repetition. Others were still unintelligible.

When the game came to a close, Annette said, "You need to take him to his pediatrician and make sure there's nothing blocking the tubes in his ears. The doctor will show you how to keep them cleaned. That often improves hearing."

"How far behind is he?"

Oh, Nick. If you could see the fear on your face.

"It's going to require some work, but I'm convinced that by kindergarten he'll be up to the others. For the time being, he should be in a class with other children who have the same problem. It's twice a week for an hour and it really helps. Your insurance will cover it. Do you have any other questions?"

Nick got to his feet. David copied him. "What caused his problem?"

"Articulation disorders can result from many different factors. Sometimes the cause is complicated because of brain patterns. Sometimes it's relatively straightforward, having to do with the thrust of the tongue and other physical problems like blocked ear tubes. I understand your wife had the same thing when she was his age."

That revelation produced a surprised look from Nick.

"Based on your son's history, I believe he falls in the latter category. It's easily fixed with patience and hard work." She stood up and reached for her bag. "He's very bright and social. With parents like you, he can't fail. I'll leave this set of cards for you. Call me if you have any other questions."

Stefanie walked her to the front door. "Thank you for coming. I'm so relieved this is something we can work on with him."

She smiled. "Shall I put him down for the class?"

"What do you think, Nick?" He'd just joined them, carrying David in his arms. Never again would she act before they'd talked things over.

"Let's do it."

"Good. I'll take care of it," Annette said. "See you again in two months."

After closing the door, Stefanie leaned against it for a moment before turning to face her husband.

"Please forgive me," she whispered. "I should've told you before she came over."

"Someone had to do it."

He pulled her against him, although David was still tugging on his pant leg. If only Nick could talk about the things that bothered him. Was it wrong of her to want to hear his thoughts, his worries?

Clearing her throat, she asked, "What brought you home this morning?"

"The party I was supposed to fly to Colorado Springs had to cancel due to illness. That gave me the excuse to come home to my family. We've both been working hard and need a break. What do you say we pick up some hot dogs and lemonade and go to the park for a picnic?"

"I'd say that sounds wonderful."

"Good. Where's my little sunshine girl?" Nick didn't know her dad had always called Stefanie that growing up. "At your grandmother's?"

"No, although I could've asked her now that she doesn't go into Grandpa's office anymore. Ellen has her. We trade babysitting."

She glimpsed the telltale fire lighting his eyes. "Do you think there's a chance David would take a nap for a little while?"

"None whatsoever. His favorite person just came home."

Ignoring their son, who'd given up trying to get his daddy's attention, Nick pulled her against his hard body. He kissed her long and thoroughly, the kind of kiss that roused her passion and made her feel desire to the very tips of her fingers.

Too bad they couldn't do anything about it right now.

Oh, Nick—I need you so much…
I'd do anything for you. I'd give my life—

"Mrs. Marsden?"

She let out a cry. "You have news for me?"

Deputy Posner shook his head, plunging her to new depths of fear. "I'm sorry. I just wanted you to know that if you're hungry, you're welcome to have some of the doughnuts and cookies."

Someone must've put them out on the table while she'd been reading. "Thank you. But I'm afraid I can't eat anything."

She glanced at her watch. Three-thirty. The snowmobilers had been gone almost two hours and still no word. Nick had been out there too long.

Keep reading. Send him your thoughts.

Maybe Nick will hear me, and it'll keep him alive until help arrives.

July 25, 1985

My dear, dear Grandma Dixon died last Sunday morning. The nurse went in to get her up and found she'd passed away during the night. Grandpa called me and Dad. We went over to their house and when we walked in, Grandpa met us at the door with tears pouring down his cheeks.

"Mappie's gone."

He always called my grandma "Mappie."

Without her loving guidance, I would've had a much more difficult time accepting my mother's loss. Grandma lived a full life, blessing everyone with her presence. I'm not sad for her now. She's gone to a better place.

I sound like Nick's grandmother, but it's true.

The funeral was beautiful. The church was full. She touched so many lives. The minister read her favorite quote from Kahlil Gibran. Grandma and I read it together many times. It could've been written for Nick and me. I've copied the last paragraph from the funeral program.

"To wake at dawn with a winged heart and give thanks for another day of loving; To rest at the noon hour and meditate love's ecstasy; To return home at eventide with gratitude; And then to sleep with a prayer for the beloved in your heart and a song of praise upon your lips."

Grandpa managed to make it through the services, but at the cemetery he fell apart. There's a huge void in the house now that no one can fill. I felt it as her granddaughter. I can only imagine how Grandpa must feel.

If I'm grieving, it's for my grandpa who doesn't seem to know what to do without her.

How on earth did my father handle losing Mom? To have a companion for years and years, then to discover that person's no longer there and you're alone…

What a selfish child I was to resent my dad for marrying Renae. She'd suffered the loss of her husband, too. How little I understood. Mine was a selfish world. It was Nick who taught me that Dad needed a new life. He's still teaching me lessons I need to learn.

August 25, 1985

"Stefanie? Are you asleep?"

"No."

"I've been thinking about your grandfather," Nick said.

"So have I. In the month since the funeral he's gone downhill. Between losing Grandma and his Parkinson's, the doctor says he's in a deep depression. The nurse told me it's a fight to get him out of bed and into the wheelchair every morning. I try to go over there every day, but it's not enough."

Nick rubbed her arm. "After my grandfather died, my grandmother lost the will to live. The hell of it was, I couldn't leave the Guard to take care of her, and she was too old to be moved closer. I arranged for her health care and paid for everything, but it was an impossible situation. Ours isn't."

Stefanie sat up, taking the covers with her. "What are you getting at?"

"We could bring him here."

She'd been thinking the same thing.

"I couldn't ask that of you, Nick. In such close quarters we'd all be on top of one another. The noise might be too much for him. And we'd need room for the nurse. Even with the basement refinished, it would be crowded."

"It's either that or we move in with him," Nick said without equivocation. "I couldn't be there at the end for my grandparents, but there's nothing stopping us from helping him enjoy what time he has left. It'll be a temporary situation. We can rent out this house."

"Oh, darling." She threw her arms around his neck. "Thank you for being you." There was nothing selfish about Nick. "I'll go over first thing in the morning and talk to him about it."

"Tomorrow's Saturday. We'll all go."

They found him in the kitchen with the nurse, who'd wheeled him up to the table, where he could watch the portable TV and eat his cereal. His hands shook so badly, most of the food never reached his mouth.

While Nick dealt with the children, Stefanie took over from the nurse to help him finish his breakfast.

"How are you feeling this morning, Grandpa?"

"Fine." His voice was a croak.

He wasn't fine. Her grandfather had always been a talker. Now he was reduced to one-word sentences.

"Nick and I've been talking. How would you like it if we moved in here with you?"

The munching continued.

"Grandpa? Do you want company? This is a big house." When he didn't answer, she looked to Nick for help.

"We'd like you to live with us, whether it's here or at our house," he said.

Contact. Her grandfather gazed at Nick with so much love. "You have your own life, but I won't forget your offer."

Somehow he'd found the words for Nick.

Stefanie put her arm around him. "You're a big part of our lives, Grandpa. We want to take care of you."

"I'm all right."

No, he wasn't, but there was no budging him. He missed his Mappie. Without her, he didn't want anyone else.

Ten months later he joined her. With his death came the passing of an era. Stefanie's father was the patriarch of the family now. He called Stefanie and her siblings together for the reading of the will at his attorney's office.

"It's your grandfather's wish that his savings and assets be divided equally between Liz and Richard. The house he has left to Stefanie to keep or to sell. Since the market value won't be as much as the other portions, he's giving his stock to Nick. His exact words read, 'If he sells it at the appropriate time, it should buy him a new airplane. He's an ace in my book.'"

Stefanie had always adored her grandfather, but the fact that he'd paid such a special tribute to Nick made the memory of him doubly precious. He'd known of Nick's deep sorrow and the fears that had dominated his life. This was his way of trying to ease the burden a little.

She looked to her husband, but his head was turned away from her.

"I can't accept that stock," he said the minute they got back to their house.

"Oh, yes, you can. No one else offered to have him come and live with them."

"Your brother and sister live away. It would have been hard for them to make those arrangements. We're right here."

"That's true, and as it turned out, Grandpa didn't want to leave the house he built for Grandma and himself. But your generosity touched his heart, Nick. I saw the way he looked at you the morning we went over to talk to him. He felt your sincerity."

She moistened her lips. "You don't know this, but after you and I came home from Eureka that February, I told him about your father and mother. He helped me understand a lot of things and always kept my confidence. Grandpa knew how much I loved you. From that time on he had a special place in his heart for you. You've had the same effect on Dad and Dries. On me…"

"Stefanie. I—"

"It's true. I'm the envy of all my friends. Since Penny's divorce, she tells me all the time how lucky I am to have met you. The other day, when I was at the park with her and Sara and the children, they both admitted to being jealous of my relationship with you in school. Sara said she couldn't believe how fast I changed the moment I met you. She said I reminded her of the girl in *Splendor in the Grass*."

"Sara made the wrong analogy. I saw that movie, too, Stefanie. The girl had a nervous breakdown and the two lovers never got together in the end. It was a tragedy from start to finish. We're nothing like those pitiful characters."

"I know. That's what I told Sara. Well, not in those exact words. I think it hurt her feelings."

"You were always more intelligent than your friends. They couldn't deal with it."

One comment like that from Nick wiped away years of feeling inadequate around her friends.

"Let's not talk about the girls. What I want to know is, what kind of plane would you want to buy next?"

"We don't need another plane yet."

"Maybe you ought to think of trading in the two-seater for another four-seater and using the stock money to make up the difference."

"You think so?" He still seemed to be in shock. Coming from such humble beginnings, he couldn't comprehend accepting money he hadn't earned.

"I bet Dries would love the idea." Through a little subterfuge, maybe she could get him to rethink his decision. "What kind of plane would *he* want?"

"Another Cessna. You can always count on them." She detected that faraway look in his eyes. He was already envisioning it.

"What model?"

"I don't know. Maybe a Skylane."

The present—Stefanie

His second Skylane.

It had gone down.

Nick had gone down with it.

Our Father who art in heaven, hallowed be Thy name. Thy kingdom come, Thy will be done, on earth as it is in heaven.

If it is Thy will to call Nick home, then give me the strength to accept it—give me the strength to comfort my children....

After Stefanie had finished her prayer, she got up and took a brief trip outside the truck. When she came back in, she checked her watch. It was twenty after four.

She called David and discovered they were almost at Mackenzie.

"Your grandfather's waiting for you, honey. I'll let you know the second the snowmobilers have a sighting."

"What the hell is taking them so long?" He sounded so much like Nick just then Stefanie couldn't believe she wasn't talking to her husband.

"It's a tedious process, David. They have to cover every inch of terrain on their way up. He could've gone down in so many places. Fifteen men on snowmobiles are out there searching for him. One of them is going to come across the wreckage." She didn't want her children to lose hope. "They'll find him and he'll be alive!"

"He has to be!" She heard her son swallow a sob. "Just a minute. Nan wants to talk to you. Here she is."

Soon she heard her daughter's voice. "How are you holding up, Mom?"

"I'm okay. Everything possible is being done to find him. I'm positive we're going to hear good news at any moment."

"I know we will. Dad's a fighter, like Uncle Dries. He made it through the war. Dad'll make it through this."

"Of course he will. Can you imagine what it's going to be like when he's back home and he and Dries start swapping survival stories?"

"I can't wait!"

"Neither can I, honey. Neither can I."

"Ben said to tell you he loves you and he's praying for Dad."

"Tell him I love him, too."

"Here's Amanda. She wants to talk to you."

"Of course."

"Mom?"

"Yes, honey?" It thrilled her that her daughter-in-law called her that.

"I think you're the bravest woman I've ever known."

"Then I've got you completely fooled."

"No way. Listen, our plan is to leave Jack with Grandpa Larkin and Renae, then the four of us will come straight over to you. David wants the phone back so he can get directions."

"Okay. Give my grandson a big kiss from me and Nick."

"I've been giving him dozens," she said in a weepy voice.

Stefanie could understand. Once she had Nick in her arms again, she'd never stop loving him.

When David said goodbye and they'd hung up, she poured herself some coffee. The men in the front of the truck still had nothing to tell her. Desperate for the waiting to end, she sat back down and resumed reading where she'd left off. Memories were all that held her together.

Chapter 14

Chapter 14

April 12, 1992
Last night the whole family got together at Dad's for Liz's fortieth birthday. Richard and Colleen flew in with their children from Helena. We invited Dries, who's part of our family now.

The toast Don made to Liz was very touching. In front of everyone he spoke of his love for her.

But as I've learned from Nick, there are other ways to show love. And yet...

"Jeff?" She turned to the staff writer from the newspaper. He'd been covering a story and she'd been sent with him to take pictures. They were on their way back to the office. "Do you mind if I ask you a personal question?"

He flashed her a grin. "Ask away."

"How long have you been married?"

"Twenty years. What about you?"

"We're going on fourteen."

With both children at school all day and Nick busier than ever, Stefanie had felt the need to go back to work part-time.

"*That's* the big question you wanted to ask me?"

She smiled. "Not exactly. You're probably going to tell me to mind my own business, but I'd really like to know how often you tell Erica you love her."

"Well…" He scratched his head. "Let's see…I say it in the morning on my way out the door. Then I say it on the phone a couple of times during the day. And I say it when I kiss her good-night. I'd catch grief if I didn't. So what are you doing? Running some kind of poll we can print in the paper?"

Her hands twisted in her lap. "Hardly."

His expression sobered. "Mind if I ask *you* a personal question?"

"Go ahead."

"You and Nick aren't having problems, are you?"

"No!"

"That sounds firm enough. But since you asked me that question, I couldn't help wondering." After a moment of silence he said, "What's the matter, Stefanie?"

"I shouldn't have said anything. Nick's so wonderful."

"But there *is* something wrong. I knew it when you came to work at the paper the first time around."

She stared out the car window. "Our first baby was stillborn."

Jeff let out a troubled sigh. "I knew something had happened. You had a look of sadness about you, but you were so private. Maybe you need to talk to someone."

"I'm talking to you."

"I'm not an expert. Ask Erica and she'll tell you."

"But you *do* talk."

He pulled over to the curb and shut off the engine. "What are you saying? That you and Nick have stopped talking?"

Tears fell down her cheeks. "It isn't that. I feel so disloyal even discussing this with you."

"Discussing what?"

"Nick has never told me he loves me, but that's not important anymore because I know he does. What worries me is that he's never talked about his feelings."

Jeff blinked. "Never as in *never?*"

She wiped the moisture from her face. "He just can't."

"How did you two ever get married?"

Stefanie gave him a wry smile. "The old-fashioned way."

"You mean show, not tell."

"That's a good way to put it. You must be a writer."

"And you're the artist who works with pictures instead of words. Except that everyone needs to unload once in a while."

Jeff understood.

"Nick's never really talked about the losses in his life. He didn't talk about the loss of our baby. The death of his father. Or his mother's abandonment."

"Whew."

She nodded. "There's a lot he keeps bottled up inside. You don't know how many times over the years I've wanted to *make* him talk to me."

The compassion in Jeff's eyes hurt. "You need to confront him about it, Stefanie."

"I can't. He's a perfect husband and father."

"Does he talk to your children?"

This conversation was beginning to sound like ones she'd had with her father years ago.

"Nick's there for them in all the ways that count. He's always shown physical affection to them and to me. Saying anything to Nick would make him feel diminished, and I won't do that." She shook her head. "You don't know what his past was like."

"But if he has no idea what this is doing to you—"

"It doesn't matter."

"It matters enough that you've broken down in front of me."

She blinked rapidly. "I'm sorry about that, Jeff. Please forget we had this conversation."

"I couldn't do that if I tried. I'm your friend, Stefanie. What you need is to talk to a professional."

"Without Nick's knowing about it, I couldn't. My grandfather was a doctor. Years ago I talked to him about Nick. He said he needed therapy. His whole family did, but they weren't the kind of people to get it and they didn't recognize that Nick needed help."

"It's not too late for him, Stefanie. What a tragedy if you never broach the subject. If you could find the courage, he'll probably thank you one day, But I can understand your fear.

"It took my mother years to confront my dad about his drinking. But she finally did it, even though it could have meant a divorce. To Dad's credit, he acknowledged his problem and started going to Alcoholics Anonymous. In his own way Nick might surprise you."

"You could be right. I'll think about what you said."

"As you know, I started out being a film critic for the paper. Growing up, I was crazy about the old '30s and '40s films. The way you describe Nick reminds me of Cary Grant's character in *Only Angels Have Wings*. Have you ever seen it?"

"No. Was it a book first? I always prefer the book."

"I'm not sure. It takes place in Ecuador. Jean Arthur plays opposite Cary. She's a visiting entertainer at the bar that's also the headquarters of Barranca Airlines. They deliver the mail under death-defying conditions. He's a pilot who won't be pinned down to anything. Of course, she's intrigued enough to miss her connecting boat and stays in Barranca for a week. He may be her ideal man— if she can just crack his code. Nick sounds a lot like him."

"I'll have to rent it at the video store."

"Maybe you should plan a romantic evening at home with Nick and the two of you can see it together. Perhaps he'll recognize some of himself in the character. It might get him thinking."

Stefanie's eyes widened. "That's a brilliant idea, Jeff!" She leaned across the seat to kiss his cheek.

By Friday night she had everything planned. Her dad and Renae had agreed to watch the children so she and Nick could have the house to themselves. She made enchiladas and lemon iced tea with mint, one of Nick's favorite meals.

In honor of the evening she wore the white Mexican wedding dress that Nick had picked out for her at a little shop in Puerto Vallarta. They'd flown down there to meet Todd— a friend from Nick's Guard days—and his wife. The four of them had spent a great vacation with all their children.

The dress showed off her tan. She'd been working hard in the garden of her grandparents' house, the house she and Nick had made into their own home.

Nick arrived home at his usual time. He came through the back door into the kitchen and slid his arms around her waist from behind. After nuzzling her neck, he pulled one sleeve down to her elbow and began to kiss the delicate hollow of her shoulder. Her legs suddenly felt weak.

"What's the occasion?" His voice sounded husky.

"I thought we'd have a night to ourselves. The children are at Dad's. As soon as you've showered, dinner will be ready. I'll meet you in the family room with our food."

"I won't be long," he promised.

Within a half hour they'd eaten. "Now for your surprise."

"Good. That's what I've been waiting for." He reached for her, but she evaded him and got up from the couch to turn on the tape. "I got an old movie for us to watch together."

"How old?"

"1939."

"That means black-and-white."

"Yes."

Nick didn't enjoy movies all that much. "Have *you* seen it?"

"No. While I was at work the other day, Jeff Sargent told me about it. He used to write the Critic's Corner movie reviews for the paper. He said it reminded him of you because you're a pilot." She handed him the case. "There's a blurb on the inside."

While the credits were running on the screen, he read it aloud in an increasingly mocking tone.

"The film's themes include 'male camaraderie and rugged, stoic bravery—the pilots' code.' So *that's* what it is," he scoffed.

Suddenly his head reared back. "Who wrote the movie? This says it's about courier aviators delivering the mail in South America."

"I believe it was the director of the film."

Nick frowned. "He must have copied the idea from *Southern Mail*."

She shook her head. "I don't know. When did Saint-Exupery write his book?"

"1926."

Stefanie smiled. "Well, I guess we'll find out."

I hope I'm not doing the wrong thing.

Twenty minutes into the film she could tell her husband was restless. Any hope that he might get some insight from the hero's characterization was lost because all Nick could do was find fault with the technical aspects of the film's aviation background.

The second it ended he turned off the TV. "The story's an absurd travesty. If Jeff ever starts doing critiques again, tell him he can quote me. I don't know about you, but without the children around, *this* pilot has better things to do."

The movie already forgotten, he picked her up as if she was a new bride and carried her through the house and down the hallway to the master bedroom. There was no chance of an in-depth discussion, because Nick proceeded to make love to her with an intensity that took her breath.

"Stefanie?" he whispered two hours later. He was leaning over her with a worried look on his face.

"I know. We should have picked up the children before now."

"You're right, but that isn't what's troubling me. I forgot to use protection. I can't believe I did that."

"I wasn't thinking either. Maybe I shouldn't have gone off the pill." She shrugged. "Well, if we're pregnant, it's too late to worry about it now."

"How would you feel about another baby?"

"Giving birth at thirty-six would make me an older mother."

"And me an older father."

"You didn't act old tonight." For once he didn't grin. "In fact, you took me back to Tortola."

"I'll take you there again one day."

"For now I'm perfectly happy to be right here. To answer your question, I'd love another baby, but I don't think I'm ovulating."

Her comment seemed to relax him. He kissed her deeply, then slid out of bed. "I'll go get the kids. Keep the bed warm for me."

"Nick." She reached for his arm. "If I did conceive tonight, are you okay with it?"

"How could I complain when it was my fault?"

While he was gone she pondered his remark. It wasn't the answer she'd wanted. What was he doing assigning fault to himself for anything? Especially when it had to do with the possibility of their having another baby?

Ten days later her period came. She experienced a pang of disappointment, but it was fleeting when she realized the news would erase the shadows from Nick's eyes. He'd never enjoyed her pregnancies. Not since Matthew.

She could understand it—and yet she couldn't. David and Nan had brought so much joy into their lives.

On her way home from work she stopped at the drug-store to buy a card. After grazing through the selections, she found something perfect. The sentiment inside said, "Nice try, but no cigar."

Why not make this a night of celebration?

She picked up the children from elementary school and announced that they were going to have a party at Daddy's office.

"What kind?" David wanted to know. Like Nick, he tended to get straight to the point.

"Oh, just a let's-make-Daddy-happy party."

Nan beamed. "Can we give him candy?"

"Of course. What kind shall we buy?"

"Snickers."

Yup. She knew her daddy.

"Uncle Dries likes black licorice."

She smiled at David. "While we shop in the deli for chicken and potato salad, we'll get some of that, too." And a couple of cold beers. And…a condom to slip inside the card.

Finally, she bought paper plates and plastic forks. Delighted with her surprise and their purchases, she drove them out to the airfield.

"Uncle Dries!" the children cried the moment they saw him in the front office. They both flung themselves at him. "We're going to have a party," Nan informed him.

"Come on in the back."

No one could light up his face the way they did. He lifted smiling eyes to Stefanie. Maybe they were even twinkling. "What's the occasion?"

"Oh, this and that."

"Uh-oh."

"It's good news, Dries. Trust me. Where's Nick?"

"He's up there."

She looked out the window to see the red-and-white plane make its approach and touch down on the tarmac. No matter how often she watched, she could never quite squelch the fear that this time something could go wrong.

While he taxied over to the hangar, the children ran outside to greet him. For a fraction of a second her gaze met the Dutchman's. He knew what she was thinking. But what he said was, "Graceful as a swan skimming the water. I taught him to do that."

Her eyes misted over. "I would loved to have seen you in action in 1942."

"Be glad that was before your time, Stefanie." Now his eyes were moist.

How lonely his life would've been if Nick hadn't come into it. Two remarkable souls who'd needed each other and had met at exactly the right moment.

A few minutes later, pandemonium reigned in the kitchen. While the men washed up, Nan helped Stefanie empty all the bags and lay out the food. David wheeled a couple of chairs down the hall so they could sit around the table together.

Her heart skipped a beat when she discovered Nick's searching gaze fastened on her. Better put him out of his misery so he could enjoy the party.

Without hesitation she got up from the table and walked over to him. "Happy unbirthday, Nick." She gave him the card. On the envelope she'd written *For your eyes only*.

"Unbirthday—you're funny, Mommy." Nan giggled.

As he took it from Stefanie, his hands actually trembled.

While everyone watched, he opened it and pulled the card out with a jerk. The force sent the little packet to the floor.

"What's that, Daddy?"

"Yeah, Dad."

He bent to grab it so no one could tell what it was.

Stefanie didn't think she'd ever seen Nick blush before. When he got up, his face had gone the same color as Dries's whenever he was upset about something.

"Drinks for everyone," she said to help her husband regroup. She handed Dries a beer. "And one for my husband."

Nick had just read the card. Instead of taking the can, he flung his arms around her and pulled her to him.

"It isn't that I don't want another baby," he whispered into her hair.

"I know, Nick." But residual fear from their first baby's stillbirth lingered in his mind.

"We've got presents for you, Daddy."

"You mean there's more?" he teased, sending Stefanie a private message that said once they were alone, he'd enjoy the present she'd given him with the greatest relish.

Evidently she'd managed to surprise her husband with her gift. And since—aside from the pill—she'd never been the one to buy protection for them, she'd surprised herself.

My makeshift sled has taken me in the wrong direction.
I can't see for the trees.
My tears are frozen.
I'm so tired. So tired…
I can't feel my body.
I keep hearing this damn buzzing in my head. It's growing louder. Something inside me must be shutting down.

* * *

"Death happens that way sometimes, Nicholas. I saw it with one of the pilots."

"Don't stop now."

"In July we were transferred to the 167 Gold Coast Squadron. Our mission was to provide air defense for the Royal Navy base at Scapa Flow. That's where the convoys for Russia were formed. We flew protection and reconnaissance missions."

"That must've been something."

"You'd better believe it. I strapped myself into a sweet little Spitfire Mk VB and thought I was the cock of the walk. In those days, I'm afraid, we strutted around like that.

"Everything went fine until the squadron was transferred to Ludham in East Anglia. My job was to escort bombers flying above occupied territory. You know, we flew right over my home."

"What was that like?"

"Surreal."

"I can imagine."

"That's where we got into our first dogfight. Unfortunately we were outnumbered by the Germans. As we came out of the turn, someone reported 'Bandits at six o'clock above.' Our CO gave the order to break left a hundred and eighty degrees.

"I followed him around, keeping station behind him. The next thing I knew, his aircraft was hit. We'd been jumped by some German Bf 109s. I took out seven before I realized he'd been injured.

"'Stay with me,' I told him.

"He kept saying, 'I can't, Dries. It's over for me.'"

Nick shook his head in sympathy.

"'You're talking nonsense,' I told him.

"'No,' he said. 'I'm hit, but no Nazi's going to take me alive. The buzzing in my head is getting worse.'

"'That's your plane,' I told him.

"'No. It's something else. Like I stuck my finger in a light socket. My whole body's quivering with vibrations. This is it. So long, Dries. Go get those bastards.'

"I tried to keep him talking, Nicholas, but it was no use. I saw him slip away from us. Then he was gone. His body was never recovered. Only God knew where to find him."

Nick could remember hearing his mentor sob only twice.

"God notices the fall of every sparrow, Nick."

I hope my grandmother's right. Only God knows where I am, and this body is degenerating fast.

Victor Hugo said it best. I memorized this passage years ago. "The human body might well be regarded as only an appearance. It hides our reality. It lies thick over our light or our shadow. The reality is our soul. To speak absolutely, the human visage is a mask. The true man is that which is beneath man."

Beneath your beautiful body lies a beautiful soul, Stefanie. A shining light ever beckoning me.

I feel you slipping away from me. Come and warm me, darling.

"The Lord is my shepherd. I shall not want. He maketh me to lie down in green pastures. He leadeth me beside the still waters. He restoreth my soul. He leadeth me in the paths of righteousness for his name's sake.

"Yea, though I walk through the valley of the shadow

of death, I will fear no evil, for thou art with me. Thy rod and thy staff they comfort me. Thou preparest a table before me in the presence of mine enemies.

"Thou anointest my head with oil. My cup runneth over. Surely goodness and mercy shall follow me all the days of my life. And I will dwell in the house of the Lord forever with my beloved."

Chapter 15

October 27, 1998

Last week Adam Wright phoned me with a job offer I couldn't refuse. It's a real coup. He's the owner and publisher of *Northwest Trails* magazine, a publication out of Mackenzie.

He wants to build up circulation around the country and make it a household name like *Arizona Highways*.

He told me he's always been impressed with my work at the newspaper but especially with the photos I've taken that have appeared in other publications. Now that the person who headed his photography department for the last ten years has been forced to retire due to unexpected health problems, the position is open and he wants *me!*

It's a nine-to-five job, five days a week, working

on in-depth articles. I would brainstorm with him and Ira Goldman, a new editor from New York, to come up with the stories and layouts. I have to admit this is what every Brooks graduate aims for—to find a forum in which to establish yourself as an artist.

As soon as Nick walked into the house from the airfield, I talked to him about it. He's pulling for me all the way. Now that Nan has left for college in Seattle, both children are out of the house. It seems I've finally got the time to dig into my career.

Adam's already asked me to come up with an idea to launch me as part of the team. Nick thinks we should fly to Eureka and take more pictures of the northern lights, then do a layout that compares them to the pictures I took years ago. His friend Hal at Montana State's Meteorology department will tell Nick which night would be the best for viewing them.

I think his idea is fabulous. Nick grew up in Eureka and is friends with a group of Native Americans whose ancestors were the Kootenai Indians of the Tobacco Plain. They lived along a trail traveled by the explorer Thompson, who was the first white man to see the area on his way to British Columbia.

This trail eventually became the northern section of U.S. Highway 93. Nick says the sighting of the northern lights is woven into the Kootenais' history. I could include it in the story.

I didn't know any of this!

My husband is a font of hidden knowledge—and the source I go to when I need to renew myself.

Adam was impressed when I presented our idea

to him. He'd never seen my first pictures because they belong to Brooks. But the Institute is allowing me to publish them on this one-time basis. Because of the nature of the subject, he wants the entire April issue devoted to my story. He'd like me to get photos of Nick's friends, too. The works!

I'm thrilled, flattered and overjoyed because Nick is going to work with me on this. He plans to fly low over the original trail and get pictures from the air. We'll do an overlay to show the past and the present. My husband is brilliant!

March 2, 1999

Yesterday Ira called me into his office after hours to celebrate the latest edition. Everyone else had gone home. To my surprise, he produced a bottle of champagne and poured me a glass. A strange feeling passed through me. Over the past months we've been working together pretty constantly. He's divorced and that's why he stays late so many nights. Sometimes I've stayed late, too, when I knew Nick was going to be delayed getting home.

Ira's a relocated New Yorker with contacts all over the globe. I think he's interested in me. It's my fault. I haven't paid close enough attention to care.

"You've only had one drink. Come on and have another with me. What's the rush?"

"Thanks, but one drink's my limit. I have to drive home, you know." She said it with a breezy smile, hoping to keep things light. She loved her job too much to risk losing it and had to find a way to work with him without offending him.

Beneath dark, shaggy brows, his gray eyes studied her. If he was waiting for her to capitulate, he was going to be disappointed.

"What's it like being married to a pilot?"

"That's only part of what Nick is. Why don't you ask me what it's like being married to my soul mate? He owns my heart and always will."

He sat back in his swivel chair, giving her the eye. "Are you for real?"

That was the second time she'd been asked that question. The first time it had been Nick's mother who'd posed it.

"What do you think?" she asked.

"I think you're the sexiest woman I ever met."

"I think you've had too much to drink."

An unsmiling Nick suddenly appeared in the doorway of Ira's office. He was still dressed in the shirt and pants he flew in. "I second that."

How long had he been standing outside in the hall listening?

Ira raised his eyebrows. "Come on in, Nicholas. We're celebrating your wife's contribution to the magazine. This issue's going to increase circulation."

"I'm afraid we're off to do some celebrating of our own."

The two men stared at each other.

"Lucky you," Ira muttered.

Before Nick could respond, Stefanie said, "See you in the morning, Ira. Better get to bed soon. We've got another layout to plan with Adam."

Nick kept a possessive hand on her neck as they walked

out of the building. He saw her to his car. "We'll come back for your car later. Right now I want to talk to you."

The second they were both inside she leaned across the seat and cupped his cheek so she could kiss him. His jaw felt like a piece of petrified wood. "I'm so glad you walked in when you did."

"You handled him well, Stefanie. I know your job means a lot to you, but I have to say I don't like the situation."

"It won't be repeated because I'll never stay late again."

"Promise?"

"How could you doubt it?"

"It's not you I'm worried about."

"Nick—he made a verbal pass at me. It backfired. He won't try it again. Everyone knows I've got a thing for this hotshot pilot."

The present—Stefanie

Sudden activity on the radio brought her to her feet. She could feel her heart in her throat as she hurried over to the cluster of men.

"…and it looks like we've got a find."

"Thank God!" she cried.

The sheriff turned to her. "Mrs. Marsden—"

"I know." She cut him off. Tears streamed down her face. "Deputy Posner told me what it means. I'm just so thankful his plane's been spotted, I can't begin to tell you."

"I'm glad you understand. It could be a while before we hear anything else."

She nodded.

"What's your location, Marv?" she heard the radio man ask.

"We're up seven miles from the command post—in the part of the saddle where the forest fire burned part of the area last year. Bill and I came up over the ridge. When we looked down, we saw the skid marks. We're following them now. He slid a long way. Judging from what we've seen, he picked a good spot. There aren't that many clear patches up here."

"Copy. We'll let the others know and send more support teams pronto."

Be alive, Nick. Please be alive.

The sheriff studied her. "It's not a lot to go on, but I'd say the first report is encouraging."

"I know it is!" He could've gone down in the trees. Nick had once told her that it was worse crashing into trees than in an unobstructed spot.

Stefanie went back to her chair to allow the men room to do their jobs. The sheriff talked with several FAA people who came and went from the truck. There were constant conversations over the radio.

Without hesitating, she phoned Dries.

"They located the crash site."

When she told him what she'd heard, he made one of those barking sounds in his throat. "That's my boy. Knew he had the right instincts the first time he took over the controls. Anybody can fly—only a few transcend."

Such praise coming from Dries. Nick would love to hear it.

"I've got to hang up and call the children. When I know anything else, I'll—"

"*Ja, ja.*"

In the next breath she was blurting everything to David. She could hear him relaying the news to everyone else at the house and heard their cries of relief.

"Listen, honey, I'm going to hang up now. Any minute we're going to learn more, then I'll call back."

"It's going to be the best news, Mom."

"Yes."

She clicked off her phone.

When she'd delivered Matthew, she'd been praying he had all his fingers and toes. It had never occurred to her that he wouldn't be alive. The horrific realization had been instantaneous.

This was a different kind of agony. Her husband had been alive when he'd made love to her this morning. Was it this morning or was it yesterday? Heavens… Time was so mixed up she couldn't keep anything straight.

All she knew was that she'd practically had to push him out the door to go to work. After being on Tortola for ten days, they were still in vacation mode.

Each minute she had to wait for word of Nick felt like an eternity. She couldn't read, she couldn't eat or drink. The rescue people were probably with him right this second. She wished she could've been the one to reach him first.

Please, God.

Static filled her ears once more. "This is Bill. We have a Code Red."

Stefanie's heart stopped beating for a second. What did that mean? She turned a terrified face to the sheriff. But it was Deputy Posner who moved closer to her.

"It means this is a rescue." He'd obviously read her

mind. "We don't know his condition yet, but your husband is alive."

"Oh, thank God." She crumpled in his arms while sobs of joy wracked her body. "I have to go to him!"

His eyebrows rose. "After the sheriff finishes giving orders, you can ask him." Judging by his facial expression, he didn't think his boss would agree. Well, she had news for him.

There was a fresh burst of activity inside the truck. She pulled away from the deputy and got on her cell phone. Her fingers were trembling so much she almost dropped it.

"David? Your father's alive!"

He let out a whoop that probably damaged her eardrum, but she forgave him.

"I don't know anything else yet. Call Dries and tell him for me." She saw Deputy Sanford leave the truck. He was the head of the EMT team. "David, I've got to go. It'll be a while before you hear from me."

As soon as the sheriff was alone, she approached him. "Sheriff Zabriskie? I'd like to go to my husband. Deputy Posner said he'd take me if it was all right with you."

He shook his head. "As a general rule, I'm opposed to it."

"I've ridden snowmobiles in these mountains for years."

"No crash site is a pretty one, Mrs. Marsden. You think you're prepared, but you're not," he said in a tone of finality.

She took a deep breath. "When our first child was stillborn, I wasn't prepared for that, either, but I survived. I *have* to be with Nick!"

The man remained inflexible.

"Are you married, Sheriff?"

"Yes."

"If you were in that crash on the verge of death,

wouldn't you want to see your wife's face one more time? If only to say goodbye?"

He took a full minute to answer. Then she heard him expel a sigh. "Go ahead. Just remember to let the men do their work."

Tears smarted her eyes. "Thank you, Sheriff."

When she turned to Deputy Posner, he gave her a quiet smile. "Grab something to eat, then put on your gear and meet me outside in five minutes."

The deputy didn't want her fainting on him.

She wolfed down the lunch Renae had made for her and followed it with another cup of coffee. Next came her ski bib and parka. Out of the duffel bag she drew the red-and-white Scandinavian hat she'd knitted and put it on. The design matched Nick's.

Once she'd pulled on her boots and gloves, she flew out the door of the truck and hurried over to the burn barrel. Before long she heard the sound of the deputy's snowmobile. He looked a lot bigger in his gear.

"Jump on the back and lock your hands in front of me."

She knew the drill. Some of her favorite outings with Nick had been on snowmobiles.

He turned his head to the side. "Are you ready?"

"Yes." She'd just put her boots in the foot wells.

"Then let's go."

The EMTs had preceded them up the logging road. The deputy followed their tracks. He was no novice; in fact, he made her feel safe. In his own quiet way he reminded her a little of Nick. She liked him for a lot reasons but especially for his willingness to be responsible for her.

Five minutes up the trail with only their headlight for

guidance, she felt a sense of isolation creep over her. Pines as tall as sentinels flanked them. The air had grown more frigid now, evidence of a higher elevation. If she didn't know better, she'd think they were thousands of miles from civilization.

"Nick? Do you ever worry about crashing?"

Long before they were married, she'd asked him that question.

"Nope."

"Come on. Be honest."

He'd kissed her nose. "Naturally I don't like to consider the possibility that I might be involved in one. Sure, there's an element of risk associated with flying, but I always figure it'll happen to the other guy. Not to me." He'd grinned but his smile had quickly faded. "Did you know that eighty-five percent of crashes happen on or near an airport, relatively close to civilization? So if I survive the crash, help will get there soon."

"But what if it's not close?"

"I'll worry about that when I have to," he'd said, "not before. Find me within the first twenty-four hours, and my chances of survival are much improved."

She estimated he'd been surviving for thirteen hours without help, a shorter time than the parameter he'd given her.

But in what condition?

He's alive, Stefanie. That's what's important.

Until they came upon it, she wasn't aware that they'd reached the ridge the man named Bill had referred to. They'd arrived at first light. The night must have seemed endless to Nick.

"He'll be down the other side," the deputy said over his shoulder. "Brace yourself. It's pretty steep."

Like a plain piece of fabric among the squares of a patchwork quilt lay a clear sweep of virgin snow. Snow that was scored by a long, deep line. Down, down, down, her eyes followed the trough carved by the belly of Nick's plane.

Her driver negotiated the incline with great expertise. When they got to the crash site she had a strange feeling of déjà vu.

Once, when David was about eight, Nick had spent several nights helping him put a model airplane together. They'd worked hard. It wasn't just any model, of course. It was a Curtiss JN, the kind she'd seen at the air show years before.

Thrilled it had finally dried, David ran outside in the snow to fly it. A few minutes later Stefanie could hear him crying. She and Nan hurried outside to see what was wrong.

"My plane hit that tree and crashed!"

Indeed it had. The nose was stuck in the snow at the base of the big hawthorn tree in the front yard. The body had cracked in two. A couple of parts had broken off and were scattered about. All their meticulous work destroyed in an instant.

That was how Nick's new Skylane looked to her. A broken toy.

He'd survived. But how?

She spied remnants of a fire he'd managed to build behind the plane. It was so small no one could have derived any warmth from it.

"I don't see him!" She felt frantic. The men on the scene

were already conducting an investigation, but there was no sign of Nick.

Deputy Posner got off the machine and gave her a hand down. "Wait here. I'll find out."

She'd promised herself not to panic. For Nick's sake she had to stand back and let the rescue people do their jobs, but she was dying inside. While she stood there trying to get some feeling back into her legs, a gust of wind carried a candy wrapper to her feet.

Her eyes filled with tears. *Snickers.* She grabbed it and put it in her pocket. His favorite candy bar had helped keep him alive. She'd frame the wrapper for their home office. A souvenir of this unforgettable night.

Except it was morning now.

In a minute the deputy returned. "It appears your husband used the door of the plane to slide farther down the mountain, possibly trying to reach a logging road, but it made a detour into the trees."

That sounded like her innovative, heroic husband. "Can you take me to him?"

"Let's go."

They climbed back on and drove past the wreckage. He followed the slide marks that gradually disappeared into the trees below.

The second they came upon the group of EMTs and she saw a body on the litter, she cried out his name.

She leaped off the snowmobile and ran through the snow toward him.

The deputy was right on her heels and held her back. "Don't go any closer. Deputy Sanford will give us an update in a minute."

She swallowed her sobs. "I'm sorry."

By now she could make out his features, so pale and drawn. A day's growth of dark beard covered the lower half of his face. His forehead had suffered a blow and was covered in blood, but he'd never looked more beautiful to her.

His eyes were shut and he wasn't talking!

The hat she'd made him lay in the snow. *Oh, Nick. My beloved Nick.*

While one man checked his vital signs, another was putting him in a neck brace. After seeing the position of the plane when it came to a stop, she knew he could have broken it or his back—or both.

They'd wrapped him in blankets, and she watched one of the men pop open the chemical bags and place them on his chest and hips to give him warmth.

A minute later the head of the team walked over to her.

"Why isn't he saying anything?"

"He's unconscious."

She moaned. "Did he speak to you earlier?"

"No. We found him this way."

"How bad is he? Tell me the truth. Please."

"He's suffered hypothermia and has a concussion. How severe, we won't know until he's had an MRI and a CAT scan. As you can see, we've splinted his arm. His hands are cut and they'll need stitches. His hip took a hard blow. They're binding his head with a clean bandage now. When that's done, we'll put him on the sled and take him down."

Sickness welled up in her. "Can I speak to him?"

"That's a good idea. A familiar voice might bring him around."

She went to kneel by his right side. She didn't dare

touch him. It seemed like every part of him was either bruised or broken. Except his lips.

She brushed hers against them. How cold they were....

For the first time in their lives there was no response.

"Nick, sweetheart? It's Stefanie. Can you hear me?"

He didn't make a sound. She choked down a sob.

"I've found you, my love, and I'm going to take you home."

Still no movement.

Terrified, Stefanie clambered to her feet. "Let's get him to the hospital as soon as possible."

For fear of injuring Nick further, the journey down the mountain took a lot longer than the one coming up. She and Deputy Posner stayed right behind the sled, where she could keep an eye on her husband.

If she hadn't seen the Life Flight helicopter waiting near the command post, ready to transport Nick, she didn't know what she would have done.

Everyone worked in harmony to load him safely inside. She turned to the deputy. "I'll never forget your kindness to me."

"It was my privilege."

"Please tell everyone thank you," she said before climbing into the helicopter. One of the attendants indicated she should sit on the bench at the back and strap herself in. During the short flight to the hospital they began an IV. She could tell they were doing everything possible to stabilize him. But her panic increased because he still hadn't regained consciousness when the chopper set down on the landing pad outside the E.R.

Someone opened the door and assisted her to the

ground. The whole family seemed to be assembled a few yards off. David reached her first. She hugged him hard. "Your father hasn't come to yet."

"We know. The sheriff's been keeping us informed. Dad's going to make it, Mom."

"He'll wake up soon, Mom!" Nan had just grabbed her. The two of them embraced.

"I know, honey."

As she watched them move Nick into the hospital, she heard one of the attendants say, "I've lost a pulse. His blood pressure's falling. Code Blue!"

"Code Blue?" she cried. "That means his heart has stopped! No!" This couldn't be happening! She was in the middle of a nightmare. A living nightmare.

David pulled her out of the way of the crash cart team running toward Nick.

"Have faith," Stefanie's father said, squeezing her shoulder while the hospital staff worked feverishly over her husband's inert body.

"Dad, they have to revive him. He has to make it. He has to come through this. I can't lose him now. I just can't!"

"Courage, Stefanie." She spun around. Dries. He was hanging on to Wes. Grant and Dena were behind them.

Something about the old Dutchman who'd been through the hell of war and was still here fighting for Nick made Stefanie pull herself together at the last second. He had that effect on her.

"*Ja,*" she whispered, reaching for his hand.

His reassuring squeeze came at the same moment she heard, "Got a pulse. Blood pressure coming up. Let's go."

The relief was so exquisite Stefanie almost fainted. With

her father and her son on either side of her, they followed the stretcher into the E.R., where the staff went to work on Nick.

Stefanie had to fill out myriad forms, but she was scarcely aware of what she was signing. Eventually one of the E.R. residents explained that they were wheeling him upstairs for a CAT scan and an MRI.

"Can I come?"

"I'm afraid not, but I promise to keep you posted on any change."

The hardest thing in the world was to see her husband disappear behind doors that said No Admittance.

Another period of waiting had begun. She had no choice but to walk to the lounge where everyone had gathered. Renae got to her first and grasped her hand. "It's all going to work out, honey."

"Yes."

"Steffie," her brother murmured. He and Colleen wrapped their arms around her. "We just got here. Liz phoned. She and Don are on the way over from the house."

"I love you guys. It means everything to me that you're here. Nick will be so touched when he sees all of you."

Ben and Amanda reached for her, giving her long hugs. Stefanie loved her children's spouses. "What would I do without my family?" she murmured.

"Come on, Mom." Nan drew her over to the couch. "You've been up twenty-four hours without sleep. You need to rest."

"I'm fine." In truth, she was horribly disoriented. She squinted at the daylight pouring through the lounge windows.

David handed her a roll and a cup of coffee. "Eat and drink or we'll have two patients in here."

While she obeyed her son, Frank walked into the room. He headed straight for her and gave her a kiss on the cheek.

"Don't move. Stay where you are. I heard about Nick and came by to tell you Ellen and I are here. Anything you need, all you have to do is ask. Nick's the best friend I've got, so he has to recover. Right?"

She smiled through the tears. "Right! Thank you for coming. It'll mean so much to Nick when I tell him."

For the next hour other friends came by, including their minister. Though she appreciated the outpouring of love, she kept waiting for the resident to appear with the news she'd been praying for. When he finally came into the lounge, she jumped up and hurried over to him.

"Has he wakened?"

"Not yet, but the good news is there's no internal bleeding from his concussion. Although his left hip is severely bruised, the only broken bones are in his left arm, above and below the elbow. They've taken him to surgery."

"But if he hasn't regained consciousness…"

"It's a waiting game now. The warm infusion to treat his hypothermia is working. His vital signs are holding."

Nick, why aren't you awake yet?

"Doctor? Could we wait upstairs? Please?"

"Sure. Go to Six North. There's a lounge for families of surgery patients. When he's out, I'll ask the doctor who operated on him to talk to you."

"Thank you."

As he walked away she caught sight of Deputy Posner, who'd just come through the automatic doors. He started toward her.

"I thought you'd want this."

"Oh—my airline bag!" She took it from him. "Thank you!"

"Your purse and journal are inside."

"I was so worried about Nick I forgot all about my things."

"That's understandable. How is he?"

"They're operating on his arm, but he isn't conscious yet."

"Don't give up."

Her throat almost closed. "No." *He's got to stay alive. He has years of living ahead of him.*

"Mrs. Marsden," he said, lowering his voice. "There's an envelope inside that bag you might want to open when you're alone. It contains something the investigators uncovered at the crash site. The head of the team said it's personal. He didn't require it for evidence. When he found out I was coming to the hospital, he asked me to give it to you."

An envelope full of what?

Maybe it contained pictures Nick had kept in the plane.

"Thank you, Deputy." She managed a glimmer of a smile. "That's all I ever say to you. One day I'm going to express my gratitude."

"Just doing my job. We're all pulling for him."

"You were angels out there." *Don't break down now.* "Do they know the reason for the crash yet?"

"I'm not at liberty to say. As soon as they've finished their investigation, you'll be contacted by an FAA agent."

She nodded.

The second he disappeared she hurried over to the others. "The doctor said we could wait upstairs while Nick's in surgery."

Nan put her arm through Stefanie's as they headed for

the elevator. Once they found the other lounge, she turned to her daughter. "Honey? I need to use the restroom."

"Do you want company?"

"No. I'd rather you stayed here. If there's any news about your father, come and get me."

"Okay."

Stefanie gave her anxious daughter a hug. Then, smiling at David, she walked down the corridor to the women's restroom. There was an adjacent room with a couch for nursing mothers and a changing table.

For the moment Stefanie had the place to herself and sat down to open the bag, desperate to know what the deputy had brought her. Anything of Nick's was precious to her.

Inside the mailing envelope she discovered maybe a dozen three-by-five-inch crumpled sheets of yellow notepaper with scribbles on them. They came from Nick's knee pad.

He always wore it strapped around his right leg when he left for work. It contained paper, a loop for a pencil and a small pocket to carry items like keys or gum. The first time she'd asked him about it, he'd explained that Dries had taught him to wear one. That way he would never have to hunt for something to write on.

Of necessity, a pilot needed to jot down coordinates and numbers or make a note to remind himself of something. With the pad attached to his body, he didn't have to think about looking for paper or a pencil while he flew.

She drew a sheet from the collection. Whatever he'd written rambled all over the page and was difficult to decipher. All of them had smears of blood, and they looked like they'd survived a flood.

These weren't numbers.

With no window in the room, she needed more light and opened her purse to get her car keys. On the same chain she kept a dispenser of mace and a pocket flashlight Nick had bought her. He worried when she went out alone to take photographs for the magazine. She'd told him his fears were groundless, but he'd said, "Humor me anyway."

After flicking on the light, she lifted the paper to see if she could make out the words Nick normally wrote in a bold cursive style. This reminded her of her children's handwriting in grade school.

To her frustration, water had left rivulets that had dried, washing out some of the writing, all of which had been done in pencil.

In...I shall be laughing. And so....will be as if all the stars were...when you look at the sky...night you and only you—

Stefanie gasped. These were words from *The Little Prince.*
Nick, darling, what were you trying to say?

She spread the sheets out on the cushion, trying to make sense of his thoughts. To sort them into some kind of order would be impossible.

Her heart began to pound with sickening speed.

If this...my last flight...worry. I'm all right...can't help... It's my body. I will never...you, my beloved soul mate.

Stefanie rocked back and forth, astounded, stunned by what she was reading.

...swear I didn't...about the babies, Stefanie...my fault Matthew died ...so sorry, sweetheart. All I...is bring...pain.

She jumped off the couch, unable to contain the emotions inside her. What babies? What did he mean it was his fault?

Her gaze flew to the next paper.

My gorgeous...sweet wife. You're...Little Princess

whose tender heart couldn't…away from…noxious weed growing…your planet. You saw beyond the spikes… thorns…tamed me.

Nick.

…I'm glad…crashed. …I may have…perfect vision all…life but I've…wandering…like a cowering blind… afraid of everything…don't know why you've…up with me, darling. I don't…how in the hell…was lucky…to meet the only woman for me.

Her entire body pulsating, she reached for the next one.

I…wait for night…if…still alive…walk alone on…highway that runs through…town till…find my tropical bird… her…green eyes. Alone and…in my beloved's arms I'll… her why is…I ought to die.

Nick was quoting from *Flight To Arras*. But Saint-Exupery had never mentioned that his tropical bird had *green* eyes. Hungry for the words she'd waited all these years to hear, she went through the rest of the notes one after another.

The last one read, *I…you to know I've…you more than any…has ever loved…woman.* More lines had disappeared except for two words. *I vow…*

She pressed the papers to her lips, then hurriedly put them in the airline bag and tore out of the room. Nan rushed toward her.

"The doctor just came in."

Stefanie could see the surgeon, still gowned, talking to the family.

"Doctor? I'm Nick's wife. Is he awake yet?"

"No."

She reeled in terror.

"But the surgery went well. Both bones were broken but not shattered."

"I have to see him, Doctor!"

"I understand. He's in the ICU. Only you can go in right now—and only for a moment."

White-faced, she handed her things to Nan and followed the surgeon out of the lounge and down the hall. They reached the ICU after passing through another set of doors. Two nurses were working over him.

It was almost impossible to associate the sight and sounds of monitoring devices, IVs, catheters and oxygen with her strong, virile husband lying there so still in his hospital gown. They'd wrapped his head and put his arm in a full cast. Pulleys raised it to prevent swelling. His hands were bandaged.

The doctor stood next to Stefanie. "We had to cut off his wedding ring before it impeded the circulation in his finger. One of the nurses will give you the pieces later."

Oh, Nick. You've suffered so much.

"May I talk to him?"

"Yes."

She approached his right side and leaned over him. "Nick? It's Stefanie. You're home now. And safe. Please wake up. Please come back to me. I can't live without you."

Tears welled up in her throat and eyes. "You're my Saint-Exupery, and I'm your tropical bird. We're the only people who know how to take care of each other. Open your eyes!"

She could hear his heart monitor. All of a sudden it was beeping faster.

The nurse over by the computer turned to her. "Keep

talking to him, Mrs. Marsden," she said urgently. "He's starting to respond."

Joy.

Whether she should or not, she lowered her head and ever so lightly kissed his lips below the oxygen tube. They were much warmer now than up on the mountain.

"I love you, I love you, I love you," she whispered.

She heard a moan.

"That's right, Nick. Wake up. You're not in Arras. You're back home in Mackenzie. I'm here, my love, and I'll never leave you."

This time she thought he said her name. She waited while he struggled.

"I—love—you—darling—"

Stefanie couldn't hold back the sobs shaking her body. His beautiful blue eyes had opened.

All these years he'd been quietly loving her. Now the long silence had been broken with those notes and his words.

She kissed his lips again. "I love you, too. You're my very life."

"Life—" he took a breath "—began—the—day—I—met—you."

* * * * *

HARLEQUIN®

EVERLASTING LOVE™

Every great love has a story to tell™

A line of deeply emotional novels that show
how love can last, how it shapes and transforms lives,
how it's truly the adventure of a lifetime.
These novels tell the whole story.
Because "happily ever after" is just the beginning....

Turn the page for a sneak preview of
OUR DAY
by Jean Brashear
An emotional novella
from the 3-in-1 anthology
THE VALENTINE GIFT

Available January 29
Wherever books are sold

"**K**itchen closed until further notice," read the note propped on the counter beneath the telephone. "The cook ran off to join the circus."

Jake Marshall squinted and read it again as he groped for a mug to fill with lifesaving coffee—

Which…wasn't there. The carafe was all but empty and stone-cold.

"Lilah?" he called, but he'd already sensed that she wasn't home. The house had a different feel without her in it—too still, somehow. Lifeless without her unbounded energy.

He glanced out the window and saw Puddin' sniffing around. Though the dog was nominally his—found by him, yes, but named courtesy of their daughter's favorite dessert— Lilah was the one who babied the old guy. If she had really run off to join the circus, she'd have taken Puddin' with her.

Jake grinned sleepily, shrugged and began assembling the makings for a fresh pot. She was pulling his leg, but Lilah's sense of mischief went down better after his brain was clicking. She was wide-awake the second her eyes opened; he hated mornings altogether.

The filters took a while to hunt down. When was the last time he'd had to make coffee? She was always up before him. He muttered a little before he finally succeeded. Was it one extra scoop for the pot or—

He set everything down, shoulders drooping. He needed caffeine, tanker loads of it. Now. Last night had been a long one, with an emergency surgery lasting until nearly 2:00 a.m. *Okay, you can do this.* He dumped in two extra scoops for good measure, then shuffled off to hit the shower while it was brewing. On the way, he passed the dining room—

Oh, hell. Their anniversary. He'd missed it. No wonder Lilah had sounded funny when he'd called her to say not to wait up.

Man…everything still sat there—wilted salad, melting dessert. His favorite pot roast petrified in congealed grease. Lilah liked her house in order; she wasn't one to leave dishes soaking in the sink, much less food going bad on the table.

He was in deep doo, no question. He'd always been lousy with dates, but this one was sacred, the anniversary not of their wedding but of the night they'd first made love. Our Day, they called it. The tradition had been special to them both. Even during the tumultuous child-raising years they'd never missed it.

He could plead the press of work, which was admittedly

crushing since he'd switched to the trauma team. He was so tired half the time he could barely remember his name.

His colleagues thought he was crazy to give up a solid private practice, but he loved this work. Medicine interested him now in a way it hadn't in a long time.

Not more than Lilah, though.

Kitchen closed. Suddenly the note wasn't quite as funny. Lilah loved to cook and was so gifted that friends had often urged her to open a restaurant or catering service. She might not be kidding, and for her to shut down her beloved kitchen…not good. He had some serious amends to make. Thank heavens it was nearly Valentine's—he could remember that connection, only three days after Our Day. He'd have to go the distance to dig himself out of this hole.

As soon as he showered, he'd get busy cleaning up the dining room as a gesture of good faith. Lilah would be home soon, surely, and he'd grovel, if necessary—

Upstairs, he heard his pager go off. And groaned. He was on call. Not a chance he could ignore it. He cast another glance at the mess, painfully aware that he'd barely have time to throw on clothes. He'd have to shut off the pot. No coffee until he reached the hospital.

Not good. Really not good.

But Lilah was a reasonable woman, and she loved him, too. They'd work it out.

Wouldn't they?

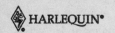

EVERLASTING LOVE™

Every great love has a story to tell™

The Valentine Gift

featuring
three deeply emotional
stories of love that stands
the test of time, just in time
for Valentine's Day!

USA TODAY bestselling author
Tara Taylor Quinn

Linda Cardillo

and
Jean Brashear

Available just in time for Valentine's Day
February wherever you buy books.

www.eHarlequin.com

HEL65427

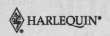

Every great love has a story to tell™

Olivia Banks and James McElroy were high
school sweethearts until James succumbed to
family pressure to end the relationship. He
unknowingly left Olivia pregnant with his
child.... But despite that betrayal, despite the
decisions they each had to make in their lives,
they never forgot each other...and eventually
discovered that love really could last.

Look for

Heart of My Heart

by
Stella MacLean

Available February wherever you buy books.

REQUEST YOUR FREE BOOKS!

2 FREE NOVELS PLUS 2 FREE GIFTS!

 HARLEQUIN®

E V E R L A S T I N G   L O V E ™

Every great love has a story to tell™

YES! Please send me 2 FREE Harlequin® Everlasting Love™ novels and my 2 FREE gifts. After receiving them, if I don't wish to receive any more books, I can return the shipping statement marked "cancel." If I don't cancel, I will receive 4 brand-new novels every other month and be billed just $4.47 per book in the U.S. or $4.99 per book in Canada, plus 25¢ shipping and handling per book and applicable taxes, if any*. That's a savings of about 15% off the cover price! I understand that accepting the 2 free books and gifts places me under no obligation to buy anything. I can always return a shipment and cancel at any time. Even if I never buy another book from Harlequin, the two free books and gifts are mine to keep forever.

153 HDN ELX4   353 HDN ELYG

Name	(PLEASE PRINT)
Address	Apt.
City	State/Prov.	Zip/Postal Code

Signature (if under 18, a parent or guardian must sign)

Mail to the **Harlequin Reader Service®**:
IN U.S.A.: P.O. Box 1867, Buffalo, NY 14240-1867
IN CANADA: P.O. Box 609, Fort Erie, Ontario L2A 5X3

Not valid to current Harlequin Everlasting Love subscribers.

Want to try two free books from another line?
Call 1-800-873-8635 or visit www.morefreebooks.com.

* Terms and prices subject to change without notice. NY residents add applicable sales tax. Canadian residents will be charged applicable provincial taxes and GST. This offer is limited to one order per household. All orders subject to approval. Credit or debit balances in a customer's account(s) may be offset by any other outstanding balance owed by or to the customer. Please allow 4 to 6 weeks for delivery.

Your Privacy: Harlequin is committed to protecting your privacy. Our Privacy Policy is available online at www.eHarlequin.com or upon request from the Reader Service. From time to time we make our lists of customers available to reputable firms who may have a product or service of interest to you. If you would prefer we not share your name and address, please check here. ☐

HEL07

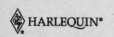

EVERLASTING LOVE™

Every great love has a story to tell™

When a long-lost file lands on Lieutenant
Colonel Anne Dunbar's desk, she's stunned
to find it contains a recommendation
for a medal for Marie Wilson, one of the
Hello Girls who served in France during
World War I. At the same time, Anne faces
dissolution of her marriage to D.C. attorney
Brian Dunbar. Marie and her lieutenant
form a bridge that helps Anne and Brian
overcome their painful past.

Look for

The Hello Girl

by

Merline Lovelace

Available March wherever you buy books.

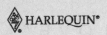

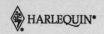

COMING NEXT MONTH

#25 THE VALENTINE GIFT by Tara Taylor Quinn, Linda Cardillo, Jean Brashear

Valentine's Daughters. The Hand That Gives the Rose.
Our Day—three special stories from three acclaimed authors. Three different versions of what Valentine's Day really represents…and how it celebrates everlasting love.

#26 HEART OF MY HEART by Stella MacLean

Olivia Banks and James McElroy were high school sweethearts—and like all young lovers, they believed their love would last forever. But they ignored the real world as it existed in their small East Coast town during the 1960s, the world of parental power and social propriety. When James succumbed to family pressure to end the relationship, he unknowingly left Olivia pregnant with his child…. But despite that betrayal, despite the decisions they made, they never forgot each other…and eventually discovered that love really *could* last.

www.eHarlequin.com